THE
ODD
JOB
MAN

N.J. CRISP

THE ODD JOB MAN

St. Martin's Press
New York

Library of Congress Catalog Card Number: 78-21410

ISBN 0-312-58114-9

THE
ODD
JOB
MAN

CHAPTER ONE

The decibel level of cheerful conversation in this pub, where most people seemed to know most people, was such that George Griffin could hardly hear himself talk, let alone the bald, resigned-looking little man with the pince-nez who was trapped beside him in the corner of the L-shaped bar.

Not that the little man seemed inclined to say anything much, but Griffin did not care. He just wanted someone beside him to make it appear that he was part of the scenery, one of the regulars, with no reason to account for his presence to anyone who might have sensitive antennae for such small things.

'And then there was this fellow,' Griffin said to the little man. 'I don't know if you've heard this one . . . he was at this fun-fair . . . he was smashed, in fact stoned out of his mind.'

Griffin took a cigarette from a large, elaborate, stainless steel cigarette case which served, when required, a useful second function. He did not stop talking.

'Not to put too fine a point on it, he was pissed as a newt.'

The man who was sitting at a table the other side of the bar finished his plate of beans, hamburger and chips, laid his knife and fork on the plate neatly, and sipped at a glass of bitter which he had bought an hour before. Since then, Griffin had enjoyed three large gin and tonics, and badly needed a fourth to deal with the fear which was nibbling at his guts.

Griffin had never spoken to the man, who had carefully placed a paper napkin across the lap of his mohair suit and delicately cut his chips into small mouthfuls, but he thought his name was Tauber, and that, by choice and training, he was a professional assassin, a calling in which he had a notably successful track record.

1

Griffin flicked a couple of times at his cigarette lighter, angling it in a particular way. The lighter sparked but failed to light.

'Damn thing must be empty,' Griffin told his uninterested neighbour. 'Where was I? Oh, yes, this fellow, who was addicted to the sauce, always carried a hip flask in case he sobered up by accident. And in that respect, his judgement was sound,' he said, draining his glass and banging it on the counter.

The barman was nearby and seemed to have been half listening to his story. 'Same again,' Griffin pleaded. 'Good men are dying of thirst here.'

'Right away, Mr Jarvis,' the barman said to a man wearing a cloth cap, and moved to draw two pints of Keg.

Griffin was not surprised, or resentful. He was used to being ignored. In his experience, barmen and waiters were frequently afflicted by unaccountable deafness when addressed by George Griffin. He always found bones in filleted fish, too. He sometimes wondered why.

'Anyway,' Griffin resumed, pinning his neighbour, who had been trying to edge away, back against the bar, 'this fellow paid his money, picked up six wooden balls, and despite the fact that he obviously couldn't focus on anything closer than half a mile away, he threw those balls and knocked down every target in sight. So the stall holder, none too chuffed, gave him this baby tortoise, which promptly withdrew its head and feet into its shell, suspecting with some reason that it was not going to a good home.'

The little man with the pince-nez was not a wholly attentive audience, probably because the bony woman who had poked him in the ribs with one bony finger while Griffin was talking, and whispered fiercely 'We're waiting,' was his impatient wife.

'Shan't be a minute,' the little man said, trapped where he was by the arm which Griffin was using to lean on the bar, and which also happened to prevent the little man from moving.

Griffin heard the bony woman say, behind him, to an even bonier and older version of herself, presumably her mother, 'He can't get away from that seedy-looking bore.'

2

Griffin supposed it was not a totally unjust assessment. His suit qualified for veteran status, and although he had been meaning to have it cleaned for two or three months now, somehow he had not got around to it. Last winter, he had nearly replaced his somewhat tatty raincoat, but it had the rare virtue among raincoats these days of being reasonably waterproof, and also there had been other calls on his purse at the time. His local off-licence had cut up nasty about the sixty-three pounds fifty he owed them. As for the old trilby which hung so comfortably on the back of his head, it was the only hat which had ever really fitted him, while serving to cover up his bald patch at the same time.

'Last orders, please,' the barman bellowed suddenly. 'Last orders, gentlemen, please.'

'Yes, definitely,' Griffin said, loudly. Surprisingly, the barman looked in his direction. 'A large gin and tonic over here, as a matter of priority.' The barman took his glass. 'I always drink gin for health reasons,' Griffin told his neighbour. 'Keeps me reasonably slim, provided I don't do anything silly like eating.'

Griffin patted his stomach, illustrating, although in truth it was not the flat, muscular torso he dimly remembered possessing at one time. Now, a half sphere was developing; an incipient paunch; to be brutally honest, a pot. That was the trouble with being average height, those few extra pounds always seemed to accumulate round the belly. Tauber, now, he had no paunch. His body under that well-cut suit would be as unyielding as steel. But then, besides being younger than Griffin, no more than thirty-five at the most, he was also six feet three, and looked as though he took as much care to keep in training as a professional athlete, which he probably did.

Tauber was gazing idly around the bar, apparently deep in thought. His eyes moved straight past Griffin without a pause or a flicker, but Griffin felt a twinge of unease. If this went wrong, it could prove painful in the extreme, and Griffin had a profound aversion to pain of any kind.

'And whatever my friend and his ladies were drinking,' Griffin called to the barman, placing a comradely arm round the

3

little man's shoulders.

'No, no,' the little man said.

'Nonsense,' Griffin said. 'I insist.'

He fished a crumpled ten pound note from his hip pocket and threw it casually on the bar. It was a good feeling, having tenners on you to chuck around, even if the original five hundred pounds had diminished sharply to the point when Griffin preferred not to count it any more. His emphasis on necessary expenses, although exaggerated, he had fondly hoped at the time, had proved to be far from fanciful. And, to face unpleasant facts, whatever was left, plus a good deal more, was already mortgaged, so that Griffin needed to collect his second half before he would have some left over to call his own for the necessities of life, such as a case of gin and what he suspected would be an extremely expensive evening out with the divorcee, who lived in a ground floor flat in Marylebone, and for whom Griffin lusted at the moment.

The barmaid, presumably the barman's wife, was rinsing glasses, bending forward to do so, and Griffin found himself presented with an astonishing view down the front of her dress. Had she been an actress, instead of a hard faced, artificial blonde, middle-aged cockney, he would have been certain he was looking at a tit job. They were much too good to be true. As it was, he supposed he was really admiring the result of some brilliant brassiere engineering, but the effect was remarkable just the same.

The divorcee had tits rather like that, but she was younger, better looking and wore expensive perfume. He wondered if her tits owed more to surgery than nature, and whether to suggest the Savoy or A L'Ecu de France, but he thought that the divorcee was a Mirabelle bird, which was going to come really expensive, especially if she wanted Dom Perignon and Napoleon brandy, which she probably would.

Still, if he collected the second half of his fee, he could afford it, and after that—well. Griffin thought, it was either into bed or not. You had to invest to find out. The trouble with growing older was that it seemed to cost more to find out all the time.

'Anyway,' Griffin said to the little man, 'this fellow at the fair-ground tottered off into the crowd and was lost ιc sight. But about an hour later, he re-appears, having clearly supped on his hip flask in no very moderate fashion . . .'

A large gin and tonic appeared on the bar in front of Griffin. 'God bless you, sir,' he said to the barman. 'You're a friend in need, you are indeed, and that sentiment comes from the heart, I promise you.'

Griffin tensed. Tauber was moving. Not towards the door, but heading for the telephone.

'Excuse me,' Griffin said to the little man. 'Must have a slash, back in a flash. Sorry. I'm a poet manqué.'

The phone was in a booth. Griffin made his way towards it, paused, fumbled for a box of matches and lit the cigarette which still hung from his lips.

Through the glass topped door, he saw Tauber insert 2p, which almost certainly made it a local call. There was no way of hearing what Tauber was saying or if he was speaking in English. Griffin did not like this telephone call. It worried him. He decided to risk a quick slash, which in fact he needed.

There were few people left in the bar when he came back. The little man with the pince-nez and his bony companions had gone, leaving empty glasses as testimony to his unappreciated generosity. Griffin scooped up his change, and put back his gin in one without bothering with the tonic.

'What happened then?' the barman enquired, propping himself up opposite Griffin. 'That bloke at the fair-ground.'

'Ah well,' Griffin said, 'by this time he was positively pie-eyed, he could hardly stand up, but incredibly, he knocked down every target again. So the stall holder, realizing there's no justice, said "What would you like this time? A teddy bear?" And the fellow said, "No. Give me another of those delicious, crunchy meat pies I won before."'

Griffin laughed appreciatively, and slapped the bar with the flat of his hand.

'Yuk,' the barman said.

'That's a good story, that is,' Griffin said. 'I inherited it from my grandfather.'

Tauber had returned to his unfinished glass of beer, and Griffin began to feel decidedly conspicuous in the nearly empty pub. 'Good-night then, squire,' he said, to the barman. 'Time I picked up a lady friend, if I can find one anywhere.'

The pub was in a North Kensington mews, which was picturesque at this time of night mostly because of the inadequate lighting.

Griffin hovered irresolutely in a deep shadow cast by the van parked next to his car. A couple left the pub, which emptied it except for Tauber, Griffin calculated as he watched them walk off up the mews. Then the place was dark and silent, apart from the growl of distant traffic.

Griffin was not certain what to do. He did not like Tauber's telephone call at all. And yet, if he left, Tauber could disappear again. Griffin might conceivably be able to find him once more, but Tauber would certainly remember him second time round and act accordingly. Griffin wanted the rest of his fee, but he did not wish to become dead or maimed.

No. It would have to be now, if he got the chance. He was certain that the man *was* Tauber, but, even if he proved to be merely an innocent bystander with a facial resemblance, the police would simply find the victim of yet another unsolved mugging and no harm would be done, except to the man who looked like Tauber.

But if it were Tauber, and if Tauber had already formed certain suspicions, Griffin would lack that vital second of surprise, which he desperately needed, before the man's reflexes came into operation. There had been a time when Griffin could have taken any man regardless of any disadvantage in weight or size, but that was before his trousers started feeling tight round the waist and when drinking meant a few pints of beer.

Griffin took a cigarette from his elaborate case and put it between his lips. He did not much care for the prospect before him. He thought it would be nice to drive home and go to bed with a good book, or better still a pneumatic blonde like the divorcee in Marylebone. Perhaps she was not a Mirabelle bird after all. Perhaps a boat trip up the Regents' Canal and a bit of wit and charm

6

over a glass of beer would do the trick. Yes, that was why she wore Joy perfume, and her hair was done at Vidal Sassoon's, because she'd enjoy sitting on a long boat with a crowd of perspiring tourists. No, it was either the Mirabelle, or forget it, and find a scrubber in some Wimpy Bar. Put that way, Griffin thought, it was like the prospect of being hanged—it concentrated the mind wonderfully.

The big man in the mohair suit came out of the pub, turned without hesitation, and walked along the mews. He moved lightly and silently. His manner was slow and casual, and Griffin recognized it as that of a man who was watchful and careful. It must be Tauber all right, no question, and for all his caution he did not know where Griffin was. Griffin felt good about that, but there would be no advantage in trying anything from behind. That was what Tauber was poised for, the unexpected, like some jungle predator which lived its life alert for danger from any quarter.

Griffin needed him thrown, just for that one second. He wandered out of the shadows, snapping his cigarette lighter vainly. Tauber's head turned, and as Griffin offered a sheepish grin, he caught a glimpse of grey, unblinking, expressionless eyes.

'Sorry to bother you, old chap,' Griffin mumbled, 'but do you think I could have a light?'

'Yes, of course,' Tauber said, coming to a stop. 'No trouble at all.' His voice was quiet, calm, and scarcely accented at all.

'Something wrong with this blasted lighter of mine,' Griffin said.

But he knew it was no use, even as he spoke. Tauber's casual turn, as he put his hand into his pocket, had taken him half a pace further away from Griffin. Only half a pace, no more than a few inches. But it meant that, in the second which Griffin needed, and had available, he would be very slightly off balance if he tried to apply that damaging combination of blows in which he had been well schooled, and which would render a man silent and unconscious for pretty well any period Griffin desired.

But in that second, because of Tauber's move, his weight

distribution was wrong, and Tauber was not in the least off balance.

Griffin swayed like a man who was half smashed, in which reality lent his imitation a helping hand, and did nothing. But he did not really expect Tauber to be convinced, and he was not surprised when he saw that the object Tauber held was not for lighting cigarettes, but was small, shone cold blue in the dim light, and was fitted with a silencer.

'Keep quite still, please,' Tauber said. He moved in close now, and dug the gun into Griffin's ribs. Nothing was going to stop the bullet entering the heart from that position if Tauber's finger twitched no matter what Griffin did, and he practically stopped breathing.

Tauber's free hand was expertly checking him for a gun or a knife. Griffin chose to place another interpretation on Tauber's movements.

'You can take my wallet, old chap, and welcome,' Griffin said. 'I don't want any trouble.'

'Shut up,' Tauber said, softly, 'and stop playing the comedian.'

Griffin shut up, as requested, until the frisking was over.

Tauber said, 'Right. Who are you?'

'Griffin. George Griffin. I must say I don't know what all this is about . . .'

'George Griffin who does what?' Tauber asked, ignoring his protestations.

'I'm an executive with a publishing company,' Griffin said. 'You'll find my business card in my waistcoat pocket.'

Tauber kept his eyes fixed on Griffin's, and the gun pressed into his ribs, as his fingers searched for and found the card.

Griffin still had his cigarette case in one hand, and his lighter in the other. He tensed himself inwardly. There had to be a moment when Tauber glanced at that card . . . but Tauber's eyes merely flickered, and the fraction of a second had gone. The man must have eyes like a bloody night owl, Griffin thought sourly.

'Major Griffin,' Tauber said, suspiciously.

Griffin cursed himself viciously. He had forgotten about that

8

'Major' in his anxiety to distract Tauber. A lapse of memory which was a sure sign of panic. Well, who wouldn't panic with this merchant, who traded in death as a career.

'Retired,' Griffin said. 'I served in the Pay Corps. I'm entitled to use my army rank in civilian life.'

If only Tauber would move away a bit, a couple of feet would do. He dared not try anything with the barrel of a gun burning an incipient hole in his chest.

'You've been following me,' Tauber murmured.

'No, my dear chap, I do assure you . . .'

'That's your car,' Tauber said, 'parked behind this van. I've seen it three times today. And then you turn up in the same bar.'

'Coincidence,' Griffin said. 'Sheer coincidence. I've never seen you before in my life as far as I know.'

'I don't like coincidences,' Tauber said. His fingers thrust the card back into Griffin's waistcoat pocket.

But there was a trace of doubt in Tauber's eyes now, and Griffin allowed a little hope to smoulder, although it did nothing to quell the terrified beating of his heart.

'Well, come to that,' Griffin said, trying to sound indignant, which was hard, as well as afraid, which was not, 'I don't like having a gun pulled on me when I've been doing nothing more than having a quiet drink, doing no harm to anyone. If you don't want money, what is it? Are you police or something?'

'That's right,' Tauber said. 'You resemble a man we'd like to question. You can drive me to HQ.'

'Where's that?'

'I'll direct you,' Tauber said. He stepped back a pace. 'In the car, please.'

Griffin had no intention of getting into his car, with Tauber sitting behind him and a gun pointing at the back of his head. Why the hell do I get myself into situations like this, he wondered in anguish. Just for a bit of lousy money. It's not worth it.

There were altogether too many places, even in the middle of London, Hyde Park being a good and nearby example, where a man could be shot dead and left in a car, until some copper wondered what it was doing there.

They were both playing the same game. Tauber was not certain, he thought it was just possible that he had stuck a gun into the ribs of an honest and harmless citizen. But even if that were so, he was certainly not about to let that citizen wander off and dial nine nine nine. Griffin had just one advantage. He was dead sure about Tauber, while Tauber was not quite sure about him.

Tauber followed Griffin the few steps to his car. Griffin put away his cigarette lighter, and took out his car keys. He kept the cigarette case in his left hand, bent down, and shakily failed to insert the car key the first time which did not take much acting.

'Give it to me,' Tauber said, with quiet impatience. Griffin handed the keys over. Tauber did not shift his eyes from Griffin's, but for a moment, his attention was divided. It was the only moment Griffin would get, and he used it.

He pressed a small, concealed catch in the cigarette case, which fired the single nine millimetre bullet with which the device was loaded. Simultaneously, and with remarkable speed for an out of condition lush, the heel of his right hand struck Tauber on a particular pressure point below the jaw with all the force of an iron bar.

Tauber collapsed silently on to the cobble-stones, without firing his gun, which was the object of the exercise. But Griffin knew at once, sickeningly, that it had gone wrong. Very wrong indeed.

The bullet fired from the cigarette case should have smashed Tauber's gun hand, as a precautionary measure, should Griffin fail to stun him first time.

But Tauber's hand was uninjured, and still held that gun. Blood there certainly was, but that came from somewhere in the region of Tauber's chest. Griffin's nervousness had made him miss, and miss badly. Now he had a seriously injured man on his hands, and he could hardly ring up the ambulance service, and say 'Oh, by the way, I've just shot this fellow, and I think he needs a bit of surgery, or possibly a coffin.' Besides, the deal was that Tauber should be unharmed. 'Christ Almighty,' Griffin groaned. He felt very sorry for himself indeed. Why the hell did things always have to happen to him?

It seemed like forever since Tauber had stepped out of that pub, but in fact it was only two or three minutes. Someone was going to come walking along this mews soon. And there was the phone call. That phone call still bothered him.

Griffin opened the boot of his car, and thanked whatever God would have anything to do with him that he had once thought that this big, old Ford would be a comfortable car to drive, without even reflecting that the boot would take the body of a man in comfort.

Griffin knew all about the difficulties of lifting the dead weight of an unconscious man. He had also been trained how to do it by good instructors.

He heaved Tauber into the boot, pocketed his gun, slammed the lid, locked it and felt slightly better.

He felt better still when he drove his car out of the mews and turned left. He was a hundred yards along the road, when, in his rear view mirror, he saw the headlights of a car swing into the mews. Griffin slowed, and parked as soon as he could. He got out, and walked back.

At the entrance to the mews, he took one look, before he about turned and headed for his car again.

There were two cars in that mews, stationary in the middle, engines running. One had entered from each end. Two men were looking at the cobble-stones, presumably at Tauber's blood-stains.

Griffin had been right about that phone call. Tauber had phoned somebody. Griffin wondered who, without any intention of ever finding out if he could help it.

In the strange world of assassination in which Tauber moved, friends of his were liable to have primitive responses towards a man who had shot him and shoved him into the boot of his car.

Someone else would be looking for Tauber now. Griffin began to wonder what the hell he could do with him.

11

CHAPTER TWO

The traffic was heavy, and Griffin concentrated on avoiding maniac taxis and grinning youths in battered sports cars, who appeared to be perversely determined to carve him up. The last thing he needed was to be involved in an accident, no matter how minor. Four double gins, plus his previous intake during the day, would most certainly lead to a firm invitation to the nearest police station, should any copper decide there was some reason to breathalyze him; an event which, with quite incredible good fortune, Griffin had so far avoided.

He wondered if the law would look inside the boot and decide that the evening looked like being an interesting one after all, and thought it distinctly likely. He had no wish to try and explain the wounded Tauber to some thick PC with sudden visions of promotion. It was becoming more difficult by the minute to explain what he was doing with the bloody man to himself, George Griffin. A thousand pounds no longer seemed like a very good reason.

Suppose he dumped him? Just opened the boot, tipped him out somewhere, and left him? Griffin was strongly tempted, but he reluctantly decided that it would solve nothing. He was, admittedly, dealing with friends, but despite their affability they were hard men who were paying good money for Tauber and expected him safely delivered. They would not be pleased to learn that Griffin had slipped up. At the very least, they would want their money back. Griffin was in no position to repay it, and he doubted if they would take kindly to any suggestion of extended credit. Besides, Griffin liked to see money coming in, not going out.

Still, he might have risked that particular piece of unpleasantness, except for Tauber himself, who was still alive. Should Tauber recover his health and strength, he would harbour something of a grievance, and he knew what Griffin looked like.

Griffin could make quite sure that Tauber did not recover, of course, and he seriously considered various silent ways of putting the man down. But then the police would have a murder case on their hands, and shrewd detectives, anxious to make a name for themselves, would be checking on the dead man's movements.

Moreover, there was that telephone call Tauber had made. A clammy film of sweat suddenly covered Griffin's forehead. Tauber had recognized his car. He was a skilled pro and would have memorized the registration number. Suppose he had given that number to whoever he had telephoned? The recipients might decide to pass on an anonymous tip to the police, and Griffin fancied life imprisonment only marginally more than the prospect of being executed by a vengeful Tauber after what would certainly be agonizing preliminaries.

No, he decided, with profound regret, his only hope lay in keeping Tauber alive and harmless, although, he thought, there seemed to be a built-in contradiction there which would prove difficult to resolve. Somehow he would have to try and go through with the original deal, lie convincingly to explain the delay and generally play it by ear.

The trouble was, that would turn him into a sitting duck, plumb in the sights of those interested in Tauber, and there was more than one deal in the air. That was the only reason why Griffin's services had been required at all. He did not like it, he wanted out but unfortunately he was too far in now. No, his best chance was a living, breathing, preferably unconscious Tauber, safely tucked away in some place which only he, Griffin, knew about.

And how the hell do you achieve that little lot, he wondered bitterly.

Griffin drew up in Elgin Place, Maida Vale, and switched off his engine. So far so good. It was quiet in this empty, tree lined,

13

residential road, and he drew a deep breath and tried to think straight.

There was no lift in his elderly block of flats, which was why they came less expensive than some, and there was no way he could carry Tauber up three long flights of stairs. Griffin knew his limitations only too well. Besides, his address was no secret and people were liable to call.

No, not here. This was merely a pause for thought and refreshment. There was a bottle of gin upstairs and Griffin needed another drink badly. This was going to be a long night.

He sat where he was, behind the driving wheel, temporarily postponing the drink in favour of reflection and lit a cigarette. Where? Portsmouth? The contented, lethargic Brenda? He rejected that at once. Unthinkable. His mother and step-father, two elderly people now, still living in the same bungalow as far as he knew? He tried to visualize waking them up at two o'clock in the morning, with the body of a man who had been shot draped over one shoulder. 'Hullo, mum. How have you been this last quarter of a century? I just thought I'd drop in, you know.'

Griffin shifted angrily in his seat and wiped more perspiration from his forehead with the back of his hand. This was closer to the nightmare ravings born of delirium than logical thought. Concentrate for Christ's sake.

Captain Drew? He was a possible. He would not regard such a request for help as being out of the way. But Captain Drew was not a man who could be totally relied on when there was money at stake. No, Griffin needed someone he could trust completely, and he rejected Captain Drew.

Maisie? That weird, fascinating, quirky, and ultimately impossible girl might play ball just for kicks. But Maisie had moved to Scotland, she had a fellow who had no good reason to help Griffin and Scotland was too far away. Griffin needed to be seen about his normal business tomorrow as though nothing had happened.

Nancy? Griffin pondered that one carefully. Nancy had another and very important advantage. On the other hand,

Nancy was straight and honest, which was why, Griffin supposed, he had come out of it looking like such a shit in retrospect, even in his own eyes. Still, Nancy was definitely a thought.

Griffin threw his cigarette away and climbed out of the car. He made sure there was no one in the road and unlocked the boot. He had heard no sound of movement, but it was in his mind that Tauber might need tying up and gagging. But the way the bastard looked, what he needed was a hospital. He taped an old field dressing on to the wound which did not look as though it would kill a man like Tauber. Griffin locked the boot again. He had the same relaxed attitude, based on experience, to men who had been shot, as a doctor had to illness. If a man was going to die, he usually did it quickly. Otherwise there was normally a certain amount of time available, and no need to panic. Just the same, something had to be done with Tauber, and he had to decide what.

Griffin climbed the three flights of stone stairs which led to the front door of his flat. The low powered bulbs, which were all the economy minded landlords felt inclined to provide, shed little light, but Griffin could walk up those stairs with his eyes closed, and frequently did.

The climb never failed, however, to render him breathless and by the time he arrived on his landing he was puffing humiliatingly. He spared a moment, as he invariably did, to swear that he really must get back into trim one of these days soon, but he had so much else on his mind that the resolve was even more superficial than usual.

That was probably why he did not even see the six feet tall, athletically built young man, who was squatting in a corner waiting for him.

The young man uncoiled himself, stood up, stepped forward, and said 'Hullo, dad.'

'Jesus Christ Almighty,' Griffin said, startled, recoiling instinctively. 'What the bloody hell are you doing here?'

'A typically affectionate greeting from doting parent,' Dick Griffin said.

15

'You silly little bugger,' Griffin said, shaking his son's out-stretched hand, and looking up into his face. 'Why didn't you let me know you were coming?'

'It was all last minute,' Dick said. 'Someone offered us a lift as far as London and we knew you'd be delighted to put us up for the night. Say hullo to Jane,' he instructed his father, pointing over his shoulder. 'You know Jane.'

Griffin looked behind him, and saw the slim, small, dark haired girl, with the duffle bag slung over her shoulder. 'Hullo Jane,' he said.

White teeth glimmered, somewhere behind the hanging curtain of long dark hair, as she gave him a smile of greeting. 'Hullo Mr Griffin. I told him he should have telephoned first.'

Griffin unlocked his front door, and let them in.

'I wasn't to know he'd be out on the town,' Dick said. He fell into an armchair with a sigh of relief. 'We got here about seven, hung about for a while, and then decided to go and have a Chinese nosh. Your landing is not designed for waiting about,' he told Griffin. 'I tried two or three of your locals, but you weren't around. What were you up to, anyway? Wining and dining some female?'

Griffin shook his head. 'Business,' he said briefly.

'Any luck?' Dick enquired casually.

'No,' Griffin said. 'More of a disaster. Why? Are you short?'

Dick received a students' maintenance grant and worked during the vacations when he could find a job, but Griffin needed no more than a grasp of simple arithmetic to know full well that while his son could get by, a simple luxury like that 'Chinese nosh' would have made a hole in his pocket, which he could not afford.

Griffin was proud of his son, and he tried to make sure that Dick usually had some spare cash which he could spend without thinking twice. Christmas and birthday presents were always cheques. The birthday present must have run out.

'No more than usual,' Dick said. 'Not to worry.'

Griffin took a couple of ten pound notes from his wallet, and chucked them into Dick's lap. 'I can spare twenty,' he said. 'But

16

try and make it last.'

'Well, all contributions gratefully received,' Dick said, fingering the notes although he did not put them in his pocket, 'but I thought you mentioned a disaster.'

'More of a temporary setback,' Griffin said. 'Cash flow is relatively healthy. Take it while it's going.'

'OK' Dick said. 'I'm not proud. Thanks very much. I'll put it in the little book.'

Dick kept a small account book in which he meticulously listed the money Griffin gave him, although Christmas and birthday cheques were excluded after a long argument which Griffin had won.

'Don't bother,' Griffin told him. 'Just keep me in booze in my old age.'

Griffin poured himself a half tumbler of gin, and started searching for a bottle of tonic.

'I'd rather fund the national debt,' Dick said. 'No thanks. I'll just pay you back. It'll work out a damn sight cheaper.'

'What are you two up to, anyway, bumming your way round the country?' Griffin asked. He discovered a bottle of tonic behind the settee. It was nearly empty, but the dregs would provide sufficient dilution in the state of mind he was in. 'I thought it was the middle of term.'

Downstairs, the body of a man who had been shot rested peacefully, for the time being, in the boot of his car. But it was important that Dick did not know about such things. This must pass off in the normal way such visits did.

'It's a reading week, Mr Griffin,' Jane said. 'No lectures. Well, hardly any.'

'Which we can cheerfully miss,' Dick said.

'You treat university like a bloody holiday camp,' Griffin complained. 'You just remember that if you fail your degree, you might have to work for a living and you wouldn't like that.'

'Fail?' Dick grinned his engaging, cocky grin. 'No chance, doting parent. No way.'

And the boy was right, Griffin thought. Dick was bright. Christ knew where he had got that from, but he was. Dick was reading Law, took a second class honours for granted, and would be mildly disappointed if he did not get a first.

That, unfortunately for the state of Griffin's cash flow, would not be the end of it. Dick wanted to be a barrister, and would no doubt become a good one, and prosperous in due course to boot. But Griffin knew that young barristers had a rough time of it financially in the beginning. It could take years before a young man was established, and in the meantime a private income was desirable. Well, Dick would not have any private income, but Griffin had established what he privately called a Sinking Fund.

The Sinking Fund was in a bank account whose existence was known to no one but Griffin, and least of all the Inland Revenue. Griffin tried to put half of his earnings from odd jobs into the Sinking Fund.

Perhaps Dick would never need it, in which case Griffin could run three mistresses at once until the money gave out, or become a complete alcoholic, or possibly both. But if, one day, as a struggling young barrister, Dick needed money, possibly to buy a house and get married for example, then the Sinking Fund would be there.

There were times when Griffin groaned under the several burdens imposed upon his income. There was Brenda, the house, the rocketing rent of this flat, Dick's education, the Sinking Fund—Griffin had been appalled when he had once worked out how much he needed to make before he could even buy himself a packet of cigarettes, let alone the gin to go with them, or the various ladies, past and future, if not present, who all cost money in the form of being taken out to dinner, perfume, presents and so on. Even the very occasional domesticated ones, who liked to cook at home and should work out cheaper, started getting ideas about decorations, new furniture, refrigerators, cookers, and the like.

Griffin could never have managed, with the small and somewhat second-hand talents he possessed, had it not been for the steady, if relatively infrequent demand for him in his capacity as an odd job man.

Griffin saw no contradiction between the actions those odd

jobs demanded of him, and the fact that his son would become a pillar of the law, conceivably, in the end, a High Court Judge. It would be nice to live long enough to see that, although Griffin doubted if his liver would hold out. But as for the odd jobs themselves, they took place in another world. They were nothing to do with Dick's world.

'Anyway,' Dick said, yawning, 'we can get through our reading programme at home.'

'Is that where you're going?' Griffin asked.

Dick nodded. Jane's people lived in Southsea. 'I shall stay with mum. She wants the kitchen painted. I can do that while I'm there.'

Griffin wondered for a moment if there was any implication that it should be dad who was at home, painting the kitchen. He sometimes thought that, possibly, Dick might understand why he was not there, but he did not know for certain. He had never discussed it with him.

'How is she?' Griffin asked.

'Fine,' Dick said. 'The same as ever.'

'I keep meaning to go and see her,' Griffin said, uncomfortably. 'It must be months now, since I was there. But, I don't know, it's hard to find the time, somehow. Anyway, tell her I'll come for a week-end as soon as I can.'

'She doesn't keep track,' Dick said. 'Just turn up when you've got nothing else to do. She won't notice how long it's been. Time doesn't mean much to mum.'

Yes, Dick loved his mother, but perhaps he did understand.

Griffin took another quick look at his watch. 'Would you two like some coffee?' he asked.

'Please,' Dick said, idly scratching his leg.

'I'll make it,' Jane said. She got up at once. She was good about things like that.

Dick looked round at the untidy muddle of the living room. 'I gather Maisie's gone for good,' he said. 'I know she only tidied up once a week, but it looks like a month's dust on those shelves.'

'I like dust,' Griffin said. 'It's homely.'

'Who's the next one going to be?' Dick asked, scratching the

19

other leg. 'Have you got anyone lined up?'

'I'm suffering from a marked shortage of volunteers,' Griffin said. 'Go and help Jane with the coffee. I've got a phone call to make, and it's private.'

Dick stood up, and grinned at Jane. 'He's feeling randy,' he said, 'and he wants to try and lay something on. It's never too late for my father.'

'Get out, you cheeky little sod,' Griffin said.

The phone rang several times, before a drowsy voice said 'Hullo'.

'Hullo, Nancy,' Griffin said. 'It's George.' There was a long silence from the other end.

'George Griffin,' he said, prodding her memory.

'I guessed that,' Nancy said. Her voice had ceased to be drowsy, and was cool, veering to cold. 'There's only one George who'd ring me out of the blue at this time of night.'

'I'm sorry if I woke you up,' Griffin said. 'But this is important.'

'To you, possibly,' Nancy said. 'Not to me. Goodnight.'

'Nancy, please. Don't hang up on me. Please,' Griffin said urgently.

He had planned how to play this, worked out how to enlist Nancy's sympathy, but he forgot the careful phrases designed to appeal to her better nature in his desperate need to stop her from hanging up on him. His voice rose in a pleading note, and contained a ring of fear as well. A moment later, he realized that she was still there. 'What's wrong?' she asked cautiously.

Accidentally, it had worked. The first hurdle was overcome. 'I must see you,' Griffin said. 'I can't tell you why on the phone. I'm leaving London now, and I'll be there as soon as I can.'

It was only after he had rung off, that he realized that he had omitted to ask if she were alone. Would she be? Nancy? Some people found her a very attractive woman, Griffin among them.

There was the sound of voices in the kitchen, and he heard Jane laugh. She very rarely said anything in Griffin's presence, but she and Dick chattered away like magpies when they were alone.

20

What they called the generation gap, presumably. He was, after all, her boy friend's father. He remembered his last one-night stand, just after Maisie had left, which had gone well in bed, and disastrously over breakfast. That girl had been no older than Jane.

Jane probably thought he was a dirty old man, who was not worth talking to.

He went into the kitchen. Jane stopped what she was saying and held out a cup of coffee.

'No thanks,' Griffin said. 'I can't. I've got to go out.'

'How long will you be?' Dick asked.

'Fathers ask sons questions like that,' Griffin said. 'Not the other way round. Mind your own business.'

'If you're going to be out all night,' Dick said, patiently, 'we'll use your room, that's all. It's more comfortable.'

'I'll be back,' Griffin said, 'and I intend to sleep in my own bed. Use the couch, as usual. See you in the morning.'

Griffin felt his way down the stairs. Bloody cheek, he thought. Taps me for twenty quid, and then wants to pinch my room, because it's got a double bed. They're soft, the present generation. Jesus wept, when you thought that the boy had been conceived on a shingle beach, with a cold wind blowing up bare arses and the smell of decaying seaweed, and did we care? Griffin fell over something in the hall, cursed, and rubbed his ankle. Some fool had left a bicycle there.

He went outside, checked for late night passers-by, opened the boot and took another look at Tauber. He seemed to be still unconscious, but Griffin thought that he was lying in a slightly different position. Perhaps he was due to come round.

Griffin opened the first aid kit again, and strapped Tauber's hands and feet together with adhesive tape. Then he taped lint across the man's mouth. If the poor bugger comes round, he thought, he'll imagine he's on some motorized ferry across the Styx. Well, the bastard had despatched enough people on that journey. If there were any natural justice, he would have followed long ago.

There was very little traffic now, but Griffin drove carefully,

21

although not with such 'undue caution' as to attract the attention of the police. He would also be interested in any car which remained behind him, but none did.

Once on the M4, he relaxed, although he kept to the inside lane, and paid a lot of attention to his rear view mirrors. But no car stationed itself behind him.

He checked the time as he drove along. Dick and Jane would be bedded down on the couch by now, and he wondered curiously if they were easy and natural together in that department too. Probably. Young people had a better deal these days.

Griffin knew that he was never entirely at ease with Dick's girl friends. His son had good taste, and the girls were always entirely fanciable, which left Griffin rigidly trying not to fancy them or even look at them in the speculative way he would normally eye such young ladies in a bar or a restaurant.

Jane was quite the most beautiful of the crop so far, and she and Dick had been together for nearly a year. He sometimes wondered if they intended to get married in due course, but he did not ask. That was their business.

He wondered if Dick ever fancied any of his own lady friends. Perhaps he did. Dick was always perfectly polite to them, took them for granted, made no mention of any of their predecessors in their hearing, in short behaved with tact and consideration.

But suppose Dick had sometimes sat there, during those noisy games of Scrabble they had played with Maisie, for example, trying not to notice how good her legs were, or how fully those young breasts pressed against the top of those low cut dresses she liked to wear? Suppose Dick too had rigidly tried not to fancy his girl friends?

Griffin laughed out loud. God, he might have led a complicated and less than satisfactory life, but out of it had come his son, and who the hell had any right to complain about that?

Griffin left the M4 at Maidenhead and headed for Marlow.

Nancy lived quite close to Marlow, but the small house was in an isolated position in a narrow lane and no one lived nearby. That was another plus in Nancy's favour. She had bought the house with her share of the money from the divorce settlement.

Griffin pulled up opposite the garden gate, switched off the engine and lit a cigarette. Now that he was here, it occurred to him that there were other, practical difficulties in the way, even if Nancy were willing. He sat thinking about how those difficulties might be overcome.

He saw the front door open a few inches. She must have heard the car arrive.

He got out, and slammed the door. 'Hullo, Nancy,' he said. 'How are things with you?'

CHAPTER THREE

Griffin had liked Nancy's house on the occasions when he had been there before. The living room was gracefully and pleasantly furnished, and he remembered it as warm and welcoming. It still was, but Nancy was not.

She had a face which could be quite movingly lovely at times, when she awoke in the morning, for instance, and the clear, early light caught her features as she turned her head on the pillow. Without make-up, that fine, severely symmetrical bone structure had stirred soft, unfamiliar feelings in Griffin.

At present, the severity dominated. She had taken the trouble to get dressed, and wore a heavy, loose sweater and trousers.

Griffin smiled. 'No need for the protective clothing,' he said. 'I haven't come with fun and games in mind. I thought you gathered that, when we spoke on the phone.'

'I had second thoughts,' Nancy said. 'I remembered how good you were at lying, and putting on an act, when you want something.'

'I suppose that's fair comment,' Griffin said, 'but on this occasion, I want something else. Your virtue is safe.'

'My virtue is on the tarnished side already,' Nancy said.

Griffin did not even try to field that one. On a wicket of her own choosing, Nancy could score as effortlessly as she wished. She was bound to win.

'The truth is,' he said, 'I've got myself into rather a muddle.' He gave her a shy, guileless look. 'I think I'll have a nervous breakdown.'

'No, you won't,' Nancy said, ruthlessly. 'You impose those on other people.'

Griffin winced. 'How anyone as kind and sensible as you,' he said, 'ever got mixed up with someone like me, I'll never know.'

'I've often wondered that myself,' Nancy said. 'What sort of muddle?'

'It would be hard to explain in detail,' Griffin said, 'and there are things you might find difficult to believe.'

'I shall be surprised if I believe any of it,' Nancy said impatiently.

'That's your privilege,' he said. 'But I've come to you for help because there's no one else in the world I can ask. Just remember that and try to take me on trust, just a little bit.'

'That poses a small problem,' Nancy said. 'I don't trust you, George, not one inch.'

Griffin sighed inwardly. She was not going to give way, no matter how she really felt about him. He was fairly sure there was more than a little still there, and he gave her a soulful, searching look, gazing deep into her eyes.

Nancy did not look away or even blink. 'In fact,' she said, 'not one millimetre, come to think about it.'

Griffin gave up, and lit a cigarette. 'Have you got any booze in?' he asked. 'Only I've practically dried out, and I don't like it.'

'You've been drinking all evening,' Nancy said. 'I can smell the gin from here.'

'All right,' he snapped. 'So I'm a lush. Either give me a drink or not, but stop nagging about everything.'

She stared at him without moving, and at first he thought he would have to go through the rest of the night with nothing to relieve his parched throat, and the need in his guts. But then she opened a cupboard, took out a quarter full bottle of gin, a full bottle of tonic, a glass, and handed them to him.

'Thanks,' Griffin said. He ignored the tonic. At this stage, tonic was superfluous.

'How's Maisie?' she enquired neutrally.

'All right, I think. She writes to me now and then.'

'Writes?' Nancy's eyebrows rose. 'From where?'

'Scotland. She very sensibly took herself off with an American oil man. They're in Aberdeen.'

'You mean some woman gave you what you deserve? That

must be the first time ever.'

'It's not,' Griffin said, grumpily. 'But I saw no point in keeping you up to date with my list of failures.'

'You could have given it a certain gloss,' Nancy said. 'Told me that you'd got fed up with her and kicked her out, for example.'

'She was screwing the oilman at his hotel when I was out at work,' Griffin said. 'That may not show me in the heroic light I'd prefer, but you've caught me at a bad moment. I've had a long day, I'm short of sleep, and I'm too tired to lie.'

'Yes, but you choose whether to speak the truth or whether to lie the way other people select trumps when they're playing cards,' Nancy said. 'What's the new lady like? There has to be one.'

'There is a candidate,' Griffin said. 'Although she's not yet aware that she's been nominated.'

He took a brief, inward glance at the divorcee from Marylebone. The way he felt just now, he'd yawn in her face. 'Nor,' he went on, 'whether she'll feel inclined to accept the honour. The fact is that I'm over forty now, and the birds don't perch quite as readily as they used to.'

'Poor old George,' Nancy said. Her tone lacked sympathy, he thought.

The way this was going, he was on to a dead loss. He should pretend to make a pass, to account for his presence, and leave. But then what? It had all seemed peaceful and quiet in the boot when Nancy had opened the front door, but something had to be done with Tauber before tomorrow morning. He was committed to Nancy now. It was too late to change his mind.

'How about you?' Griffin asked, pouring himself another slug of gin. 'Still nursing for that agency? You haven't gone to some hospital full time yet?' Which was more of a prayer than a question.

'I decided against it,' Nancy said. 'I prefer to work when I choose. It's nice to have some free time now and then.'

Thank God for that. 'Like now, by any chance?' he asked.

'Until next week. Why?' she enquired suspiciously.

'Someone I know needs a bit of private nursing, for a few days.

It'd be worth, say, a hundred quid,' he suggested. Christ, he was spending money like water. What a lousy job this had turned out to be.

'Well . . .' Nancy hesitated. She was a practical lady in some ways, if not in others. Money, she was practical about. 'Where would I have to go?'

'Nowhere,' Griffin said. 'He's outside now. I'll bring him in.'

He was out of the door while her mouth was still open in surprise, and before the protests were formed. Get the bastard indoors. At least that would be one bridge crossed.

Griffin ripped the adhesive tape from Tauber's hands and feet, and removed the lint from his mouth. Getting him out of the boot proved to be a problem. Finally, Griffin managed to sit him up, and heave him over one shoulder.

'He's passed out,' Griffin remarked, as he staggered into the living room, and kicked the door closed. 'He was in an accident. He's been bleeding a bit.'

Nancy became brisk, professional and dextrous. Griffin helped her remove Tauber's jacket, and lay him out on the settee.

While Nancy cut off Tauber's shirt with a pair of scissors, Griffin quickly searched his jacket. There was a passport, bearing Tauber's photograph, but it appeared that his name was Eric Groman and his nationality was American.

That foxed Griffin. If they had provided Tauber with a passport in readiness, that implied agreement on his part. So why had George Griffin been brought in?

Unless his cover was Eric Groman, citizen of the USA, and it was mere coincidence. But for some reason, Griffin had assumed that his cover would be continental, probably West German or Austrian.

'This man's been shot,' Nancy said sharply. She had got the dressing off. Griffin was glad to see that Tauber was bleeding very little now, and congratulated himself on his first aid.

'That's right,' Griffin agreed. 'It was a shooting accident.' Nancy stood up. 'I'll send for an ambulance.'

'He can't go into hospital,' Griffin said hurriedly. 'He got mixed up with the wrong sort of people. I tried to warn him, but

27

he thought he knew better. He was in this shooting gallery, and a bullet ricochetted. Quite unintentional, but it would look bad if anyone started asking questions.'

'It'll look a damn sight worse for him if he doesn't get proper care and treatment,' Nancy said sharply. 'I'm not a doctor.'

'For Christ's sake,' Griffin said tiredly, 'you're an experienced theatre sister. You're as good as most doctors, and a bloody sight better than some. It won't do any harm to have a look at him. I don't think he's badly hurt.'

That was by Griffin's definition. If he had been badly hurt, he would be dead or dying by now and this merchant was still breathing, and a slight trace of colour was returning to his face.

Nancy stared at him mutinously. 'Do the angel of mercy bit,' Griffin said. 'Pretend you found him in the front garden, and your phone's not working.'

Nancy bent over Tauber again, and then went into the kitchen. Griffin lay down wearily. The world was taking on a definite haze and sound was blurred. He must not close his eyes, but if only he could . . .

Nancy came back, wheeling a trolley on which were a number of shining instruments. She's going to bloody operate, he thought light-headedly.

He watched the moving trolley through half open eyes. The number of times he had shoved a different sort of trolley around at Portsmouth. One dozen cardigans, stroke thirty-three, blue, for knitwear; six dozen nylons, stroke forty-nine, bronze, for hosiery; two dozen shorts, grey, lined, stroke eighty-one, one dozen shorts, grey, unlined, stroke twenty-two, for boys' wear . . .

Griffin was not aware of any passage of time. He sat up with a jerk. Nancy was looking at him. Her lips were compressed.

'How is he?' he asked, unable to suppress a yawn.

'Apart from the wound,' Nancy said, 'he appears to have sustained a severe blow, which is why he's still unconscious. In fact, I'm surprised his neck's not broken.'

'He fell downstairs,' Griffin explained.

'Where?'

'At this shooting gallery.'

'I see,' Nancy said. 'Well, I don't think his condition is serious, though he'll need rest. It was a very shallow wound, and I've got the bullet out.'

That lousy cigarette case must be faulty, Griffin thought. Shallow wound? It was supposed to be suitable for a quiet assassination. He was glad that Tauber was not going to die, but he felt aggrieved just the same. He objected to weapons that did not work properly.

Suddenly, he saw what Nancy was doing. Galvanized into action, he sprang across the room, took the telephone receiver from her, and replaced it. 'There's no need to make any phone calls,' he said.

'I've done all I can,' Nancy said firmly.

'You said yourself he was all right,' Griffin argued. 'He could stay here. You'd be paid . . .'

'I don't want to be paid,' Nancy said. She lifted the receiver again.

'Nancy,' Griffin pleaded, 'if he goes into hospital, I'm in all kinds of trouble.'

She stopped dialling, and looked up at him. 'Were you in the shooting gallery when it happened?'

'No, but . . .'

'There was no shooting gallery,' Nancy said. She bent over the phone again. 'Perhaps you know that, perhaps you don't. Either way I can't get involved in something like this.'

'I'm only asking you to take care of him,' Griffin said.

'They use very small bullets in shooting galleries,' Nancy said. 'This was much larger.'

She had finished dialling. Griffin could hear the ringing tone. 'Nine millimetre,' Griffin said.

Her eyes widened. Griffin heard the squawk as the ambulance service answered. 'You send for them,' he said, 'and I'm in it right up to here.'

'Hold on,' Nancy said into the phone. 'I must,' she said to Griffin. 'I think he'll be all right, but suppose something went wrong? Suppose he died?'

'Then you'd see me tried for murder,' Griffin said.

Nancy stood, holding the receiver, her hand over the mouth-piece. Griffin heard the squawky voice, 'Hullo . . . hullo . . . hullo . . .'

Nancy replaced the receiver, and shook her head helplessly. 'Are you lying to me again?'

Griffin showed her the cigarette case, and how a nine milli-metre bullet was fired from a concealed aperture. He explained that it was a souvenir he had acquired during his army days and that he had forgotten it was loaded.

Then he talked very fast. 'I swear it was an accident,' he said 'but the police wouldn't believe that. His name's Eric Groman. He's an American.' He showed her Tauber's forged passport. 'I think he's Mafia. I don't know what they're doing over here. I only got mixed up in the whole thing by chance at a drinking club I use, but it'll take me a day or two to contact his friends and explain what happened. You'll be all right,' he added hastily, 'no one'll know he's here. I can't force you to help me, but it's prison or worse for me if you refuse. I can't say "for old times' sake", be-cause I expect you wish we'd never even met, although why the hell I ever fancied Maisie at the time, I'll never know. There's one more thing I have to tell you, darling, if you can look after him for a couple of days. You'll have to keep him doped up. Don't let him come round. He's a dangerous bastard.'

Griffin nearly went to sleep on the motorway on his way back to London out of sheer exhaustion. He did not suppose that Nancy believed all that stuff about the Mafia, but then she would not have believed the truth either. The main thing was that, reluc-tantly and nervously, she had agreed that Tauber could stay, on the strict understanding that, if his condition deteriorated, he must go into hospital come what may. Griffin had agreed to that, since he thought the risk was marginal. Tauber was as strong as a bull.

He had, to be honest with himself, panicked over nothing. Tauber would be fit to travel in no time. All he had to do was explain the slight delay.

It was six o'clock when Griffin crawled into bed in the silent flat. He set the alarm for nine am and closed his eyes. Then he remembered that he had not developed those bloody photographs. Oh, hell, that could wait until the morning. He must have three hours sleep.

But his head was pounding and throbbing relentlessly. He tottered into the bathroom, took three aspirin, went back to bed and waited for them to work. As long as you go on getting hangovers, he told himself, you're not an alcoholic. But he did not know whether to believe it or not. If you used those standards, he thought, as he slid into delightful oblivion, he had not been an alcoholic since he was seventeen years old.

CHAPTER FOUR

George's father was a coal merchant. He had borrowed every penny he could to set up his own business, and achieved this aim three weeks before the Second World War broke out. His assets comprised one cart and two weary cart horses which were kept in the tumbledown stable at the back of the house.

'And the goodwill,' George's father would add, during the not infrequent discussions on his failings as a business man.

'Goodwill,' George's mother said scornfully. 'Good nothing. You were cheated over that. They saw you coming.' She did not approve of her husband's entrepreneurial ambitions.

Sometimes, during the school holidays, when George was a small boy, he used to go with his father on his rounds, sitting on the back of the cart between the sacks, while the horses clopped and plodded their blinkered way forward. When they stopped to deliver coal, George would help his father heave the hundred-weight sacks on to his back, or at least his father allowed him to think that he was helping, and gave him a grin, his teeth flashing white in his blackened face.

But that came to an end. 'It's not good enough,' his mother said angrily. George was sitting sulkily, stripped naked on the kitchen table, while his mother scrubbed him furiously with carbolic soap and water and a rough flannel.

'Ow,' George said, wriggling. 'That hurts.'

'You be quiet and sit still,' his mother said.

'The boy enjoys it,' his father said.

'Yes, and then I have to try and get him clean,' his mother said, rubbing until George thought his skin would come off. 'Well, I'm not doing it any more. If you want to drag him round on that filthy old cart, you can wash him in future.'

His father shrugged in resignation, and went out to bed down the horses.

At the time, George did not realize that they were poor. Everyone else that he knew was the same, and it did not occur to him that it was possible to live differently. Arguments which he drowsily heard when half asleep only made sense to him later.

'I was always against it,' his mother said, her voice tight. 'You and your daft ideas. We've been in debt ever since, I'm fed up to the back teeth with trying to make ends meet.'

'I wasn't to know war was going to break out,' his father's deep voice said.

'All right, but you could have gone into munitions. You still could. You'd make twice as much money, you'd work regular hours, no dirty horses to clean up after, it'd be clean . . .'

'I've always wanted my own business,' his father said obstinately.

'Oh, yes, I've heard all that,' his mother said, shrilly. 'Be your own master. You work like a coolie, doing coolie's work. You can never get yourself clean, you're always tired, the back yard smells of dung but you don't care, you've got your own business. Suppose you had to go into the army? What then? Do you expect me to carry sacks of coal around on my back?'

George's mother always won these arguments. She had a fluent gift of words which his father lacked.

'The war might end before then,' his father said sullenly. 'It can't go on for ever.'

George was sleepily surprised at this talk of his father going into the army. He thought that only young men went into the army, like Leslie's brother, Maurice. His father was old. He must be, since he was his father.

But not long afterwards, his father came into George's bedroom one night and sat on the bed. 'Your dad's got to go away for a while,' he said. 'I've been called up. Your mother's a bit upset about it.' He brooded silently for a while. 'So mind you're a good boy,' he said, at last.

Men came and went, looked at the horses, studied dog-eared account books, sucked their teeth, and shook their heads.

Finally, his father clasped hands with one of them and the horses disappeared along with the stocks of coal and the cart.

George was rather excited, and looking forward to seeing his father in uniform, but he simply left the house one day in his ordinary clothes carrying a suitcase, and did not come back. A few days later, the suitcase was delivered. It contained his ordinary clothes.

George's mother looked pinched and strained for a while, and her temper was short. It was no use talking about comics or toys, she said. There was no money for things like that.

One day George felt ill, the doctor diagnosed mumps, and he was sent to bed, where he was quite happy to stay and be waited on. When he was allowed up, he found that they had acquired a lodger, Stan, a skilled worker at the Supermarine factory.

Comics were allowed again, and Stan sometimes bought him little presents, took him to the Sports Centre and paid for him to take a paddle boat out on the boating lake.

George's mother seemed happier and relaxed. She started using lipstick again, and wore nice clothes which George did not remember seeing before.

Stan installed a splendid radio set with a short wave. Occasionally, George was allowed to stay up and twiddle the knobs, straining his ears to see if he could receive America through the hissing and crackling.

'Come on,' Stan said. 'See if you can get the Jack Benny show.'

'How old are you, Stan?' George asked one night.

'What a question,' his mother said, smiling, her voice almost girlish.

'Well, my dad's in the army,' George said. 'Why don't they make you go into the army?'

'Someone's got to stay at home and build the aeroplanes,' his mother said.

'Yes,' Stan said. 'We can't make cigarette lighters all the time.'

His mother laughed as though that were funny, although George did not see the joke.

One Sunday afternoon, his mother was busy in the kitchen, rolling and slapping pastry, flour up to her elbows. She was preparing Stan's evening meal. Stan always worked on Sundays.

'Oh, for goodness sake, get out from under my feet,' she said, harassed. 'Go and play with Leslie.'

He walked out into the sultry, summer air, along the street, taking care not to tread on the cracks between the paving stones, past the corner grocers' shop, down the hill, past the gap, where some of the houses had been bombed and along the cut which led to Leslie's back garden.

He pushed open the wooden gate, walked by the patch of sooty vegetables which Leslie's father grew, and stopped to look at the rabbits which scuffled nervously in clumsy wooden hutches. One hutch was empty. Leslie would have had rabbit for Sunday dinner.

The little house seemed very quiet and he wondered if there was anyone in. A large mangle stood outside the open back door, and he turned the handle experimentally, and watched the big wooden rollers, as the cogs groaned round. His mother had a mangle with small, rubber rollers, which she thought was an improvement. George liked this one.

He went through the scullery and into the kitchen. There was no one there, but they might be in the front room. They sometimes sat in there on Sundays.

He wandered into the airless, narrow passage. He was right. There was someone in the front room. He went in.

Maurice was on the sofa with a girl. It was a few moments before they realized he was there, and he watched them curiously.

Maurice's khaki tunic hung over a chair. The girl was making soft noises. Her fingers picked at Maurice's broad braces.

When they saw him, the girl sat up, her face flushed. Maurice looked startled, and then his lips twisted in a wry grin, and he said 'Hullo young George.'

'Is Leslie in?' George asked.

'No. Mum and dad took him to the recreation ground. They won't be back till tea time.'

35

'Oh.' George thought of going to the recreation ground himself but there was a comic on the armchair. George picked it up. 'Can I look at this until he gets back?'

A look passed between Maurice and the girl, which he could not interpret. Both seemed to be breathing heavily, which George thought was odd, since they had only been lying down.

'You'd better go on home,' Maurice said.

'Mum told me to come and play with Leslie,' George said. Maurice fished in his pocket. 'Here's a tanner,' he said. 'Go and buy some sweets.'

George took the sixpence. 'What do you want me to bring?'

'Nothing,' Maurice said, laughing for some reason. 'Eat 'em all yourself.'

'Coo, thanks,' George said, and went quickly before Maurice changed his mind. He left, as he had come in, through the back door. He had never known anyone use the front door in Leslie's house.

He forgot that it was hot, and ran to the nearest sweet shop which would be open, although, since it was in the main road, by the tram stop, that was not very near.

There were still a number of sticky, sweet objects which were not on ration, and he browsed carefully, before buying. He decided he had better eat them all before he went home. His mother had a tiresome habit of equating lack of sweets with dental health. But, as so often in George Griffin's life, his precautions were inadequate.

'Who's been giving you money for sweets?' his mother demanded, looking at his fingers.

'Maurice,' George said, falling back on the truth. 'Leslie wasn't in.'

'Don't blame me when all your teeth fall out,' his mother said. But it was an abstracted automatic response, and George knew that she was not really angry. 'I don't suppose you want any tea now.'

'Yes, I do,' George said. 'I'm hungry.' He sat down, and spread jam on his bread and butter. 'Mum,' he said, thinking of something else.

'What?' his mother said, tiredly.

'Maurice was there with a girl, and he had his hand up her skirt, and she was making funny noises. What were they doing?'

That was when his mother's face flamed scarlet and she lashed out, catching him a stinging blow across the face. 'Don't you ever say anything like that again,' she cried, in a high pitched voice.

George fell sideways off his chair, and landed on the floor, clutching his piece of bread and jam. He was so astounded that he almost forgot to cry although the pain soon reminded him.

Later, he related these puzzling events to Leslie, who was able to explain. 'They were having a fuck, stupid,' he said.

George rather resented being called stupid, especially since he instinctively suspected that Leslie's smug air of knowledge was new found, or he would have heard about this having a fuck, whatever that might be, before. 'I know that,' George said condescendingly. 'I was just testing you.'

'No you weren't,' Leslie jeered. 'You didn't know.'

'Yes, I did.'

'No, you didn't.'

It ended in a scuffle, after Leslie, who was slightly less quick-witted than George, had been provoked into relating precisely what a fuck was.

Some time later, George realized that Leslie had got certain details wrong, but by then the whole subject had become a matter of deep personal interest.

'Oh, my God,' George's mother said. 'Have you two been fighting again?'

'Leslie started it,' George said. He was awed and impressed by the blood which had suddenly poured from Leslie's nose, and stained his shirt, by the way the much bigger, curly haired boy had crumpled and wept.

The blow itself had been largely accidental, no more than another of the vague, windmilling swings which they were accustomed to fling at one another. But there had been something different about this one. It had landed with a frightening smack, stinging George's knuckles, and Leslie's head had jerked back, and he had cried out with pain.

They never fought again, after that. They remained friends, but there was a new element in Leslie's attitude, one of cautious respect, which George found satisfying and pleasant.

He saw his father in uniform when he came home on leave. George chattered, and wanted to know all about the army, but his father only gave brief answers. His thoughts seemed to be elsewhere.

One night, George woke up, briefly. Voices were raised in the room below. There was a thumping and clattering, and then silence. George dozed off again.

In the morning, his mother and father ate breakfast in silence. It was an important day for George. He was going to play football in the junior trial game. He chewed his spam fritters and indulged in his favourite day dream in which he scored the winning goal. Only when he got up to fetch his football boots, did it occur to him.

'Where's Stan?' he asked.

'He's gone,' his father said.

'Gone where?'

'Just gone,' his father said. 'Listen, what time's this match of yours? I might come and watch you.'

His mother took the plates away and started to wash up.

George's father was killed in Germany, in April 1945. George cried when he was told. When the tears dried, he set out to remember his father, concentrating fiercely on some image of the man, which he could preserve, and keep with him.

What he saw was a burly figure, dressed in khaki battledress, standing on the touch-line, shouting 'Come on, George,' a few seconds before George ignominiously missed an open goal.

'Good heavens, Griffin, a crippled old lady could have put that one in,' his sports master remarked.

George turned, and looked at his father, ashamed. His father gave him a huge wink, and said, 'Never mind, my son. There'll be another time.'

But there was not, and George never did play football for his school.

In May, a sergeant arrived who had served with his father. He drank tea, and spoke quietly to his mother and patted her consolingly on the shoulder. He gave her a large envelope containing personal odds and ends belonging to his father, and about something else, he said, 'Perhaps the boy should have this.' His mother nodded.

The sergeant took George aside, and said, 'How old are you, laddie?'

'Nine,' George said.

'Old enough to have a watch,' the sergeant said. 'This was your dad's.'

He handed George a wristwatch. George strapped it on his wrist in silence. The watch was loose.

'You'll have to make another hole,' the sergeant said.

'Yes.'

'I don't suppose it makes much sense to you,' the sergeant said, 'but your dad was a brave man. You can take my word for that.'

'Were you there?'

'I saw what happened,' the sergeant said. He lit a cigarette and inhaled deeply. He blew out a long stream of smoke, and watched it rise lazily into the air. 'The funny thing is,' he said at last, 'I think they'd had enough, but your dad wasn't having any. It was as if he wanted to kill every last one of them himself.'

George swore a private oath then that he would wear his father's watch for the rest of his life. But it had only cost five shillings, and was not designed for life long service. Two years later, it stopped for good, worn out. George kept it in a drawer for a while, but when he left home he forgot about the watch, and when his mother cleared out his room she threw it away.

Stan moved back three months after the sergeant's visit. Early in 1946, George's mother said, 'We're going to move. It's a lovely modern bungalow, just outside town. We're ever so lucky to get it. You'll like it there. Much better than this horrible little house.'

George did not know what she was talking about. 'I like it here,' he said.

'Well, you'll like it there better,' his mother said. She fiddled with the broad, gold band of her wedding ring for a few seconds.

'You'll have a dad again too,' she said. 'Stan. You like Stan, don't you?'

The sprawling and unlovely conglomeration of Victorian houses and scattered bungalows unjustly dignified by the name of village was on the outskirts of Southampton. It was there that George Griffin moved with his mother and new step-father.

George could not trace the course of the transition, but over the next few years, Stan changed. He lost his jokey affability, completely with George, and partly with his mother. There came a time when George could not remember an evening when Stan's breath did not carry the heavy, sickly smell of beer. Sometimes, his mother went to the pub with Stan, but usually she did not.

George tried to keep out of Stan's way when he came home from the pub. Then, his manner was surly and his temper short. George was quick on his feet, but he could not always avoid the slamming, heavy blows which Stan would sometimes aim at his head as punishment for some wrong-doing, fancied or real.

His mother never tried to intervene. To her, Stan could do no wrong, and even on those days when her face was pale, her lips were pinched tight and there was a bruised swelling on her face, she never uttered a word of complaint about Stan, at least not in George's hearing.

When he was eleven years old, George took the entrance examination to the grammar school, and failed to achieve the required standard, to nobody's surprise, least of all George's or his teachers'.

George, it was deemed, would benefit most from an education at a secondary modern school, and that was where he went. He left, four years later, at the age of fifteen, totally unremembered, except for one thing.

George discovered boxing at school, and took to it like a duck to water. He was fast, moved well, studied the art with the intensity of a scholar and loved it.

For a time, the sports master crowed with delight. He had never come across a boy with such a natural built-in talent. He had visions of coaching George for the county championships, and more than that, of basking in reflected glory as

George became schoolboy champion, and possibly, who knew, of travelling abroad with George who would be the white hope of his country's boxing team.

George could do it. George had it.

George, for his part, revelled in this new found approval and worked earnestly to increase it. But he learned too much, too fast, partly from instinct and application, partly from going to see every professional fight he could.

A tinge of doubt entered the sports master's mind, and he spoke to George, man to man, which was his way. But when, before the whole school, George took part in the boxing tournament, he was disqualified for persistent rabbit punching.

For a boy, George's armoury had become extraordinary, and he practised and mastered not only those punches authorized under the Queensbury Rules, but such variants as the rabbit punch, the kidney punch, holding, butting, pulling an opponent on to a punch, gouging his eye with the thumb of his glove and the use of his elbows in unexpected ways.

The sports master was distressed, but being a nice man, he had another long talk to George, man to man, and gave him a second chance. George boxed for his school against another school in Bournemouth which prided itself on its prowess in the noble art.

They duly lost, as expected, every bout except one, and that was George's. George won, and was vigorously booed out of the ring. He left his opponent not knowing which day it was, dazed and bleeding slightly from a cut at the corner of his eyebrow, inflicted by George's head, and freely from the nose, where George's elbow had found its mark.

George could not understand the anger and disgust which his victory generated; why his headmaster expressed cutting, contemptuous distaste before going off to apologize to his opposite number; why his sports master could hardly bear to speak to him.

George knew that he had taken in everything which his sports master had said to him. He had been careful to turn his opponent so that all his illegal tactics took place on the referee's blind side, and shown great skill in doing so. What was more, it had worked.

The referee had been unable to fault him, and had declared him the winner. He had won! So what was all the fuss about?

Sport? Boxing was not a sport, it was a contest. It was beating the other man, it was winning. Your opponent had the same chance, it was up to him. George could not see it at all.

Later, when his sports master had calmed down, he tried to explain to George, using words like sportsmanship. George listened, and then endeavoured to put his point of view.

'Look, sir,' he said, 'you were in the RAF. You flew bombers, didn't you.' George much admired his sports master's war record, which included collecting the DFC.

'What's that got to do with it?'

Like all the children of his time, George knew a lot about the war. All adults talked about the war, there were comics about the war, books about the war, things on radio about the war, newsreels about the war.

'Well,' George said, 'I was only a little kid, but I can just remember when the Germans bombed Southampton, and being woken up, and taken to the Anderson shelter, and the noise and everything. And my mother saying what devils they must be, flying up there, and dropping bombs on women and children. And my father—my real father—saying that it was a dirty game, but we were doing exactly the same thing.'

'Not intentionally,' his sports master said. 'We were given particular targets, and we bombed them as accurately as we could.' He did not seem to like George's line of argument.

'Oh. I'm not saying it was wrong, sir,' George said, hastily. He gazed at the fresh faced, auburn-haired young man with obvious and genuine admiration. 'I mean you must have killed thousands of Jerries personally. Thousands of them. But when you see the newsreels, you know, all the damage and that, they're all houses, aren't they, all flattened, places people lived, miles of them?'

'We weren't responsible for the targets we were given,' his sports master said. 'And anyway, it's got nothing to do with what happened at Bournemouth.'

George strove eagerly to convey the connection which was in his mind. 'Well, we had to do more to them than they did to us to

42

win the war,' he said. 'And then there was the Atom Bomb,' he said, warming to his theme. 'That place in Japan. A whole city wiped out, people burned walking along the street, their clothes on fire and all that. But it did the trick, didn't it, sir? It won the war.'

'We're not talking about a war,' his sports master said, irritably. 'We're talking about boxing. There's no comparison.'

George could not see the difference. If you were in a fight, you won, if you could, any way you could, and people like referees were there to be circumvented. If they caught you out that was your own fault.

But George's philosophy found no favour and he never boxed for his school again. They could not stop him using the gym, but none of the other boys would spar with him and after a while he stopped going.

When he left school, it was without regret, either on his part or anyone else's.

Stan had left Supermarine at the end of the war—and now had a well paid job at a large factory in Eastleigh. George started work there as an apprentice, Stan having used some influence.

'I've done as much for you as I would if you were my own,' Stan said, unctuously. 'Keep your nose clean, look out for the foreman, and you'll be all right.'

It was a long cycle ride to Eastleigh, but George rather enjoyed it in the early morning, the chill, fresh air on his cheeks as he free-wheeled down the long hill which led past the 'White Swan', and over the Itchen river. From there on, past the airport and through Eastleigh, it was reasonably level, and he could hurry or dawdle, according to the time, so as to clock in at exactly eight am.

George soon decided that he would like to get into the Testing Department, where young men appeared to do nothing but smoke and twiddle mysterious knobs all day, but Stan looked doubtful, and reminded George of his negligible academic qualifications. He was lucky to be in as an apprentice. Later on, he might be able to ask for a transfer, but in the meantime it was up to George to make a good impression.

43

It was far from clear to George how one made a good impression at his lowly level. He was eager to learn, but no one seemed to be teaching him anything of any interest. He spent most of his time fetching and carrying whatever anyone else wanted, including cups of tea, and falling for ancient gags like being sent to the stores for a 'long stand'. George waited for half an hour before one of the storekeepers said, 'OK son, you've had your long stand. You can piss off now.' They all thought that was very funny.

'You're in too much of a hurry,' Stan said. 'It takes years to learn a trade that'll stand you in good stead for the rest of your life.'

And keep you out of the Army if there's a war, George thought, but he did not say it.

The evenings at the Social Club were the best part. George played billiards and snooker with a few others, smoked cigarettes, as befitted a working man at leisure, and drank half pints of bitter.

The barman who served him when he bought his rounds of drinks, never queried his age. At fifteen, George was a big lad, and looked older. He was five feet eight inches tall, well built, and weighed ten stone. The trouble was that he never grew much after that, until his stomach began to expand, many years later.

The women in the factory bothered George in all kinds of ways. There were so many of them. In some sheds, nearly all the operatives were women, mostly in their twenties and married. They were loud and laughing and bold eyed with the confidence born of numbers and the effect they well knew they had on youngsters like George.

For some time now, the sap had been rising vigorously in George, but he had failed to find a girl at school willing to show a personal interest in this phenomenon. The women disturbed him, and induced reckless, blatant fantasies.

Eventually, one such fantasy nearly came true. One of the women, shapely and buxom under her overall, paused, stared into his eyes, and said, 'What are you looking at? Haven't you seen a pair of tits before?'

44

George mumbled incoherently and tried to retreat, but a small, giggling group had formed around him. Piles of packing cases hid them from the rest of the area.

The woman grinned at him, with arrogant pride in her sexuality. 'Go on,' she said. 'Have a feel.'

She grabbed his hand, and clamped it to her left breast. George tried to take it away, but she held it there, watching his face through half closed eyes, her lips parted in a smile which showed her white teeth and the tip of her tongue.

George lost any sense of where he was. The breast under his fingers was warm and soft and rounded, and he could feel her nipple slowly rising.

'He likes it,' the woman told the others.

'Too bloody true he does,' one of the others said, looking at George's trousers.

'He walks around like that, this one,' the woman said. 'It's all he thinks about.'

She looked down at his trousers herself, and slowly traced a pattern with the tip of one finger. George stiffened, and moaned indistinctly. He did not care that he was in the middle of a factory, that he was a spectacle, the subject of their game. All he knew was that he was being driven frantic.

'We'd better do something about it,' the woman said. 'Put the randy little bugger out of his misery.'

They took hold of him, and forced him against a packing case. George struggled. Their hands were rough, as they grabbed and pushed him, and at first he did not realize what they were doing.

And then, suddenly, there was a flutter of alarm, they released him and were gone.

George shakily pulled himself erect. Why had they stopped? He wanted them to come back for the last, glorious pulsating seconds.

He found himself looking at the foreman. The foreman was standing a few feet away. The foreman watched him in silence.

'I didn't like the job, that's all,' George said. 'So I left.'

Stan roared with laughter. 'That's not what I heard,' he said. 'I heard the foreman caught you having a wank.'

'Oh, Stan, no,' George's mother said. 'That can't be true.'

'I swear to God,' Stan said. 'He was behind some packing cases, looking at the women and tossing himself off.'

George caught the look on his mother's face, and a cold controlled, vicious fury took hold of him. 'That's not what happened,' he said tightly, 'but even if it were I think that's better than screwing another man's wife when her husband's been called up into the army, don't you?'

He was addressing Stan, who stopped laughing. His mother turned pale, and shrank back. There was a moment's silence.

'What's he talking about?' his mother enquired plaintively, looking at Stan.

'Oh, mum,' George said. An unutterable sense of hopeless sadness was interleaved with his fury. 'Did you think I didn't know? Even little kids have got eyes and ears.' He pointed at Stan. 'Dad came home on leave and threw him out. Then he went back and killed himself.'

'Your father died in action,' his mother said. Her voice was querulous.

'The Germans would have surrendered,' George said. 'But dad kept on firing. The sergeant told me. He wanted to be dead. He didn't want to come back after what had happened.'

A coal fire was burning in the living room, and it was hot and stuffy. There was too much furniture, and little space to move about.

Stan said nothing. He took off his jacket and threw it down. With his foot, he started to push chairs aside, his eyes fixed on George.

'Perhaps there were reasons for you, mum,' George said. 'Perhaps you couldn't stand being alone. Perhaps there were things about dad I don't know. If it had been another soldier even, I might have understood it. But not him.' He looked at Stan, who pushed a table against the wall. 'He could have gone, he was younger than dad, but he didn't. He'd rather do essential war work, go in on Sundays and get paid double time, and then take Monday off and flog the cigarette lighters and ashtrays he'd made round the pubs. He'd rather let other men do the fighting,

46

and be able to flash his money around, and screw their wives.'

George had finished. He had assembled these thoughts gradually over the years since his father died. Only slowly had it all dropped into place as he grew older, as he learned more, as he understood that men and women lie and cheat and need feel no shame if they deceive themselves as well as others. And that his mother was not only a person who cared for him, and no doubt loved him, but a woman as well.

Stan spoke for the first time. His voice was quiet, deadly, and measured. 'You're an evil-minded little shit,' he said. 'I've been too soft with you. Now you're going to get what you deserve. After that, you can get out. We've finished with you.'

Stan began to advance. He was in no hurry. He intended to enjoy himself. George retreated. It was like a replay of those occasions when Stan came home in a surly mood from the pub. But this was different. This would be no back handed swing across the face, although even that made George's head swim, and his eyes water. Stan meant to beat him half to death.

George skirted the settee as he moved back. Stan reached out a hand, and shoved it away on its castors. He was bigger, stronger and heavier than George, who now had nothing between him and Stan, and only the window behind him.

For the first time, for real, George tried using the element of surprise, which was to serve him well in later years, and other places. Stan was expecting him to behave as he always had done before, to crouch, to cower, to hide his head behind his arms in an attempt to protect himself from the big man's superior strength.

Instead, George suddenly rushed at Stan, ducked under the swinging fist which Stan, taken aback, was late in releasing, and butted him in the stomach.

Stan grunted, and stumbled back, off balance. Then he yelled and fell over a chair, as George kicked him in the crutch.

But the man was strong, and began to claw himself to his feet almost at once. George spared the time for one more punch, more for his own satisfaction than anything else. It landed on Stan's nose, and he felt the bone break under his knuckles. Stan roared with pain, and George flung open the door and left as fast as he could.

He had no intention of seeing the fight through to a conclusion. Stan was hurt, but not badly enough, and there was murder in his face now. If George remained, he would be on the receiving end next time, and he cared for that idea not at all. Then, as on later occasions, George was a good judge of when to use his legs, and depart from the scene.

Outside, George ran until he was exhausted. The first bus that came along happened to be going to Portsmouth.

CHAPTER FIVE

It was the store Christmas party, and the staff manageress, who conceived it to be her duty to induce a suitable degree of merry-making all round, smiled at him sweetly and said, 'Not dancing, George? Come on. There are enough girls to ask. Or do you expect them to ask you?'

George was painfully aware how many girls there were in the store. He looked at their trim stockinged legs disappearing under their trim skirts every day of his life as he bent down and replenished the under counter stocks.

'I can't dance, miss,' George mumbled, blushing.

'Of course you can. There's nothing to it. I'll show you.' And she took his hand and led him on to the dance floor.

The staff manageress must have been all of forty, but she had a small, neat figure, and her blouse was nearly transparent. She wore her red hair swept back, which showed that she had no lines on her forehead, even if the skin over her prominent cheek bones was rather tight.

'We'll start with the night club shuffle,' she instructed George. 'Just move your feet a few inches, and I'll follow you. No, don't look down. Put your arm right round me. That's it.'

Everyone knew that the staff manageress was having it off with the district superintendent, Mr Bull, a bald, broad shouldered, pouchy faced man, who had Mrs Bull with him that night, since it was a warm, happy, social occasion for one and all, even Mrs Bull. In view of her liaison with Mr Bull, the staff manageress had been privately christened by the staff, not surprisingly, the Cow.

George soon learned the trick of shuffling more or less in time to the music, and concentrated on the fact that the Cow was

49

rotating herself against him in a slow and interesting kind of way.

When the dance ended, the staff manageress kept hold of his hand until a new one started, talking continuously in her rather high pitched, Lancashire accented voice about the store, and George's work, and how well he was doing.

George's hands became clammy, and his heart was pounding like a piledriver. She rested the back of her right hand, still clasped in his, against his chest, and smiled at him knowingly while talking about the forthcoming stocktaking.

When George thought that his trousers would burst under the strain, he huskily remarked how hot it was in here, and perhaps they could go for a walk outside.

The Cow laughed at him, said, 'Don't be a naughty boy, George,' and left him to talk animatedly to Mrs Bull.

George walked stiffly back to the bar, where Jim, the head porter, was amused but sympathetic. 'She's a prick teaser, that one,' he said confidentially in George's ear. 'She does it to everyone, son. She only wants to make you want it, she doesn't want to give it, except to that bald, bad tempered old bugger.' Like all the men in the store, Jim had suffered under the lash of Mr Bull's tongue.

The assistant manager, a nice, plump, well meaning man who was not temperamentally designed to be an ambitious chain store executive, practically quivered with fear whenever Mr Bull walked into the store.

'Have a drink and forget it,' Jim advised, handing George a half of bitter. George already had a whisky which someone had bought him, but he did not refuse. It seemed convenient to tip the whisky into the beer. The mixture went down easily, he discovered, and induced a pleasant glow.

George bought the next round, pouring the whisky into the half empty glass of beer. More rounds followed. George stuck to the agreeable concoction he had discovered.

After a while, he grew red faced, and started talking loudly and confidently. 'Time you called it a day,' Jim told him.

'One for the road,' George said, and ordered another round.

His recollection became patchy after that. He remembered holding the waist of some unknown girl, and roaring 'Conga!' as the line of people snaked away around the building in front of him. Later, someone, George himself, he suspected, started a breakaway movement aiming for Clarence Pier, and a nude midnight dip. George was the only one who arrived there.

He wondered whether to wait for the others where he was, or if they would expect to find him in the water.

'You'd better go home, son, before you get into trouble,' a kind policeman of the old school advised him.

George nodded, put his shoes and socks back on and set off. He was beginning to feel tired.

He was surprised when the pavement pivoted upwards and hit him. He lay where he was for a few moments, puzzled. Clearly he had not fallen, since he was unhurt. Strange. He scrambled back to his feet and moved on, keeping a close eye on that aberrant pavement. But although it happened twice more, it took him aback both times and he could not see how it was done.

George slithered into bed, but this time it was the bed which was moving. He spent the night in the lavatory clutching the WC like a long lost brother.

He lay in bed the whole of the following day, and gradually the will to live returned. His landlady did not disturb him, or ask any questions. She was used to lodgers who spent Sunday in bed. In any case, she rarely spoke to him. She provided clean bed linen at intervals, and collected his rent weekly, and that was it. Lodgers got a room. If they wanted home comforts, they went home.

George did not go home. Nor, to his knowledge did his mother ever try to find out where he had gone.

He had been lucky when he got off that bus in Portsmouth, since that was as far as it was going, and looked at the bombed-out shell of the Guildhall. He had two weeks pay in his pocket, one in lieu of notice, enough to pay a cautious landlady a week's rent in advance.

The first lady who took lodgers, to whom he was recommended, looked at his hands hanging at his sides, asked a question and slammed the door in his face. George learned from this experience, and bought a cheap fibre suitcase at a street market. Armed with this empty proof of his respectability, he found a room in a dingy terraced house near the dockyard.

The next thing he needed was a job and again, next day, he was lucky. JUNIOR PORTER, the notice said, in the window of the chain store near Commercial Road, AGED 18–20. GOOD PAY AND STAFF CONDITIONS. APPLY WITHIN.

George applied within, adjusting his age from fifteen to eighteen. It so happened that the warm-hearted assistant manager interviewed him. He did not query George's age, but was clearly worried by his inability to provide references. George felt that it would worry him even more, should he write to the factory in Eastleigh, and learn why they had parted company, and stuck to his story which concerned a wholesaler, for whom George had laboured hard and willingly, who had unfortunately gone bankrupt and moved up north, George knew not where.

The assistant manager was on the verge of making regretful noises, clearly loth though he was to do so, but he was won over when George revealed that his father had been killed in action and that his mother had died in the air raids on Southampton. The assistant manager's prominent eyes glistened slightly, and George got the job, which was not a bad job at all, as such jobs went.

The firm provided a heavily subsidized canteen on the premises, and George ate all he could at work, which saved him a fair bit of money. There was a staff discount on purchases in the store, and he was able gradually to build up a modestly serviceable wardrobe. The work itself was not unpleasant and George found it easy. He did not make mistakes, and he was popular with the department managers since he made it a habit to warn them when particular lines were running low in the stockroom. This gave them the chance to re-order in good time, and thus avoid Mr Bull's wrath and his acidly phrased annual reports which would damage their chances. Mr Bull regarded running out of a colour or size as the equivalent of high treason. In his terms, it probably was. Directors of the company were liable to wander in anonymously, unannounced, and browse round the counters, studying the displays and any gaps in sizes or colours which should not be there.

Should one of the all-powerful discover any such omission in any of the stores in Mr Bull's district, he could kiss his ambition to become national superintendent at Head Office goodbye. Consequently, Mr Bull was in a daily, constant state of nervous tension, continually on the alert for the errors of any manager or department manager who might ruin his chances of promotion.

On the Monday after his debauch, George returned to work ready to sign the pledge and devote himself to a life of sobriety and good works. But, oddly, he noticed that some of the girls looked at him with a certain respect and admiration which had been lacking so far. One of them was called Brenda. George casually asked her out, and she accepted.

He thought at first that Brenda was shy. Later, he discovered that she had very little to say. However, it was not her thought processes he was interested in.

For a while, George's career with the company bloomed. Everyone thought well of him. Even Mr Bull, having inspected his section of the stockroom, wrung out a grudging word of praise. 'You're going to be all right,' Jim said, as if he knew something. 'You mark my words.'

George did not quite see how. He supposed that, possibly, he might become head porter in twenty years time, when Jim retired, but that was an eternity, as impossible to comprehend as the extent of the universe.

It was the assistant manager who threw some light on Jim's cryptic assertion. Every night, the manager and assistant manager carried leather bags of money, the takings for the day, to the bank, and put them in the night safe. The porters acted as escorts.

On Saturdays, they adjourned to the nearest pub. The manager, a remote man, bought one round of drinks, his entertainment duty for the week, and then disappeared. On this Saturday, the assistant manager stayed on and detained George, who was due to go and meet Brenda.

'Something you might think about, George,' he said. 'You're

53

doing well. You're a bright chap. You've got brains. Mr Bull's noticed your good work. The thing is, have you got ambition?'

He rapped on the counter for another round of drinks. George lit a cigarette. He was not sure if he had ambition or not. He thought it would be pleasant to have a lot of money. Presumably that was the same thing.

'It's not often,' the assistant manager went on, 'that the company promote porters to department manager trainees, but if a man's clever, and young, and keen . . . well, it has happened. Do you follow my drift?'

'I think so,' George said, blinking at the new horizons which had suddenly opened up.

'You're not quite twenty-one yet,' the assistant manager said. 'But once you are, it so happens there's a new training course starting soon after. If you were to apply, and Mr Bull were to endorse it . . . this is all unofficial of course.' He tapped the side of his nose with his finger. 'I haven't said a word. I'm just dropping a hint that it could happen. So bear it in mind, and don't do anything to spoil your chances. A word to the wise, right?'

The assistant manager was a bit pissed, but that was nothing unusual. As he ran to meet Brenda, George thought that the world was turning into a pretty good place after all.

He had never dreamed that it was remotely possible for him to be trained for an executive job. Even the department managers were well paid. It was said that the manager of the giant store in Oxford Street earned more than ten thousand pounds a year, an incredible fortune to George Griffin in the 1950s.

Life was really handing it out to him on a plate. He was going to become rich, and he had found a girl who would. She had not yet, but he was sure she would before long.

She did. It was on George's eighteenth birthday, although, of course, Brenda thought it was his twenty-first. They sat in the pub most of the evening. George tried gin for the first time, and Brenda drank *crème de menthe*. There was a look in her eyes and she smiled at him a lot.

Afterwards, they went for a walk along the sea front. When they got to the quiet end, George led her down on to the beach.

He knew instinctively that she was ready.

Even so, he was taken aback by her urgency, then delighted, and responded to it in full.

Afterwards, he lay, panting heavily. Brenda pushed at him. 'Get off,' she said.

George rolled over on to the shingle, which crunched and slithered under his weight.

'You're heavy, and my bum's cold,' Brenda explained. She wriggled into her knickers, sat up, and pushed at her hair. 'Well, I suppose we'd better go then,' she said at last.

George continued to look forward to what became the regular climax to their meetings, but the preceding hours in a cinema or a pub, or on Sundays, in a bus into the country, seemed to drag a little.

Brenda had a round face and short dark hair. None of her features were outstanding in any way, but if you took the assembly all together, she was reasonably attractive. Her figure, delicate and well proportioned, was her best feature. But, George began to think, until she was lying down, she was, to be brutally frank, somewhat boring.

He was rather attracted to the girl in the tobacco kiosk near the dockyard, who joked with him when he bought his cigarettes every morning. But if he asked her out, he would have to lie to Brenda, who might get suspicious. And of course, he did not know whether the girl in the kiosk did or not, whereas Brenda definitely did, and he did not feel inclined to forgo this new found regularity yet.

He was surprised when Brenda sought him out one morning in a corner of the stockroom. 'Mind out,' he said, heaving boxes on to a trolley. 'Menswear are screaming for these shirts.'

'She wants to see us now,' Brenda said. Her face was pale and strained.

'What? Who? What's the matter with you?'

'You are quite certain, Brenda?' the staff manageress enquired. Her nose was wrinkled as though some unpleasant odour were emanating from the region of her desk.

'Yes, miss,' Brenda sniffled tearfully. 'I saw the doctor again this morning.'

The assistant manager was sitting uncomfortably in a corner. He disliked scenes like this, and said nothing.

'You might at least have had sufficient commonsense to take precautions,' the staff manageress said tartly to George.

George was the one who had been left standing. 'We did,' he said sullenly. 'Except for the first time.'

Somehow, as Brenda drew him urgently to her on the beach, it had not seemed possible to break off and fumble with the packet of Durex which he had optimistically bought from a barber some time before and hopefully carried around in his wallet.

'Do you love each other?' the staff manageress asked.

'Yes, miss,' Brenda said.

George's mouth had opened to say something else. He closed it again.

'Will your parents give their consent, Brenda?' the staff manageress asked. 'You are only eighteen, of course.'

'I think so, miss,' Brenda said tearfully. 'Things being what they are. But I don't know if you could talk to them, miss. Come with me, and say . . .' Her imagination ran out at that point, and her voice expired into a sob.

'Certainly,' the Cow said briskly. She would no doubt know exactly what to say. It occurred to George that this scene had been rehearsed when Brenda was in this office before. The staff manageress had the advantage of him. She not only knew her lines, but what her cue would be as well.

George cleared his throat. 'The thing is . . .' he began.

'Fortunately, there's no problem in your case, George,' the staff manageress said. 'You're twenty-one. There's no reason why you shouldn't get married.'

George opened his mouth again to point out that he was only eighteen and a few weeks. But somehow it seemed a bit late to start correcting that mistake.

'Did you say something?'

'No,' George said.

'Well, I think that's all,' the staff manageress said. 'George, you can stay for a few moments, please. I'd like a word with you.'

Brenda gave him a tremulous smile. 'I'll see you after work,' she said. The assistant manager looked unhappy, and avoided meeting George's eyes. He closed the door behind him.

George waited. The staff manageress began to write busily, as though she had forgotten George was there. Finally, she put her pen down, and looked up. The smell from her desk seemed to have got worse. She dusted her nostrils with a lace handkerchief.

'The welfare of the girls is my first concern,' she said. 'It's also my duty to provide whatever help and advice I can if they have any problems. You've taken advantage of Brenda, and now it's up to you to make it up to her. She's a nice girl, and in my opinion, you're luckier than you deserve.'

George shifted uneasily, and shoved his clenched fists deeper into the pockets of his brown overall. 'Is that all?'

'Not quite,' the Cow said. 'I believe someone misguidedly advised you to apply for executive training. For Brenda's sake, I wish that were possible. But I'm afraid you're quite unsuitable, George. I wouldn't bother to apply, if I were you. It would be a waste of time.'

'That's not up to you,' George said. 'It's nothing to do with you.'

'This company does not like immorality,' the staff manageress said piously. 'It demands high standards of conduct from its executives. You obviously don't know how to keep your hands to yourself. We have to safeguard our female staff. If you apply, you'll be turned down. You can take my word for that.'

George stared at her. The skin over her cheek bones was stretched more tautly than ever. It looked like parchment.

'You hypocritical old bag,' George said. 'Is that what you're going to tell old fat-guts in bed tonight?'

She smiled at him sweetly. 'Find another job, George,' she said. 'You have no future in this company whatever.'

Later, there were times when George thought that he should have run away, there and then, as far from Portsmouth as he could get. But Brenda clung to him, her vulnerability daring him to hurt her. And her mum and dad, although somewhat tight-lipped and artificial, did their best to pretend that it was all very romantic.

They were even married in church, and Brenda wore white. George stood beside her in his best suit. 'I will,' he said throatily, and sick apprehension lay in his guts like an iron weight.

That had passed. George had shaken it off on the train to Torquay for the honeymoon which Brenda's father was funding. So he was married. So what? Everyone got married sooner or later. In his case, it happened to be sooner, that was all.

Since George was only eighteen, he needed permission to get married. He wrote to his mother, explaining what he wanted, and added, by way of a PS, an invitation to the wedding. She returned formal permission, but did not write a letter. There was a note from Stan, though. 'Your mother will not be there. And keep your tart away from us. You're not wanted, neither of you.'

Brenda was put out when he told her the truth about his age. 'You told me you were twenty-one.'

'Well, I'm not.'

'You said you were.'

'Oh, for Christ's sake shut up about it,' George said.

Brenda sulked, but not for long. She needed George. Having a child without being married happened to other girls, but Brenda could not imagine it for herself. That gold ring was essential. Even now, the neighbours would raise sceptical eyebrows when the word 'premature' was casually dropped into the conversation later on, after she gave birth, but that was all right, good for a few days gossip, but no more. It was not like being stared at all the time as you grew fatter, with no ring and no husband.

The honeymoon dragged. There was a lot of sex, even if Brenda seemed a little less fervent than previously, but once they had done it night and morning, there were still twelve hours in between, only about four of which were occupied with eating.

It was chilly, and the beach was bleak and unwelcoming. They went out drinking one night, and Brenda was sick for the whole of the following day. George loyally did not suggest a drink again. They went to the cinema once. Halfway through, Brenda complained that it was stuffy. They got up to go, and she became dizzy in the foyer, and fainted into George's arms.

They talked desultorily now and then, but Brenda rarely initiated a conversation, and George became tired with passing remarks about the view, or the weather, and took to reading paperbacks.

'You're always reading,' Brenda said edgily. 'Talk to me.'

'What about?'

'I don't know. Anything. The way you act, people would think we were an old married couple, instead of being on our honeymoon.'

There were other moments, close together at night, huddled under the eiderdown.

'You do love me,' Brenda whispered. 'Don't you? Say you love me.'

'I love you,' George said.

'I love you,' Brenda said.

That, George knew, was the way it should be, and he could feel the truth of it when he held her slim, naked body pressed against him under the bedclothes.

It was during the day when an apprehensive lump seemed to settle in his stomach, trivial occasions, meaningless in themselves, like after breakfast in the small boarding house, when Brenda would finish her third slice of toast, dab her lips genteelly with her serviette, look at him, and say, 'What shall we do today?'

What was there to do? George could think of nothing to do. Something else bothered him too. He found himself looking at the chambermaid as she made the bed, and her skirt rose high over her girlish flanks. He was just married, and getting all he wanted. He should not be looking at girls like that.

According to all the films, books and stories which formed George's vicarious background to life, he had reached the ultimate in his emotional experience. He was married to a good-looking girl, who loved him and he loved her, and they were going to have a baby. 'The End' came after that, because no one could wish for anything more. This was it. At eighteen, he had got there already.

Admittedly, George's observation of real life to date did not entirely support this simplistic, idyllic version of the course of human happiness, but George shared the normal opinion of youth, that whatever trifling mistakes he became involved in early on, he would sort them out effortlessly, being more gifted and worthy than his elders and incapable of stumbling into the messy traps they had fallen for.

It was perhaps a daunting thought, as they sat silently together in the tiny 'resident's lounge' of the Torquay boarding house, and watched the rain run down the windows, that if he reached his biblical span of three score years and ten, he still had fifty-two years to go. Something, presumably, would happen in those fifty-two years. George looked at the umbrellas passing by outside, and struggled to visualize it. For one thing, that as yet unborn child would be more than fifty years of age, nearly three times as old as he was at this moment, sitting in Torquay with the smell of steak and kidney pudding drifting up from the basement kitchen.

But although he could put the words and the thought together, the idea that his child, its presence still invisible inside Brenda's slim body, could become fifty, on course for old age, was as unreal as the conception of personal death. The notion was totally incomprehensible, and George gave up. They would be all right when they got back, he decided. Torquay was a boring hole. The fault, if fault there were, lay in the place where they had by chance decided to stay, not in themselves.

Brenda's father ran a small corner grocer's shop, and hence had many acquaintances, who, with persistent optimism, he regarded as friends.

Through one of these friends George and Brenda acquired what was called a flat, but was really only two ill-furnished rooms, with a shared kitchen and bathroom. Something less than pure altruism appeared when it came to the rent, which George could not really afford.

He left the store, and took the first job he could get, which was as an unskilled labourer in Portsmouth dockyard. The rate of pay was low. It was a naval dockyard, and even skilled men did not command the same wages which were paid in the commercial ports like Liverpool or Southampton. But George worked all the overtime he could get, and they made ends meet.

Brenda lost her edginess, and became calm, placid and contented. She did not expect much in the way of conversation any more when George came home late in the evening, and he was too tired to try. His supper was always ready, never quite burned, never quite not. She was quite happy to sit and knit innumerable baby things, while he dozed in an armchair over the evening paper.

She grew very large, and sex became technically difficult to accomplish. In any case, Brenda now found the idea repellent, which George supposed was normal in the circumstances.

Some time, George would have to do his National Service. As a married man with a baby, he could get deferment, and everyone assumed that he would, including George. Sometimes, however, he used to watch the naval ratings as they passed through the dockyard on the way back to their ships. Whether complaining or laughing, there was a certain vitality about them. They seemed to enjoy the life on the whole, and George could see why. The idea of setting sail for Singapore, Port Said, or Gibraltar, had its attractions. But not, he told himself hurriedly, when there was a baby on the way.

The birth was an easy one. George looked at the boy child, and wondered how he and Brenda could have made, between them, something so incredibly complex as another human being.

He was nearly nineteen. He could not vote, or enter into hire purchase commitments, but he was a father. George felt rather proud, as he looked at Brenda's cheerful, smiling face affectionately.

He began to answer advertisements in the local newspaper, looking for a better job.

The future was beginning to clarify. George could see it. There was Brenda, slim and loving again, in a proper flat, or even a small house, with decent furniture and their own bathroom, where the lavatory was not always stained with someone else's excreta. There was young Richard, growing into a toddler, curious and energetic, and then a schoolboy, and George would teach him cricket, and football and boxing, and how to win. There was another child, perhaps a girl this time, not for a few years yet, but later, and the excitement of watching a girl of his flesh grow into a beautiful young woman. Meantime, George himself, having got his better job, would be studying, remedying his negligible education, working for promotion, well regarded, respected. Eventually, he would move his family to the downs, high above Southsea, looking over the sea, where detached houses in their own grounds had central heating, and cars in their garages. He was bright, he had talent, they had thought so at the store, until the Cow had put the boot in. He could do it. He could do it all.

Many years later, an older George Griffin, snorted with sad amusement at the young man's brief dreams, which he only recalled very occasionally, when too much gin put him to sleep with the efficacy of a hypodermic injection, and then, perversely, woke him up at four in the morning, sandpaper-mouthed and wakeful.

There were two things wrong with those dreams. First, the better job did not materialize. Employers were not impressed by an unskilled labourer, with no educational qualifications, whose only previous reference, from the store, was ambivalent. The Cow had had a hand in that.

Second, the slim, loving Brenda bore no relation to reality whatever. She was never slim again, and, although she was uncomplaining if passive when she could not avoid it, she had no need nor any desire for George's kind of love, much less any wish to stimulate it.

Much, much later, George Griffin realized that Brenda, by her own terms of reference, was one of the lucky ones. At eighteen, she had indeed achieved her ambition which, with gentle modifications, would last her for the rest of her life.

Brenda had wanted him, but like a bitch on heat. Once she had a young one to bring up, she had no further need for a mate, except to provide food and shelter. She did not spoil young Dick. She treated him with an animal-like sense and simplicity, but he comfortably filled her life, and was quite enough. She found the

trivia of everyday existence satisfying, and once commercial television arrived on the scene, she envied no one, and coveted
nothing.

She took pleasure in small things, a glass of sherry ac-
companied by a cigarette, talking about Dick, being warm on a
cold night. Her one great enjoyment was food, which was nice for
her, since she rarely let more than three hours pass between
meals, and always had something interesting to look forward to.

But all this dispassionate wisdom was not available to the
young George Griffin at the time. He enjoyed watching Brenda
suckle the baby from breasts which had grown large and glo-
bular, but the sight gave him ideas, which did not meet with
approval.

'Not when she's nursing, George,' Brenda's mother reproved,
apparently being the recipient of intimate confidences. 'You'll
have to be patient.'

George patiently waited for Brenda to regain her figure, but
nothing happened, except that her beam grew broader, and her
legs and arms thickened a little more.

'Girls always put on a bit of weight when they've had a baby,'
Brenda's mother said, a jolly woman, built like a captive balloon.
'It's only natural.'

George tentatively recalled a diet which he had read about in
the paper.

'She's got to eat to keep up her strength,' Brenda's mother
said. 'Anyway, she's got no need to diet. She's nice and buxom,
that's all. I like it.'

George was willing to demonstrate that the buxom Brenda
was still desirable, but small obstacles tended to arise at the cru-
cial moment.

'I don't like those nasty rubber things,' Brenda said. 'They feel
all cold and horrible.'

'All right,' George said, pulling it off. He made ready again.
'Don't worry. I'll be careful.'

'No,' Brenda said. 'It's not safe that way.'

George rolled over onto his back. Talking about it like that
always made him lose interest.

'Well, why don't you do something?' he grumbled.

'What?'

'You could go to the doctor, and be fitted for something you could put in.'

'I'm not having anyone messing about with my insides, thank you very much,' Brenda said firmly.

George took advice at a shop which sold trusses and aids for incontinence, among other things, and walked out with a small cardboard box. He read the instructions and tried it. Brenda did not like it.

'I feel all greasy inside,' she said. 'And it's running down my legs, too. Look at the sheet. I'll have to wash it now.'

George could not help but sympathize. He was not too keen on the experience either. Dick woke up, and started to cry. Brenda got up, and lifted him out of his cot, cooing lovingly. 'Who's a naughty boy then? Who's a naughty boy?'

Dick was another problem. He was always liable to wake up and start yelling, just when George was getting carried away. After a while, George fell into the negative habit of doing nothing unless his needs were overpowering. It was simpler. It was also trying.

George began to stop at the pub on the way home for a few pints of beer. Brenda tacitly approved the new routine. It made George more cheerful, gave him something to do. As the weeks went by, George stayed longer at the pub, and his consumption escalated from a few pints to more than a few.

One night, he found himself part of a group, which included a girl provocatively dressed, with eyes which held George's all evening. She steadied his hand with cool fingers when he lit her cigarette, and crossed her legs so that the slit in her skirt showed her slender thighs for his benefit. All George's unwillingly suppressed desires flared into anticipatory life. Unless he was barmy, she was enjoying working him up, and had every intention of winding him down.

The group thinned out during the course of the evening, and at closing time, George was sitting next to the girl. The only two remaining men were talking football at the other end of the table. He wanted that girl so much that it hurt.

'Are you with one of them?' he asked.

'I'm not with anyone,' the girl said. 'Why?'

George swallowed. 'Nothing.'

'Oh, well, in that case, I'll ask one of them to see me home, shall I?'

'I'm married,' George said.

The girl smiled. 'I guessed that,' she said. 'You're used to it, and you're not getting it.'

George slid into bed beside Brenda. She was asleep. He caressed her urgently, willing her to wake up. The girl probably thought he was crazy. He had abruptly said 'Goodnight' and walked out, but the effect she had had had stayed with him, was with him now, in bed beside his young wife where he should be. He knew that she was awake now. Her breathing had changed, and there was a tenseness in her body.

'Brenda,' he whispered.

'You smell of beer,' she said. 'You woke me up. I was fast asleep.'

'Brenda.'

'Oh, all right.'

George paused. 'All right?'

'Well, what do you expect? You know I don't like being woken up like that. I was just in the middle of a lovely dream.'

'Never mind,' George said. 'Forget it.'

He stared blankly into the darkness. The silence in the bedroom was as though they were muffled from the rest of the world.

He knew that Brenda was not asleep, but she did not say anything for a long time. At last, she sighed, and said, 'There are more things in life than that, George. It's not as important as you make out.'

George made his decision a month later. One of his mates at work was getting married. The stag party began in the pub, and continued after closing time in someone's house.

George was bleary-eyed and unsteady when he got home. The party had gone on too long. George had sunk into a black depression, and only been restrained with difficulty from spoiling the bridegroom's good looks, over some light-hearted remark which George took as an insult. All he wanted to do was sleep, and yet he knew that he had to be up in a few hours to go to work.

Brenda was asleep, wheezing gently, but he could hear Dick stirring in his cot. He undressed as quietly as he could, but staggered when he was pulling off his trousers. He steadied himself on the open wardrobe door, which closed with a bang. Dick started to cry, winding himself into a continuous yell.

'Shut up,' George whispered. 'Be quiet.'

The yell turned into an ear splitting bellow. Something snapped in George. He snatched Dick from his cot, and shook him savagely. The child screamed with terror, and suddenly George stopped. He could feel the little boy's sobbing gasp as he inhaled, the warm breath on his cheek as Dick cried. What was he doing? What the hell was he doing?

The light went on. Brenda sat up, blinking.

'What's wrong?'

'He woke up and started crying,' George said.

'Give him to me.'

George handed over the bundle, finished undressing, and crawled miserably into bed.

'There, there,' Brenda said, rubbing Dick's back, as he hiccupped and cried at the same time. 'What was it, my pet? Did you have a nasty dream? Is that what it was?' She glanced at George sleepily. 'Was it a good party?'

'Yes,' George said.

He lay awake long after Dick was quiet, back in his cot, filled with disgust and self-contempt.

He was thinking of Stan, whom he hated. Stan who spent every evening in the pub, and came home smelling of beer. Stan, who lashed out, for no reason but black ill-temper, at the child in his care. And he, George Griffin was behaving like Stan. Already, at his age, not yet an adult under the laws of his country, acting like that bastard, coming within an inch of hurting his own son.

George took the next afternoon off, although he did not go home. Two weeks later, when he was accepted, he said to

Brenda, 'I've joined the army.'

She was puzzled. 'You mean you've been called up? I didn't know you'd got your papers.'

'No. The regular army. I've signed on for fifteen years.'

He was afraid she would be upset, and he did not want to hurt her. He talked rapidly about lack of opportunity for him in civilian life, about learning a trade, about a career, about promotion, about the possibility of getting married quarters in due course.

Brenda listened, but her mind was on something else.

'I don't suppose you'll want to go on paying for this flat,' she said. 'I never did like it really. I think the best thing is, if I go back and live with mum and dad. There's enough room, and they're both ever so fond of Dick, and you can come and stay when you're on leave, and it'll be lovely. Much better than living in this place.'

George realized that he had been concerned about nothing. Brenda was not in the least upset. A pleasant vista of almost continuous peace and quiet had opened up before her. She was delighted.

CHAPTER SIX

Griffin started awake, his heart pounding violently. Outside his bedroom door, something was howling continuously. Jane, he realized, as some of his senses returned. She was using the vacuum cleaner. The well-meaning little fool had decided to leave the place bright and shining in return for his hospitality. He cursed her thoughtfulness.

He looked at the alarm clock. Half past eight. He had managed just over two hours' sleep.

He staggered into the bathroom. He felt like death. He caught sight of himself in the mirror. God in heaven. What a sight. Lined, bleary eyed, unshaven, he looked like those old buggers who hung around Waterloo Station at night stewed in meths.

He sat on the edge of the bath, head bowed, and closed his eyes. Mercifully, the howling outside stopped. Perhaps if he went back to bed for an hour . . .

There was a sharp rapping at the door. Griffin's head jerked up. He realized that he had dozed off.

'Breakfast'll be ready soon, Mr Griffin,' Jane's cheerful voice said.

'Bacon and eggs, mushrooms, fried bread, sausages and fried tomatoes,' Dick said.

Griffin looked at the plate, and his stomach curdled. 'I usually just have a piece of toast,' he said.

'Jane's cooked it specially,' Dick said. Jane smiled at him. Griffin wondered if she did like him after all, or if she merely tried to be kind to everyone.

'Ah, well, in that case . . .' Griffin said. 'I don't bother for myself, but this is a rare treat . . . oh, yes, a rare treat . . . marvellous.'

Somehow, he forced the revolting mixture down his rebellious throat. Afterwards, he locked himself in the bathroom, although he resisted the impulse to throw up. Instead, he reloaded the cigarette case, took the film out of the lighter which would not light, but was an ingenious little camera, and developed it. Those of Tauber in the pub were rather good, he thought.

Griffin sometimes met people whose faces he wished to study carefully later, at his leisure, or perhaps show to various acquaintances who might be prepared to search their memories about whoever it was, sometimes out of friendship, more often for money.

Taking these bloody snaps had become a habit, he thought, a kind of nervous tic. Still, you never knew.

He was half-way through, when Dick knocked on the door, and said. 'The plumbers are here about the overflow.'

'What? I haven't got an overflow.'

'It's upstairs, or something. You'd better come and talk to them.'

'Oh, tell them to wait,' Griffin said, harassed.

A couple of minutes later, he heard the phone ring. 'Take a message,' Griffin bawled.

He finished off as quickly as he could, reloaded the lighter with film, and put it in his pocket.

The two plumbers were waiting. 'We've checked the kitchen and the loo,' the spokesman said, 'and it's not there. All right if we take a look in the bathroom?'

Griffin watched, as they ran taps, and examined the cold water tank.

'There's an overflow at the back,' the spokesman said. 'We're trying to find out which flat it's coming from.'

'Why don't you try looking at the plans, and tracing it that way?' Griffin grumbled. 'Or is that too obvious?'

The spokesman laughed. 'Plans? For a block this age? You tell me where they are, mate, and I'll do it like a shot. It'd save us a lot of trouble. Well, it's not your flat,' he said, closing the door to the tank cupboard. 'Sorry to have troubled you.'

'It was your office on the phone,' Dick said. 'An appointment with someone who's dying to buy. Eleven o'clock. I've written it down.' He gestured vaguely.

'Oh, hell,' Griffin said, looking at the note. He did not feel at his most persuasive this morning. Still, if it was a hot prospect, it might not be too difficult. And if it was a real sucker, he might be able to push the luxury leather, gold engraved edition, on which he got nearly twice as much commission. The way this Tauber thing was going, he thought, glumly, he would need it. The gross figure had sounded nice and round and attractive, but by the time he deducted all his expenses, a substantial amount would have been whittled away. Too much erosion altogether of that nice round sum, considering all the trouble it was causing. Perhaps Nancy really would not take that hundred quid, he thought hopefully. But she probably would.

The radio was tuned to Capital Radio at full volume. Dick was stretched out on the settee, reading Griffin's newspaper. Jane was intently polishing furniture.

'When are you two going?' Griffin enquired.

'I don't know,' Dick said, vaguely. 'Some time. Not in your way are we?'

'No,' Griffin sighed. 'Only turn that radio down a bit.'

Dick stretched out a lazy hand, and the Job Spot voice extolling the attractions of life in the world of show business as a trainee bingo hall manager dropped from a shout to a whisper.

Griffin dialled a number. He wondered why a man like himself who spent so lavishly in some directions was so unaccountably mean in others, like clothes and telephone extensions. He had once worked out how many bottles of gin the rent of an extension would cost per annum, and decided to put first things first. After all, you could only talk on one telephone at once. But at the time, he was not to know that his living room would be infested with sons and girl friends, he thought, grossing up for the sake of simplicity.

'Hullo,' he said. 'It's George. How's our friend?'

'All right,' Nancy said, 'but . . .'

'Still quiet and peaceful?' Griffin cut in.

'I can't go on giving him drugs all the time,' Nancy said.

'I think he should go on getting the same dose,' Griffin advised. 'It might be risky to vary it. Look, I can't talk now . . .'

'George,' she said, agitated. 'I must have been out of my mind last night. Whatever trouble you're in, I'm sorry, but he can't stay here.'

'It won't be for long,' Griffin said.

'It's been too long already,' Nancy said. 'I must be half-witted, letting you con me again . . .'

'Look,' Griffin said, 'everything I told you is true. About the consequences, I mean.'

There was a slight pause. 'All right,' she said, reluctantly. 'But suppose I phoned the police, and said I'd found him in the lane. I wouldn't mention you at all.'

'For God's sake don't do that, Nancy,' Griffin said, sharply. 'Please. Look, I'll come and deal with it later today.'

'When?' she demanded.

'As soon as I can. I'll check with you first. This evening at the latest. We'll see about getting him moved then.'

Griffin hung up. He opened his pocket diary, and looked for the note he had made of the phone number of the River Park Hotel.

'Are you seeing the lovely Nancy again?' Dick asked, interested.

Griffin cursed himself for letting that 'Nancy' slip out in his alarm. 'Not exactly,' he said.

'Is that where you were last night?' Dick enquired.

'We have a mutual friend who's not well, and that's all there is to it,' Griffin said. He began to dial.

'I gave her a ring not long ago,' Dick said.

Griffin stared at him. 'Why?'

Dick shrugged. 'Just to see how she was. I liked Nancy.'

'Mr Robert Dalton, please,' Griffin said into the phone.

Dick opened the newspaper again. 'There's no doubt about it,' he said, judicially, 'you should have stuck to Nancy. What Maisie had was all too obvious, but she was a mistake. You'd have been happy with Nancy.'

'I'm blissfully happy now,' Griffin said, bitterly. 'What's

71

more, it's my job in life to make mistakes, so that you learn from my bad example and don't do the same. Now shut up. This is business. Hullo, Bob,' he said into the phone. 'George Griffin.'

'Hi, there, George,' Dalton said in his warm, friendly, American drawl. 'We were expecting to see you personally. We were getting worried.'

'I'm afraid there's been a little bit of a hitch in our arrangements,' Griffin said. 'Nothing serious, a small delay.'

'What kind of a hitch, Georgie boy?' Dalton asked, his tone abruptly losing its warmth and friendliness.

'A hold up in packaging and delivery,' Griffin said. 'I hope to get it sorted out today, but . . .'

'Just a minute,' Dalton said. 'Have you got someone with you?'

'Yes,' Griffin said. 'I'm pretty sure tomorrow'll be all right . . .'

'Well, tomorrow's not all right with me, George,' Dalton said. 'You get your ass over here right now. I want to hear about this.'

'It won't be much before twelve,' George said. 'I've got an appointment.'

'You be here,' Dalton said. 'Unless you want to be collected.'

Griffin hung up, and lit a cigarette nervously. He had not expected Bob Dalton to be pleased, but the man's harsh anger had taken him unawares. What was so bloody important about a few hours? He wondered whether to tell Bob Dalton the truth, but he decided to treat that idea with caution. Best if he took the temperature of the water and played it by ear.

A cough started with a tickle in his throat, and turned into a racking hack, in the depth of his lungs. 'Too many fags, and not enough sleep,' Griffin remarked, inhaling smoke deeply. 'Well, cheerio, you two. See you another time.'

'We may look in on the way back,' Dick said, turning to the sports page.

'Well, give me a bit of warning another time,' Griffin said. 'And I'll buy enough newspapers to go round.'

'OK,' Dick said. The penny dropped, and he held out the newspaper. 'Want this one? I've nearly finished it.'

'Too late now,' Griffin said.

He drove across Hyde Park, left his car in a parking bay strictly reserved for residents of an apartment block, checked the address Dick had given him and walked to the street entrance of the flat, which was round the corner from Queen Anne's Gate.

A friendly voice on the ansaphone let him in, and he humped his heavy case up the stairs. The door to the flat was open and a cordial, big man of about forty-five, with greying hair, was waiting.

'Major Griffin?' the man said. 'Good morning. My name's Bradley. Tom Bradley.'

'How do you do,' Griffin said, using his Major's voice.

'Come on in,' Bradley said. 'I was just thinking of having a morning snort. Care to join me?'

He held up a bottle of whisky.

'As a matter of fact,' Griffin said, 'I'm a gin man. Don't really know why. Staple drink in my particular mess, I suppose.'

'Nothing simpler,' Bradley said. 'Selection over there. Probably easier if you helped yourself, yes?'

'Right,' Griffin said. A stiff drink would set him up. Act as a stimulating substitute for all that sleep he had failed to get.

'I should be a gin man myself,' Bradley said. 'I was in the navy for a while, and my guts were pickled in gin before I came out. For some reason I can't stand the stuff now, so I've switched to scotch. Too much gin at an early age, I suppose.' He laughed.

'Probably,' Griffin agreed, politely echoing his amusement.

He could not quite place Bradley, which was annoying. Griffin believed he could ticket most men after a few seconds conversation. But Bradley did not sound like regular Royal Navy, Dartmouth and all that. He could have been RNVR, of course, served during the Korean War at 'an early age', the phrase Bradley had used.

'What bunch were you with?' Bradley asked. He was looking at Griffin with smiling, superficial interest.

'The paratroopers,' Griffin said, which was a cautious approach to the truth, if not quite accurate.

'A tough body of men, that lot,' Bradley said. 'Were you in

Northern Ireland?'

'No, I retired around then, thank God,' Griffin said.

'You must have retired rather young,' Bradley said, who was apparently good at mental arithmetic, and guessing ages.

'Golden handshake,' Griffin explained. 'One of those defence cuts, so I had no option. The Government needed to save money on the armed forces to pay out more in social security to layabouts who prefer not to work, or perhaps it was to pay civil servants' salaries in some new department they were setting up, I forget which.'

'Both, probably,' Bradley said, sympathetically. 'I don't know. I sometimes think this country's gone collectively potty. Can I top you up before we get down to business? Ice and not much tonic, I think, isn't it?'

'Thank you,' Griffin said, handing over his glass. 'You're very observant.'

'I always think you can tell something about a man from the way he drinks,' Bradley said.

Bradley took his whisky neat, and in large helpings, and from his reference to a morning snort, at regular and frequent intervals. Griffin thought that Bradley was either a lush who did nothing much else, or a man who worked long hours under intense pressure, and used scotch to keep him going.

The man certainly had money, judging from this flat. The furniture was expensive, the fittings, curtains and carpets of high quality, books covered the whole of one wall. Bradley's casual, relaxed manner did not indicate the presence of any pressure. A moneyed lush then? On the face of it. And yet there was something about this flat, a certain austerity, not in the sense of any lack of comfort, but everything was just a little too precise and well chosen. It bore a resemblance to a luxury hotel suite when the staff had just finished cleaning it, and the bowls of flowers had been added as a final touch.

'I need an encyclopaedia,' Bradley said, giving Griffin his drink. 'I've studied the brochures, and I think it's yours or Britannica.'

'Britannica used to be quite good in their own way,' Griffin said; he had no scruples about knocking the opposition. 'Not as good as ours, we could always fault them in several ways, but just the same, quite stern opposition. Yes, indeed. Quite stern. But since they changed their format . . .' He sighed, and shook his head sadly. 'Well when I tell you that we process applications weekly from their salesmen, who want to come and join us . . . weekly, without exaggeration. They know that our encyclopaedia doesn't have to be sold, you see. It sells itself.'

George took his demonstration volume out of his case with practised ease.

'I suppose you took up this game when you left the Army,' Bradley said.

'After one or two executive appointments,' Griffin said. 'But I find this much more satisfying. One's helping people, you see, giving them advice. Every client is different. May I enquire if you require an encyclopaedia as a personal work of reference? Your line of business is . . .?'

He left the question hanging in the air, and Bradley answered at once, without hesitation.

'I'm a director of a number of companies,' he said. 'Which probably sounds like a cushy number, but one of them, frankly, is in dire trouble, and I'm practically living on the job. This is a company flat,' he added, waving idly at his surroundings. 'My home's in the country.'

'Ah, I see,' Griffin said. A company flat was exactly what it looked like, on reflection. 'So the lucky recipient will be one of your children, perhaps?' There were no family photographs anywhere around, Griffin had noted.

'My godson,' Bradley said. 'He takes his common entrance exam soon, hoping to get into Harrow. I've known brighter boys to be honest, but his birthday's coming up and I thought an appropriate gift might be . . .'

'In that case,' Griffin said, 'educationally, ours is unsurpassed.' He always liked to know which aspect to plug. 'And I won't detain you unduly with any talk about the excellence of the print, except to assert that your old maiden aunt could read this easily, without her glasses. Nor about the illustrations,'

Griffin said, flicking the sample pages deftly, 'practically three dimensional though they may be. Or even the quality of the binding—I refer to the special luxury leather, gold engraved option—except to point out the splendid value from your point of view, and the lifelong joy the possession of such a beautiful set of books will give your godson. No. Such things you can see for yourself. But as a well read and educated man,' he said, glancing at the wall of books, 'you will know the work of our distinguished and highly qualified contributors, and I would add that each section is revised every year . . .'

Griffin continued with his spiel, Mark 2, well heeled and educated prospects for the use of. In council flats, he would appeal to snobbery, the advantages a child would gain over its deprived fellows by sailing through his or her exams once the encyclopaedia was installed ('No doubt you'd like the glass-fronted bookcase as well?') and a mesmeric explanation of the advantageous easy terms which practically meant they could acquire the set ('for your instant enjoyment') for nothing. Griffin got his commission on sale, and was not concerned with what happened when they failed to keep up the payments. The bad debts department took over then.

Bradley listened intently, without saying anything apart from an occasional 'M'm'. But something about the man continued to bother Griffin.

He could not put his finger on it, but he had the weird feeling that he had come across Bradley before in some previous incarnation. Not the man himself. Griffin was certain that he had never seen Bradley before in his life. But some doppelganger, some faintly related type. Only just what was Bradley's type? Griffin did not know.

Perhaps he was jumpy, or perhaps it was mere habit, but he found himself opening his cigarette case, putting a cigarette in his mouth, and flicking his lighter, taking care to angle it in a certain way.

Bradley snapped a table lighter into flame, and held it out. 'Run out of fuel?' he asked.

'Yes. Looks like it. Thank you. Oh, do you mind if I smoke?'

'Not at all. Not just now thanks,' Bradley said, declining the offered cigarette.

Griffin continued with his sales pitch, allowing fervent enthusiasm and transparent belief in the product to mount until, at the psychological moment, he ended by urging, 'So if you'll just sign this order form, sir,' placing the form on the table between them, and his gold-plated Parker in Bradley's fingers.

'Oh, I've no intention of making a decision now,' Bradley said, returning the pen. 'I have an appointment with the Britannica man this afternoon. I shall make up my mind then. Thank you for giving me your time, Major Griffin. I'll let you know.'

Griffin was in a surly mood as he went out into the street. What a waste of effort. He could forget his commission on that one. Griffin had no faith in prospects who were going to let him know. If they did not sign on the dotted line before he left, the odds were that they were not going to buy.

Griffin employed a degree of hyperbole when he extolled the virtues of 'his' encyclopaedia, but he really did believe that it was not a bad set of books at all, and arguably the best around in its own particular corner of the market. It was certainly less learned than Britannica, but although actually over-priced for what it was, it came out cheaper than its rival for those to whom an encyclopaedia represented a big investment who, happily for Griffin's commission-only earnings, were most people.

Unfortunately, the Bradleys of this world did not belong to the great majority and Griffin's only hope with them was to get them signed up before the Britannica man appeared on the scene.

Oh well, win a few, lose a few . . .

Griffin retrieved his car, and meandered around South Kensington for a while. He had thought it quite likely that he would be followed when he left his flat that morning, but he had not bothered to take any precautions. Tauber's friends, or whoever they were, could watch him call on prospects all day, and bloody good luck to them as far as he was concerned.

But Bob Dalton was another matter. Griffin wanted the second half of his fee, and he did not wish to screw that up by leading anyone to the man with the money.

Griffin's car had wing mirrors and door mirrors, as well as the conventional rear view mirror, and they were carefully adjusted so that there were no blind spots anywhere behind him.

'Good God,' Dick had said, when he turned up one Sunday unexpectedly, and found his father bolting on the final door mirror. 'Your car sprouts mirrors like an allotment grows cabbages. Are you hoping they'll breed or something?'

'I'm a road safety buff,' Griffin told him.

Griffin was satisfied that no car was tailing him, and was about to head for the River Park Hotel, when he suddenly noticed something that gave him a nasty turn. The same moped had been there behind him for some time, although he was not sure how long. It was drifting inconspicuously from one lane to another. The rider wore a crash helmet and goggles, and Griffin could not see his face.

Griffin turned into the King's Road, and swore, his heart bumping with alarm. He had been alert for following cars, not stupid, slow-moving little mopeds. And yet, of course, it made sense. A moped was the one thing which could always filter through the traffic and keep up, in the car-jammed streets of London.

Griffin drove to Sloane Square, right round it, and back up the King's Road. The moped followed him three-quarters of the way round, but then turned left, and pottered off towards the Thames.

Either the moped rider was a pro, who knew he had been spotted, or a harmless citizen who had temporarily lost his way to Battersea, and finally found it.

The first possibility continued to worry Griffin, and he left his big, conspicuous, old Ford in a multi-storey car park. He was probably paranoid about being followed, but identifying the ailment did nothing to quell the nervous spasms in his stomach. Much though he loathed public transport, he jumped on the first bus that came along. He went upstairs, travelled three stops, got off, crossed the road, and caught another bus at random.

Buses had two great advantages. Not many people boarded the loss-making monsters at this time of day, and it was easy to

78

check out his travelling companions. And anyone in a vehicle who was trying to follow a bus as it lumbered casually from stop to stop had to stick out like an orchid on a cricket pitch.

By the time Griffin entered the River Park Hotel, he was late, but his mind was easy. No inquisitive eyes were noting his movements.

The concrete-clad tower of the River Park Hotel was similar to the post-war type of luxury hotel which infested every major city in the world. Its close relations sat outside airport perimeters, doubleglazed against the screaming jets, in deserts, on the fringes of jungles, and soon no doubt in the tundra. They all appeared to have been designed by the same architect with a youthful addiction to piling one matchbox on top of another.

Dalton opened the door to his suite.

'Sorry I'm late,' Griffin said, cautiously.

'Hullo, George,' Dalton said, smiling. He either had perfect teeth, or perfect crowns. 'Think nothing of it. Come on in.'

Griffin stepped inside. He was glad that Dalton had got over his burst of bad temper.

Dalton was about forty, tall, broadshouldered, easy, smiling, immaculately dressed, a typical WASP in appearance and manner. He gave the impression that he would have fitted naturally and comfortably into the Kennedy scene, and he might have done, as a young man, for all Griffin knew.

'It's good to see you,' Dalton said, shaking Griffin's hand warmly.

Griffin returned the warm handshake and the smile. He was accustomed to the American habit of shaking hands every time you met, as though all men in the world were long lost brothers.

Dalton continued to give him that big, affectionate grin, to hold Griffin's right hand tightly. For rather longer than was necessary, Griffin thought, even if the man did want to kiss and make up.

Suddenly, Griffin snatched his hand away, and started to duck, but he was a fraction of a second too late. The blow caught him on the column of his neck.

Griffin blinked, and studied the carpet, which was a few

79

inches from his nose. His head still seemed to be attached to his body, but it was connected by a burning, throbbing column of fire.

He pushed himself up on to his knees, and looked at the yahoo who had felled him from behind the open door. Dalton casually pushed the door closed.

Another yahoo wandered into Griffin's field of vision. He knew them slightly as colleagues of Dalton's, although Dalton had done all the talking and bargaining.

Griffin stood up. They were all three smiling at him in their affable American way. Dalton leaned comfortably on the door, and folded his arms. He seemed to intend merely to supervise the proceedings.

Griffin tried to keep the fear out of his voice. He loathed pain. He hated pain.

'We either leave it at that,' he told Dalton, 'and I forgive and forget, or else you're going to have two damaged yahoos on your hands.'

Dalton thought about that, and then shook his head. 'I think he's bragging,' he informed his friends.

Griffin had been afraid he would think that.

In fact, it went quite well, in the beginning.

It had to be quick, Griffin knew that. He modestly believed that he could beat the hell out of practically anyone in the world, no matter what his disadvantage in size and weight. But, these days, it had to be over in thirty seconds, or he was in trouble. After that, he ran out of wind. He could no longer keep it up the way he used to be able to.

The first yahoo flew through the air, with a yelp of surprise, and hammered his head against the wall. The second yahoo collected Griffin's knee in his mouth which was, unfortunately for him, open at that moment. There was a crunching sound, and the yahoo fell down, blood suddenly pouring down his chin.

Griffin supposed later that Dalton had decided to intervene after all. All he knew for certain at the time was that the toe of an elegant shoe kicked him in the stomach, which was softer than it should have been, and left him retching and winded.

80

The two yahoos grabbed him viciously, and Griffin knew that it had not come off. His time had run out. He would have done better to have taken his beating in the first place without inflicting painful but not crippling damage. The yahoos were injecting a personal element into it now.

The one with a bloody mouth smashed a tumbler, and drew his hand back, aiming carefully at Griffin's face.

'Cut that out,' Dalton said. 'I don't want him bleeding all over the floor.'

The yahoo, who had blood dripping freely on to his shirt, appeared inclined to disobey orders.

Dalton stepped up to him, said something softly into his ear, took the jagged glass from his hand, and threw it into the waste-paper basket.

So they concentrated on his body and, as a connoisseur, Griffin recognized that they knew what they were doing. They did nearly as good a job as if they had been using rubber batons. Pain flared all over Griffin's body, finally joining up until there seemed to be no part of him which was not crying out in agony. When he was on the verge of passing out, Dalton said 'OK. That's enough', and they threw him into an armchair.

Griffin knew that it would get worse now, as his muscles contracted and protested, and it did. Even to take a shallow breath caused a sharp jab of pain, and he wondered vaguely if they had broken some of his ribs.

Finally, he forced himself to open his eyes. Dalton was sipping a glass of bourbon, filled with ice. He smiled, and said, 'I've just fixed myself a drink, George. How about joining me?'

Griffin eased himself painfully into a somewhat more upright, slightly more dignified position. He said, 'As a matter of fact, old chap, a small stiffener would be much appreciated.'

Dalton poured him a large glass of neat gin, and handed it to him.

'Keep the bottle at the ready,' Dalton said, standing the bottle of gin beside Griffin. 'What the hell, it all comes off my expense account, anyway.'

The yahoo with the bleeding mouth was standing in front of a mirror, trying to look at his teeth. The other yahoo was easing his hands, and studying them carefully to see if they were damaged. I'd like to feed his fingers through the wringer of a bloody wooden mangle, Griffin thought, an inch at a time.

Dalton raised his glass in greeting. 'Well,' he said, 'here's to completion day. Which is today in my book. And yet, Georgie boy, you don't seem ready to deliver. Instead you make evasive phone calls. Let's talk about that, shall we?'

CHAPTER SEVEN

It was not at all like the first meeting. All had been sweetness and light on that occasion.

The phone call had come out of the blue, and at a very good time. Only that morning, Griffin had received a less than friendly letter from his bank manager, which tersely suggested he should call at his earliest convenience. It was an invitation which Griffin was not eager to take up. The previous incumbent, who had unfortunately retired, would have listened tolerantly to Griffin's inflated expectations concerning commission due, plus hints of one of those mysterious cash bonuses which turned up from time to time, agreed to increase his overdraft, and then they would have adjourned to the neighbouring pub for a boozy lunch.

The new bank manager was made of colder, harder stuff. He was a fish-faced teetotaller whose opinion of human nature appeared to be on the low side. Griffin had only met him once before, when the man had asked awkward questions, taken copious notes, and totted up figures.

'Mr Griffin,' he had said. 'You have no salary, nothing we can rely on. It is true that your commission has been reasonably substantial over a considerable period but there is no upward trend, if one ignores the effects of inflation, to support your contention that you expect a sharply increased income in the near future. As for the irregular cash deposits you have made from time to time I cannot, I am afraid, take those into account unless you can provide some evidence, in the form of a letter, for example, from whatever source such a payment may arise, confirming when you may expect to receive further monies.'

Christ, Griffin thought, what a load of gobbledegook over one miserable little overdraft. He especially liked the idea of getting a letter of confirmation from one of his sources. That was good. He knew what the stupid burke believed. He thought that Griffin frittered his money away in gambling, and that those occasional lumps of cash represented his rare winnings. He looked into the new bank manager's unblinking, goldfish-like eyes, and knew that there was no way they were ever going to communicate.

He wondered if he could take his overdraft to some other bank, but thought there might be a shortage of takers. The branch which harboured the Sinking Fund probably thought he was a good guy, but he had prudently opened that account in a false name and could hardly now turn up as someone else.

There was a pile of bills in his desk awaiting the addition of the final demands, when he would have to pay for his gas, phone and electricity. The rates he could leave until they threatened to issue a summons, although they seemed to do that much sooner than they used to, the thieving bastards.

In short, Griffin was strapped for money. He usually was to some extent, but this was as bleak a financial position as he had experienced for a long time.

Maisie's departure had left a hole, both in his pocket, since she took the contents of his wallet, and in his personal life. Not that he cared very much about her, as a person, the whoring cow, but at least there had been someone in the flat to fight with and the occasional reconciliation was relaxing and satisfying.

Griffin had no belief in natural justice. He had seen too much random cruelty, too much pain inflicted on the innocent, too many nice, ordinary people killed for no reason. But in the Maisie affair, he had got what he asked for, he really had.

Beguiled and fascinated by Maisie's lyrical effervescence, he had cheated on Nancy, who had been buying her house near Marlow at the time, and lied about it in the first place with the honest gaze of a devoted spaniel. In her turn, Maisie had denied her assignations with the oil man, her wide, beautiful, green eyes hurt and indignant. 'I don't know where you get these horrible suspicions,' she had said plaintively. 'There must be something wrong with you. Perhaps you're getting the male menopause

84

early. Perhaps you should see a doctor.'

It was neat, Griffin had reflected later, after Maisie had departed for Aberdeen. Very neat, no doubt about that. Almost enough to make you believe in the intervention of some just Almighty being, if it weren't for the recollection of his father and the memory of helplessly watching those children gunned down at dawn as they approached the border and the expression on their mother's face as she turned and looked back.

But the loss of Maisie—God, if only there had been no Maisie, no lies to Nancy—had left him feeling screwed up and lonely. He was spending more than he should, that was true, chucking his money around in bars and clubs and restaurants, which sometimes led to a night with some girl whose name he promptly forgot, in her flat or his. It was necessary, a kind of crude therapy, which at least dealt with the symptoms if not the disease, but the result was that his new, gaping goldfish of a bank manager desired him to call at his earliest convenience.

Griffin was seriously considering raiding the Sinking Fund. He had never done it before, but he could see no alternative, short of changing his nature which he could undoubtedly do the day he discovered perpetual motion. And then, out of the blue, came that godsend of a phone call.

'You won't know me,' the warm, American friendly voice said, 'but my name is Bob Dalton. A friend of mine in the States speaks highly of you. Suppose we meet for a drink?'

The drink certainly appealed, but Griffin liked the sound of it, in any case. The man most likely to dish out references for him in America was John Irving, and John was not only likeable but had paid Griffin a fair bit of money in his time. He had some reason to hope that Dalton might be interested in making an offer.

They met at six o'clock the following evening in the cocktail bar of the Dorchester Hotel. It was nearly empty, and they talked in a corner, undisturbed.

After the opening pleasantries about British weather and the relative merits of dry martinis shaken or stirred, Dalton said 'OK George, I know a little about you, but I hope you won't mind if I get personal. I understand you sell encyclopaedias for a living.'

'Well, that supplies the bread and butter,' Griffin said. 'But a little less jam than I like.'

'How much do you make in bread and butter?'

Americans. They always liked to place a man in a financial bracket. 'About seven thousand a year,' Griffin said, exaggerating a bit.

Dalton converted that into dollars, and inhaled thoughtfully on his cigarette. 'That's not bad, by Brititish standards, Georgie boy. Not bad at all.'

'Don't forget income tax,' Griffin told him.

'Could I ever?' Dalton sighed.

'Just the same,' Griffin said, 'it's the only steady job I can do which would gross that much, I admit that. But I have this problem.'

'Which is?'

'Booze, women and personal commitments,' Griffin said, revealing nothing that Dalton would not already have been told by John Irving. 'I need to make at least ten grand, not seven.'

'So you do a little moonlighting.'

'I do a few odd jobs,' Griffin said. 'As a salesman, I'm on commission only. If I don't work, I don't get paid. That means I can take time off whenever I want it, if I get a good offer. I emphasize the words, good offer.'

'I heard you,' Dalton said. 'I guess some of these odd jobs,' he went on thoughtfully, 'could entail, shall we say, some personal discomfort?'

'When people want me to do something,' Griffin said, 'it means they'd rather not risk doing it themselves. I take that into account when we start talking money.'

Dalton grinned. 'Well,' he said 'from what I hear, you could be suitably qualified.' He cocked his head, and gazed at Griffin thoughtfully. 'Although you're not as heavily built as I'd expected. Not as tall.'

'I have to compensate,' Griffin said. 'So I don't play fair.'

He fingered his cigarette lighter, but the light in here was poor, even for the film he used. He decided to photograph Dalton later, somewhere else. If Dalton was going to make an offer, it would not be here.

'Your friend in America,' Griffin enquired, 'what was his name?'

'I don't think I recall,' Dalton said.

'John Irving, by any chance?'

'Never heard of him,' Dalton said. He smiled at Griffin and lowered one eyelid slightly.

'So consequently, he's never heard of you,' Griffin speculated.

'Right,' Dalton said. 'Nor the project I have in mind.'

Dalton finished his dry martini. 'What do you say we go to my hotel and do some serious drinking in private?' They took a taxi to the River Park Hotel. The American had been playing it safe. Griffin had been vetted on neutral ground, and only now was Dalton prepared to allow Griffin to know where he could be contacted. It looked good.

Griffin was introduced to the two yahoos who, on that occasion, nodded good-naturedly and sat in discreet silence, nursing drinks, as well-trained minions should.

'Tell me George,' Dalton said, 'would you say you were a good patriot?'

'I expect I'm as patriotic as the next man,' Griffin said.

'Yes, but who's the next man? He might be some guy who'd sell his country down the river. What then?

'Can I help it if I'm standing next to a shit?' Griffin asked.

'Come on, George' Dalton said. 'Come the crunch is it the Union Jack and God Save the Queen? Or is it send George Griffin victorious?'

'I hate moral problems,' Griffin said. 'I prefer not to know. Just do the job I'm paid for. Ours not to reason why, ours just to be paid and forget about it. That way, I don't have to worry and my conscience remains unsullied.'

'This time, you've got to know,' Dalton said. 'Because if I didn't tell you, you'd guess anyway. The British wouldn't approve of this particular odd job. So does money have a biological cleansing effect on your conscience or not?'

Griffin thought about it. He compared the bills in his desk with the state of his bank account. He assessed the likelihood of his new bank manager being persuaded to extend his overdraft.

'Let me put it this way,' he said. 'I cannot be bought, except for cash. When confronted by the dilemma you mention, I try and arrive at an intellectual rather than an emotional conclusion. In that event, I'm forced to admit that the man who said that patriotism was the last refuge of the scoundrel knew what he was talking about. Doctor Johnson, wasn't it?'

'So you're not a scoundrel,' Dalton said. 'Only don't try backing out later, George, when you know what it's all about. Friends and allies we may be, but we wouldn't like that, and nor would you.'

That was the first hint of any kind of threat, but it was said with such smiling joviality that Griffin took it to mean that he would collect a black mark and no more odd jobs from the CIA, which was a thoroughly professional attitude, and fair enough. He nodded.

'OK' Dalton said. 'Does the name Tauber mean anything to you?'

Griffin shook his head, and filled up his glass. 'No.'

'He's a hit man' Dalton said. 'He's good. One of the best. A quiet, efficient operator.' There was a note of reluctant admiration in his voice.

'Who's he with?' Griffin asked. 'Executive Action Group?'

'Well, that's what the West call it,' Dalton said. 'But Tauber's an artist. He works alone. He's carried out some first class eliminations, in his time,' he reminisced, like a football player talking about an old opponent. 'A Ukrainian emigrée leader in Frankfurt, the editor of an influential Moslem newspaper in the Sudan, the Chief of Police in Vienna, oh, any number of slick operations. He's a hard man, is Tauber.'

'So I gather,' Griffin said.

'Now he's arrived in London,' Dalton said casually. 'He's supposed to deal with an East German defector.' He looked at Griffin as though he expected some comment.

'Supposed to?' Griffin queried.

Dalton nodded. 'Tauber's still a young man,' he said, 'but it's a hard life in the Executive Action Group. Maybe he's just tired, or maybe he's realized what a valuable property he is. Maybe both, I don't know. Whatever.' He gestured with the hand which was not holding a dry martini. 'Anyway he's opened negotiations with the British. Given the right terms, he's willing to do a cross-over deal. Now, that's great for the British. Tauber knows a lot, like which targets the Executive Action Group have pro-grammed, and who's being moved where to deal with them. It's like a chess game,' Dalton explained. 'These people have to think ahead, and plan their moves. Targets are OK'd at the highest level these days, in accordance with long term policy.'

'As distinct from short term policy, like detente and co-existence,' Griffin suggested.

'Right,' Dalton said. 'So suddenly, Tauber's an important man. He knows more than he thinks he does. Upcoming targets just mean a few future funerals to him. But while there's no ap-parent connection between a bullet here and a prussic acid cap-sule there, in fact there's a link. Given that programme, which Tauber knows, a careful analysis by specialist intelligence offi-cers could show up what long term policy is really envisaged in the East. As distinct from the sweet talk in Helsinki,' he said with a smile.

'I doubt if anyone believed in all that crap,' Griffin said.

'Oh, you're wrong, Georgie boy,' Dalton said. 'Believe me, you're wrong. There are important and influential people in my country and yours who believe it because they want to believe it. It would be nice to believe it. It would be convenient to believe it. Christ, look at your sensible, intelligent trade union leaders. They managed to convince themselves that the former head of the KGB had turned respectable, become the leader of the Russian trade unions, whatever they may be, and could be invited to England to discuss common problems. Like getting a miner's strike called in Russia to bring down the government maybe?' Dalton laughed. 'Come on. Anyone who'll believe that will believe anything. So they fawned on the guy. They shook his hand as though there was no blood on it, as though the persecu-tion of Russian Jews, writers and protest groups was nothing to do with him. They crawled on their bellies and licked his boots. OK, they behaved like fools, nice fools if you like, but they're only as stupid as a whole lot of politicians who are dying to settle for the easy option: kid themselves that the West is going to be left alone now; that it's safe; that riots, demonstrations, and strikes in key industries happen spontaneously; that Solzhenitsyn is a religious fanatic, and the concentration camps aren't real, he just imagined them. They're all around us, Georgie boy, in your parliament, in our congress, eager, sincere, busting a gut to deceive themselves and everyone else. What about that female politician of yours who maintained the real danger in Portugal was from fascist reaction?' Dalton roared with laughter. The two yahoos chuckled appreciatively.

'And you think Tauber might spoil the happy scene,' Griffin said.

'Given a sober appreciation of genuine Russian long term policy,' Dalton said, 'not even the wettest of innocents in our respective cabinets could avoid facing the awkward truth. Well, maybe they could,' he qualified. 'Politicians do have a superb talent for avoiding reality, you must grant them that. But it would be more difficult. The military could lean on them harder. Maybe get some of what they need, anyway. But there's one great problem, George. Tauber approached the British, not us.'

'Friends and allies,' Griffin said. 'Don't they share and share alike?'

'Bullshit,' Dalton said. 'We'll get told what the British think we should know, and no more. OK, we'd do the same, and that's the way we want it. We want Tauber and all he knows complete. With all respect to our allies, we don't want to be fed whatever scraps the British feel inclined to throw our way. That's where you come in George. You find him.'

'If British Intelligence have got him,' Griffin objected, 'he'll be under armed guard somewhere.'

'Tauber won't deliver himself that easy,' Dalton said. 'He'll be negotiating at arms' length. Brief phone calls that can't be traced. Intermediaries, maybe. I don't know. But he'll take every precaution. He won't want the British to pick him up before he's screwed the best possible deal out of them. He's somewhere in London, that's for certain. You've got at most seven days. Can you find him?'

'I can try,' Griffin said. 'It'll cost a lot in expenses . . .'

'And then deliver him,' Dalton said.

Griffin liked the additional task a lot less than the first, and he said so.

'Both,' Dalton said, briefly. 'I'll pay you an advance on your fee now, and the rest on delivery.'

Griffin considered. He thought about his role in all this. He looked at Dalton and wondered about a few things.

'I wonder,' he said, 'why you don't go to British Intelligence, tell them you know about Tauber, and demand equal access.'

'We wouldn't get it,' Dalton said. 'There are areas where British foreign policy isn't the same as ours. We want Tauber ourselves. We'll do the deciding about access, equal or otherwise.'

'Who's we, exactly?'

'Come on,' Dalton said wearily. 'I don't have to spell it out, do I?'

'Is there any reason why not?' Griffin asked.

'Central Intelligence Agency,' Dalton said. 'Do you want to see some identification?'

'Yes,' Griffin said.

Dalton held out his right hand. The nearest yahoo opened a drawer, took out two bundles of ten pound notes, and placed them in Dalton's hand.

'There it is,' Dalton said. He laid the tempting bundles on the table. 'And that's all you're going to see. Come on, George, you're not dumb, and you're not naïve. When you leave this hotel, you're acting on your own. There's no connection with the CIA whatever.'

'In case I foul it up,' Griffin said.

'Yes,' Dalton said. 'But don't.'

John Irving had not been so ultra-cautious but then his operations were reasonably above board as CIA activities went. On those occasions, no one was doublecrossing an allied intelligence service.

'So why pick on me?' Griffin enquired.

'You've got good references as a ferret man,' Dalton said. 'And I was told you could take most men, even someone like Tauber.'

'Provided he's not expecting it,' Griffin said. 'And he won't be. Not from me.'

'Because you look like a clown?' Dalton asked cruelly.

'That's me,' Griffin said. 'The pub bore, a figure of fun.'

'Well, I was told on good authority,' Dalton said, 'so I'll believe it. But a man with Tauber's training and experience? Where did you learn to cope with someone like that?'

'I used to be in the SAS' Griffin said.

'The Special Air Service? That bunch of thugs?' Dalton seemed impressed. Then he grinned widely. 'And you had the gall to sit there talking about your conscience.'

'Mine is of the residual variety, and easily quelled,' Griffin said, looking at the bundles of ten pound notes. 'All right. You want Tauber. Why don't you take him?'

'We'd never get near him,' Dalton said. 'We've all worked in the field. He knows what we look like.'

'London's crawling with CIA men,' Griffin said. 'He can't know all of them. Use some of them.'

'I thought it was obvious,' Dalton said impatiently, 'that we can't. For Christ's sake, the British are going to know exactly what's happened, and they're going to squawk loud and long. Washington has to be able to deny any responsibility, hand on heart. We three are dispensable, let alone you. This is not only unofficial, it never happened. How the hell can we use any of our men stationed in London, when British Intelligence know who the bastards are? Come on George,' Dalton said plaintively. 'Please.'

That all seemed to make sense. Griffin said, 'How did you know about Tauber being here in the first place?'

'Various bits of information,' Dalton said. 'Some from the East, some from right here in London.' He studied the chandelier, which almost looked like crystal. 'Even in

British Intelligence,' he said quietly, 'there are one or two who like to earn a little on the side.'

It all added up to the kind of dirty, ruthless tactics which Griffin was accustomed to, and he was satisfied.

He memorized a full description of Tauber's habits and ways, studied photographs of the man and pocketed them. He learned that Tauber had arrived in London on a Swissair flight from Geneva, checked into a hotel in South Kensington, paid his bill in advance and disappeared with his luggage the following night.

Then they haggled like Arab market traders over how much the delivery of Tauber would cost. Dalton offered five hundred pounds. Griffin rejected the offer indignantly, and demanded two thousand. Dalton told him that in that case the deal was off, and he would find someone else.

They finally settled on a thousand pounds, five hundred now, five hundred on delivery, the figure, Griffin suspected, which both men had decided on before the bargaining started.

He walked out of the River Park Hotel with a light heart, and a wallet stuffed with ten pound notes. The bank manager could screw himself. Now all he had to do was find Tauber.

It took six days, and a lot of time and money. Griffin knew a lot of people, just below the surface of society, who liked to make a quick few quid, and he cast his bread upon the waters wide.

Among them was a taxi driver who worked at nights, and chauffeured his hostess girl friend. If she was unlucky at the club and failed to find a punter, he drove her around in the early hours of the morning, looking for men who seemed lonely and only had money to keep them company.

The middle-aged driver of a Mercedes or a Rolls Royce might find a taxi alongside him at a junction or a traffic lights. In the back of the taxi sat a slim feminine figure, a loose, silver satin scarf showing off her blonde hair. She looked beautiful in the dim light.

'Excuse me, guv'nor,' her taxi driver pimp would say, 'but you don't happen to be looking for a lovely young lady, by any chance, do you?'

Quite often, by chance, they were.

Griffin thought that a man who left a South Kensington hotel at night with luggage and wanted to get to a safe hole fast would take a taxi.

His taxi driver friend, palmed the ten pound notes and, having dropped his hostess girl friend in Soho, spent the evening contacting his fellow night hawks with the news that the CID were offering five quid for information about this geezer. 'South Ken mate. Could have been the rank, could have been a pick up.'

Griffin knew that Tauber would be an elusive customer. It was the man's trade to arrive in a city, disappear, remain out of sight, surface briefly alongside whoever was due to die, go to ground again, and depart unobtrusively when the fuss had died down.

But Griffin thought that there were certain factors in his favour. According to Dalton, the East German defector was living in Camberwell. Tauber would normally settle in that area so that he could observe his victim's routine and decide on the best method to remove him. But if Tauber had lost interest in his way of life in favour of lusher pastures in the West, Griffin thought it unlikely that he would go anywhere near Camberwell. That was where his colleagues and superiors in the Executive Action Group would start looking for him once it dawned on them that something had gone wrong. Psychologically, Griffin thought it likely that Tauber would stay north of the river.

On the other hand, he would not stray as far as residential areas like Kilburn or Chiswick, where a stranger might be more prominent than in central London.

That still left a large chunk of the city to comb, but Griffin guessed that Tauber would feel exposed in any of the great hotels in the West End. Altogether too many people wandered in and out of those hotels, and you never knew who they were. No, if he were in Tauber's position, it would be somewhere small, with a fast turnover in overnight trade, where they were not interested in you so long as the bill was paid.

Finally, Dalton had been positive that, although Tauber spoke good English, he had never visited London before and had no known contacts outside his embassy. The embassy was the last place he would go near, and another good reason for avoiding the West End, where one of the KGB men who were on the books as trade advisers, counsellors, or cultural attachés, might happen to recognize him.

Griffin thought he would try his luck at the South Kensington Hotel. He ignored reception, and had a quiet chat with the hotel porter who, like most of his breed, had an addiction to ready cash.

Griffin was, he said, a solicitor, who was trying to trace a client for whom he had some good news. The porter's belief in this yarn firmed up when he saw the ten pound note which Griffin took from his wallet, and he racked his brains anxiously.

'I remember him walking out with his suitcase,' he said. 'Late it was, about eleven o'clock. I asked him if he wanted a taxi, but he said no . . .'

Griffin shrugged, and started to put the ten pound note away. The porter developed withdrawal symptoms.

'Hang on,' he said, hastily. 'Let me see if anyone else knows anything.'

Griffin went into the bar, and refreshed himself with two large gins. The porter reappeared, and they conferred in low voices in a corner of the foyer.

'One of the chambermaids,' the porter said, 'she remembers him asking about somewhere to stay for a friend of his. A cheap sort of hotel, he said, where you get lots of tourists. She advised him to try the Paddington area.'

Griffin relinquished the note, which disappeared, apparently, up the porter's sleeve. His hand remained cupped expectantly.

'I had to tell the chambermaid,' he said, 'that it would be worth ten quid to her.'

'Hard luck,' Griffin said. 'That leaves you with sod all.'

Paddington, he thought, as he drove back across Hyde Park, made sense. There were whole streets where you would be hard pressed to find anyone conversing in English. Tauber would be as prominent in Paddington as a blade of grass in a field.

On the other hand, that was no more than a reasonable guess, and there was no word from his taxi driver friend yet. Griffin

95

went back to his flat and passed the time developing the photographs of Dalton and the two yahoos. The phone remained obstinately silent. Griffin decided to look up someone he knew just in case he might need him and telephoned Bayswater police station.

They met in a dimly lighted, tatty drinking club off Praed Street which was full of assorted villains of one kind and another. Among the villains was Nick, who was a Detective Sergeant in the Bayswater Division.

The two men had first met in the army, when both were young. Nick dabbled in every racket there was, from flogging leave passes to knocking off NAAFI supplies, and selling them to the Germans.

Unlike Griffin, his misdemeanours never came home to roost, and he left the army with a clean record. Just the same, Griffin was astounded when he ran into Nick one day by accident, and discovered that he had joined the police force. That seemed rather like one of Satan's minions entering the Church of England as a curate.

Later, Griffin realized that it made sense. Nick was a good copper in his own way, tough and hard working. He rapidly found his niche in CID where, apart from acting as a guardian of law and order and protecting the community, he began to make a good deal of money on the side, in those ways which are open to policemen with a knack for business, and their own private opinions on right and wrong and what they can safely get away with.

'My definition of a straight copper,' Nick told Griffin once, 'is the man who accepts a bribe from a villain, and then does the bastard just the same.'

Under various pseudonyms, Nick had money invested in a shady club, a mini cab firm catering for prostitutes and six greyhounds, in which latter enterprise his partner was a night club owner at present on bail, and shortly to face conspiracy charges at the Old Bailey.

'I warned the silly bugger,' Nick said, 'to quit before West End Central nobbled him, but he wouldn't listen. Thought he was cleverer than Old Bill.' Nick snorted with derision. 'I can't run six bleeding dogs on my own. They'll have to go. Still, they're due to win two big races next month. At least they'll fetch a good price after that.'

Griffin enquired which races, only too willing to break his non-gambling rule and stake whatever cash he had in hand at the time. It would be no gamble. If Nick said they were going to win, win they would, and how that would be arranged was none of Griffin's business.

'Don't ask stupid questions,' Nick said. 'The odds'll be short enough as it is without you shoving all your spare cash on. Get stuffed.'

Griffin felt regret but no surprise. Nick was sentimental about money.

They spent two hours in the club, and neither of them paid out a penny. Nick knew every hard-looking villain there, and they all appeared anxious to demonstrate their politeness and affection by buying drinks. 'Same again?' someone said, as their glasses approached the half-empty mark. 'What's your friend drinking?'

'Large gin and tonic,' Griffin told one villain after another.

'Half the bastards are informants,' Nick said. 'And the other half, I'll have them by the short and curlies one of these fine days. The streets'll be a bloody sight cleaner when I've put some of this lot away, I can tell you. Oh, thanks, Charlie, good health,' he said, as another round of drinks arrived. 'Especially that bloody pervert,' he said vindictively, eyeing the retreating Charlie. 'And once I get the evil sod in the nick, he's going to fall down a flight of stairs, too.' He sipped his fresh drink. 'Probably twice,' he added.

Griffin showed him Tauber's photograph, explained that he might want to find the man, and asked Nick's advice.

'Could be difficult,' Nick said. 'Unless you know what area he's likely to be in.' He did not enquire why Griffin was interested, and nor would he.

'As yet,' Griffin said, 'it could be anywhere. But suppose it was around here?'

'Then you've got chances,' Nick said, 'if you play your cards right.' He looked at the crowd of men in the club. 'Take this lot

for instance. You've got street traders, bookies, gamblers, pick-
pockets, unemployed layabouts, waiters, porters, cab drivers,
pimps, and that bloke calls on hotels selling bum paper when he's
not knocking off cars. They're all out and about around Paddington, day and night. It'd be like having a private army of
spies, if they felt like doing someone a favour.'

'Like who?'

'Like me,' Nick said.

'I thought it might be,' Griffin said, grinning.

'They wouldn't give you the time of day,' Nick said. 'Me, it's
run of the mill. They wouldn't even be shopping one of their
mates, though most of the bastards would sell their virgin daugh-
ters to a sadist for a few nicker.'

'How few for this merchant?' Griffin asked, referring to
Tauber.

'Call it a hundred quid,' Nick said.

Griffin winced. 'You always were a thieving bastard,' he said.
'You'd offer fifty, top weight.'

'I've got expenses,' Nick told him.

'Well, he might be somewhere else,' Griffin said. 'I'm not sure
yet.'

'Let me know,' Nick said.

Not bloody likely, Griffin thought, as he blearily drove back to
his flat. Bent coppers were altogether too much of an expensive
luxury. He had reluctantly paid a hundred pounds into his bank
account to keep that creep of a bank manager quiet, and he had
been peeling off ten pound notes like autumn leaves already. He
tried to remember how much he had paid out, and failed, driving
absently through a red light as he searched his memory. God, he
must be stoned out of his mind. Fortunately, it was two in the
morning and there were no other cars around at that moment.

He was pulling back the sheets when the phone began to ring.
Moaning, he dragged himself back into the living room.

'Hullo,' he croaked into the phone.

It was his taxi driver friend. 'Susie's got herself a punter,' the
cheerful voice said, 'so I thought I'd give you a tinkle.'

'Fantastic,' Griffin said. 'Susie's getting screwed, and that's news?'

'You never know,' the taxi driver said, good-naturedly. 'This one's an MP. I've picked him up at the House of Commons after late night sittings, several times. Seen him on television too. Dead against the permissive society, he is.'

'For Christ's sake,' Griffin said, 'have you got anything or not?'

'Yes. Have you got a pencil?'

In the morning, Griffin drank black coffee, swallowed aspirins, wished his head would stop aching and tried to read his wandering scrawl of the night before. Finally, he managed to decipher it.

Three taxi drivers had picked up men with suitcases, any one of whom might be Tauber, near South Kensington Station that night.

One at midnight, had gone to London Airport, Terminal One. Forget that one. Tauber could have flown to anywhere in Europe or the UK from Terminal One. But why should he? No.

The second, at ten forty-five, had gone to Waterloo. No. The hotel porter was sure Tauber had left the hotel after eleven o'clock.

The third one, at eleven fifteen, had been dropped at a hotel in Sussex Gardens.

Griffin's headache began to recede, his spirits lifted. He even felt like a cigarette, and coughed on it contentedly.

Sussex Gardens fitted the bill perfectly. Rows of small hotels, converted from Victorian houses, catering mainly for the lower priced tourist trade. Hundreds of people in and out daily. Exactly the sort of place Griffin would have headed for himself.

The thought gave him confidence. Perhaps he was like this man, Tauber, whom he had never met. Perhaps he could read what Tauber would be likely to do.

He thought about that as he drove to the hotel in Sussex Gardens. He was not put out to find that no one resembling Tauber had checked in there. If he were Tauber, he would dismiss the taxi, and then walk somewhere else. But with a suitcase, it would not be all that far.

Griffin began to comb the area, again talking to porters, and not proprietors or receptionists. He was still a solicitor looking for a lucky client.

He found the hotel in a side road, a hundred yards away. Tauber had left the following morning, but it was only a question of time now, Griffin thought happily. Screw bent coppers and their outrageous demands.

Three days later, Griffin was tense, jumpy and irritable. He had failed to find any further trace of Tauber whatever, despite the increasing desperation and frequency with which he peeled off notes which disappeared into willing palms with negative results.

Suppose he was wrong? That would be a disaster, and Griffin preferred not to think about it. He had to be right. He was positive that he knew what Tauber would do.

Because if he were in Tauber's position in a strange city, and apart from being a paid executioner, Griffin could well imagine it, he would first go to ground before making contact. Check. Tauber had left the South Kensington Hotel, and headed for Paddington, where he would be anonymous.

Griffin would then stay no more than one night in any one place. Check. Tauber had stayed overnight in the hotel near Sussex Gardens, and then moved on.

After that, Griffin could not prove that he was right. But he thought he would stay in the same district. Move on daily, staying at some hotel within walking distance, arriving without notice or pre-booking.

Phone calls would have to be made to whoever was his contact at British Intelligence, but Griffin would never make them from a hotel, where you had to go through a switchboard. He would use public street telephones.

In that event, if he were right, Tauber must be on the streets of Paddington two or three times a day, moving from one hotel to another, going out to phone boxes. But if that were so, neither Griffin, who haunted the area like a harassed ghost, nor the people he was paying, had caught sight of him.

And time was running out, Griffin thought, as he brooded over a gin and tonic in a pub off Queensway. He sighed, got up, made a phone call, bought another gin and tonic and a large scotch and sat down again.

Half an hour later, Nick walked in, sat down beside Griffin, picked up the scotch, and said, 'Cheers.'

'I think he's in Paddington,' Griffin said. 'So I'd better take you up on your offer.'

'OK' Nick said. 'I'll get around to it as soon as I can.'

'I've only got forty-eight hours,' Griffin said, urgently.

'In that case, it'll cost two hundred quid,' Nick said. 'I'll have to put a couple of my DC's on it as well, and they'll expect fifty quid each.'

'You bare-faced liar,' Griffin said, shocked at the way his expected profit was being washed away. 'All you've got to do is walk up to that bloody club, and show some photographs around.'

'All right then,' Nick said, unruffled. Forget it.'

'A hundred now,' Griffin said, 'and another hundred if and when you find him.'

'Two hundred now, or I don't even bloody start,' Nick said.

Sadly Griffin counted out twenty ten pound notes. He had no choice and he knew it.

'I hope your dogs all catch the mange,' he said.

'Serves you right,' Nick said. 'For trying to be clever and go it alone.'

On the morning of the sixth day, Griffin was in his flat. This must be what a corner of hell was like. He had nothing to do but wait. He had run out of gin, and dare not go out to buy some more in case Nick phoned.

He made coffee, and smoked restlessly. The phone rang. It was, not for the first time, an increasingly impatient Dalton. Griffin fended him off with what he recognized were singularly unconvincing tales of hot leads and the imminent tracing of Tauber, hung up, and then discovered that he was out of cigarettes as well.

This, he thought, was more than any man should be asked to bear. At one o'clock, he decided that he could stand it no longer. The gin he could just manage without. Cigarettes he could not.

So he might as well buy both.

He was locking the door of his flat when the phone began to ring inside. He nearly fractured his key in his eagerness to get back inside.

'Come and have a jar,' Nick said.

Griffin drew thankfully on the cigarette Nick gave him, and sank his gin in one. He must remember to buy a bottle before he left.

'Take the packet,' Nick said.

Under the flap was written the name of a hotel. Griffin breathed a deep sigh of relief.

'Is he there now?' he asked.

Nick nodded. 'Thank a compulsive old gambler called Freddie,' he said. 'At twelve noon, he backed a horse at a betting shop off Craven Terrace. Then he propped himself up outside. He saw your man make a phone call from the call box opposite. He had a suitcase with him. Freddie followed him to that hotel.'

'If he'd placed his bet, what was he hanging about for?'

'The result of the three o'clock,' Nick said. 'What else? He's got nowhere else to go.'

'You said "old" gambler,' Griffin objected, hardly daring to believe it had come right after all. 'If his eyesight's dicky, he might have got it wrong.'

Nick laughed. 'When he's not backing horses,' he said, 'Freddie combines pleasure with business. He's a peeping tom. When he strikes lucky, that can lead him to a bit of petty blackmail. He's got eyes like an eagle and a photographic memory. I use him as an informant and he's never let me down yet. If that's not your man, it's his twin.'

'Would you take any bets on that?'

'Yes,' Nick said. 'Two hundred quid.'

'OK' Griffin said, 'I believe you. How much did Freddie get out of it? Twenty quid?'

'He's not greedy like me,' Nick said.

Just the same, Griffin's doubts grew again as he sat in his car and looked at the hotel, one of a row with identical porticos, identical steps leading up to them from the road, and identical brass knobs on their half open doors.

He dare not make enquiries in the hotel this time, he was too close to Tauber now—if Tauber was there at all.

He only had Nick's word for that, no, not even Nick's, but a second-hand identification from some bleary old bugger who hung around outside betting shops, staring vacantly into space and who was supposed to have keen eyesight because he could see a woman undressing in her bedroom when he had his nose pressed up against the window.

And for that, he had paid two hundred quid, to a bent copper who could easily, Griffin thought with sick apprehension, have invented the whole thing. Suppose Tauber was not there? What could he do about it?

He could tell Nick that he had sold a bum lead, and talk about having his money back. But Nick would not even discuss it. He knew Nick.

'What money?' Nick would say. 'I don't know what you're talking about. Have you got a receipt?'

He could sort Nick out privately, and work off the debt that way. He could take Nick any time and had always been able to, and Nick knew it. But regrettably, Nick now had a heavy mob at his back, paid for by the taxpayer, who would cheerfully wheel him along to the police station any time on Nick's say so.

Griffin did not mind the prospect of appearing in court on some trumped-up charge, but he had no taste for what would happen the night before.

'The accused had been drinking, and was unsteady on his feet,' Nick, or some lying colleague would say with grave honesty, when asked in court to account for Griffin's injuries. 'When proceeding to the cells, he fell down a flight of stairs.'

No. If Nick had cheated him, there was nothing he could do about it. All he could do was hope that Nick had played it straight. Which was possible, but by no means certain, he thought gloomily.

Griffin smoked one cigarette after another, until his throat grew parched and dry. He got out and fed the parking meter at intervals, easing his stiff legs, and wondering if he dare slope off for a drink.

Why had he taken that bottle of gin home? Stupid idiot. How long would it take to fetch it?

But no, he must not take his eyes from the entrance to the hotel. If he was right about Tauber, and so far he had been, he told himself in an effort to restore his wilting confidence, then some time he would walk out of that hotel. That could be today, if he had to make another phone call. If not, it would be tomorrow when the man would appear with a suitcase, ready to move on again.

All Griffin could do was to wait, all night if necessary. But Tauber might not be there at all, in which case he was wasting most of the few precious hours left, assuming Dalton had meant what he said. Seven days, no more. It was the second five hundred which Griffin needed. The first five hundred would pay for his search and temporarily get him off the hook at the bank, but only the second half of his fee would provide that pleasant glow which came from having sufficient money to contemplate an evening, or possibly two if she proved difficult, at the Mirabelle.

Tauber came out of the hotel, and walked away from the parked car. Griffin slid from behind the driving wheel, and followed, happy and remorseful. Good old Nick. Fancy harbouring those miserable, unworthy suspicions about his trustworthy old friend Nick. What a nasty bastard George Griffin was.

He was sure it was Tauber. The man's face was far from distinctive. He would pass in any crowd, unnoticed. But Griffin had studied his photograph like a botanist examining a rare plant, and he knew every detail of those nondescript features.

There was something else which added to Griffin's certainty. The man walked lazily, casually, lightly, almost aimlessly. But under that well cut, mohair suit was a body which moved as effortlessly as an efficient machine, an engine with reserves of power no ordinary man would ever dream of. Griffin knew what he was looking at. He had once had a body like

104

that.

Griffin was careful, he was also lucky. A coach drew up outside a neighbouring hotel and disgorged a party of Scotsmen. Griffin disappeared into the throng, moved invisibly with a dozen or so who were wandering about, gaping and exclaiming in Glaswegian accents as though they had never seen London before, caught a glimpse of Tauber as he entered the phone box round the corner, and went back to his car, satisfied.

Tauber re-appeared, returned to the hotel and disappeared inside. Griffin looked at his watch. He estimated that Tauber had spent no more than thirty seconds on the phone. That could be a good sign, he thought. Tauber was still being careful about phone calls being traced. The final arrangements had not been made yet.

And yet, of course, they might have been. That could have been the last phone call, the one where they reached agreement, in which case Tauber would be packing, even now.

It was unlikely, Griffin thought. Tauber was not the sort of man to accept promises without something tangible to back them up. He would certainly want a written guarantee of immunity, on official notepaper, counter-signed by somebody with public standing and a career to think about, and that meant a minister of the Crown.

Tauber would want that letter first, so that he could lodge it somewhere safe, besides spraying a few copies around to make sure, before he walked into the spider's web of enemy intelligence.

All that would necessitate preliminaries: a safe drop where Tauber could collect the letter. Unless he were using an intermediary, someone who would betray neither Tauber nor intelligence. Dalton had said that Tauber had no friends in London but he could have made an arrangement with some neutral go-between, a Swede or a Swiss.

Tauber had arrived from Geneva, Griffin remembered, and he nibbled at his lip nervously. The whole affair could be nearly completed. He had no way of knowing. He did not want to risk taking his eyes from Tauber's door for one second, but he needed to make a phone call.

He got out of his car, and glanced quickly into nearby hotels. One of them had a phone where everyone could hear what was said, but it adjoined a window from where he could see Tauber's hotel.

'I've identified the package,' Griffin said into the phone, and I'll try and deliver by tomorrow morning.'

'What's wrong with now?' Dalton enquired.

'Not possible,' Griffin said. 'It's tucked away with a number of others. It may take a while before it's in a position where I can lift it.'

He hung up, and went back to his car. It grew dark and a light drizzle began to fall. There was no sign of Tauber.

The owners of the cars near Griffin arrived, and drove them away. The street was not especially well lighted, but Griffin felt as though he were in the beam of a searchlight. He backed his car up until it was concealed by a coach.

People came and went from the hotel at irregular intervals. One of them could be the Swiss go-between, Griffin thought. They might be wrapping the whole thing up, delivering the Swiss bank statement showing the agreed amount standing to Tauber's credit in a numbered account. No minister was going to admit in writing that Tauber had been paid. If it ever got into the press, which was unlikely, he would be a defector, overcome by sudden admiration for democracy.

The next thing that could happen, Griffin thought, was the arrival of Tauber's escort, when he could kiss the rest of his fee goodbye, and here he was, sitting in his car, tired, hungry, dying for a drink and doing nothing. He looked at the windows of the hotel, and wondered if he should try and do it now. In a hotel, with staff and guests wandering about? He grimaced with distaste.

The next thing that happened was that Tauber walked out of the hotel, hailed a taxi, got in and drove off.

Griffin started his engine. He hated the idea of following, but he had no choice. Tauber might be going to a meet.

The taxi dropped Tauber at a pub in a mews in North

Kensington, and drove off. Tauber went inside. Griffin parked, and thought about it. He had no great desire to go into that pub, except for the prospect of a few fast gins, but suppose Tauber was meeting someone? This could be his last chance.

And if Tauber could disappear into a crowd, he, George Griffin was perfectly camouflaged in a pub. Not in the same inconspicuous way, certainly, but the pub bore who inflicted his company, drank too much, and regaled deaf neighbours with old stories was as near as damn it invisible, and definitely no danger to a watchful man.

Griffin was certain that Tauber had not seen him. Just the same, he hesitated for a moment, but the thought of those gins flowing down his throat decided him.

He opened the door, and pushed his way into the noisy, warm, friendly bar. Tauber, he was relieved to see, was sitting alone, with a glass of beer and a knife and fork. All the man had wanted, probably, was a bit of air, a drink and something to eat.

There was a small, bald man tucked into a crowded corner of the bar. Griffin squeezed in.

'Double gin and tonic, as soon as you like,' he said to the busy barman. He turned to the small, bald man. 'Evening squire,' he said, with a friendly smile. 'Lovely weather for the time of year, isn't it?'

CHAPTER EIGHT

Griffin gave himself another gin from the bottle standing at his elbow and reflected that whatever its other merits, alcohol was a pretty poor anaesthetic. He had propped himself into a position where, apart from the pain every time he drew breath, the rest of his tortured body had lapsed into stunned quiescence. But when he stretched out his arm for the bottle, the frayed, hostile nerves in his shoulder reacted so violently that he nearly cried out.

Dalton observed the involuntary twist round his mouth, and asked sympathetically, 'The muscles playing up a little, George? Maybe you should try moving around, get some exercise. Loosen you up.'

The bastard. He knew this game backwards. He knew, as Griffin did, that all movements would be slow and agonizing for the next twenty-four hours, a constant reminder that more of the same was available, only worse.

The yahoo with the dental problem was exploring his broken teeth with his forefinger.

'Try Guy's Hospital,' Griffin advised him. 'They run an emergency service. I should think you'd offer a fascinating problem. An ideal exhibit for their students.'

The yahoo glared at him. 'Careful, George,' Dalton said. 'Your sense of humour jars sometimes, do you know that? I might decide to let him return the compliment after all.'

'No you won't,' Griffin said. 'When I leave here, you don't want my face marked. I'd attract too much attention.'

Dalton lit a cigarette, and studied him thoughtfully. 'OK,' he said. 'Under that flab, you're a hard number. So why haven't you delivered Tauber? You found him. What went wrong?'

Griffin stuck fairly closely to the actual events, in case Dalton

108

knew more than he was letting on, although he altered the ending. He was absolutely certain that he had not been followed to Marlow.

In the revised version, Griffin retained Tauber's telephone call, but then, he said, a mini cab had turned up, and driven Tauber away.

'You mean that's who he phoned?' Dalton enquired. 'Are you sure it was a cab?'

Griffin shrugged, forgetting, and winced with pain. 'Mini cabs aren't licensed in London,' he said. 'It could have been genuine, it could have been a phoney. There's no way of knowing.'

'Where did he go?' Dalton asked. 'I'm sure you followed him,' he said sarcastically.

'The Royal Garden Hotel,' Griffin said.

'You're a goddamn liar,' Dalton snapped. 'Tauber wouldn't go near a place like the Royal Garden.'

'He went to a suite which is occupied by a Swiss businessman,' Griffin said, 'and he stayed there.'

He doubted if Dalton believed him, but then Dalton would not believe anything Griffin told him. All he could do was to hope to create a little uncertainty. From the way Dalton was nibbling his lip, a certain doubt had set in, probably brought on by the mention of a Swiss businessman, which, had it been true, could have indicated that Tauber's negotiations were nearly complete. He had chosen the Royal Garden because it had a private car park, reached by a sweeping, circular ramp, which Dalton evidently knew about. There was direct access to the hotel from the car park. Had Tauber in fact followed this plan, which Griffin modestly thought was quite a good one in view of his battered condition, a car containing husky, armed Special Branch men could have used that car park to spirit Tauber away to a safe place, and there was nothing anyone could have done about it.

'George,' Dalton said at last, 'the only thing I'm going to buy is Tauber. On the strength of your phone call, we made certain arrangements to get him out of the country, and back to the USA. The British aren't going to let us buy an airline ticket for him, you know.'

'No, I realize that,' Griffin said, playing the game as best he could, and fervently wishing it were over. He desperately needed to think, and there was no hope of concentrating with the ever present fear that Dalton might decide to let the two yahoos go round again.

'Those arrangements can't be changed,' Dalton said. 'You say you know where he is, so deliver him.'

'He'll be harder to get close to now,' Griffin said. 'It'd be easier if you weren't so concerned about his health.'

'He's no use to us if he isn't alive,' Dalton said. 'We want him alive. You were paid to deliver him alive. If he dies, so do you, believe me.'

'Come on, old boy,' Griffin said. 'Despite the earlier piece of horseplay, deep down, we're all friends and allies and all that stuff, you know.' Even as the words came out, he was afraid that he had gone too far in his effort to keep up the pretence. But Dalton did not seem to notice.

'Don't give me that old boy crap,' he said, viciously. 'You can have until tomorrow morning, and that's it. If you haven't delivered Tauber alive and well by then . . .' He turned his head, and looked at the yahoo with the damaged teeth. 'What would you most like to do to him, given the chance?'

'Castrate him,' the yahoo said, thickly. 'Eventually.'

Griffin stood, swaying, outside the hotel, while a porter found him a taxi. A thin film of icy sweat born of pure, elemental fear covered his face. The porter came back, and looked at him curiously.

'Are you all right, sir?'

'I think I'm sickening for the flu,' Griffin said.

The porter helped him solicitously into the taxi. 'Go to bed, sir,' he advised, 'with a strong, hot whisky and lemon. Thank *you*, sir,' he said, accepting the handful of change which Griffin could not be bothered to sort out.

The taxi took him to the multi-storey car park, and Griffin drove home. He did not check if he was being followed. He would have been astounded if he were not being followed. At the moment, he did not care. He had to do something about this racking, crippling pain, which contracted his muscles in fiery spasms, and rendered him fit for nothing.

Dick and Jane had gone. A folded piece of paper with DAD printed on it was under an ashtray on the coffee table. Griffin put it in his pocket without looking at it, and limped to the bathroom.

A year before, during one of his more strenuous odd jobs, Griffin had over-exerted himself and developed back pains so severe as to be incapacitating. His doctor prescribed Paramol 118 to kill the pain, and referred him to the hospital. It turned out to be severe muscle strain, not a slipped disc, but he still had half a bottle of Paramol 118.

Griffin swallowed two tablets, and resisted the temptation to take a couple more for luck. The stuff was an effective pain killer, but he remembered that it had a tendency to make him drowsy. He dare not sleep until he had got rid of Tauber. But just how did he do that, he wondered, without signing his own death warrant?

He decided to see if a hot bath would help, while the tablets were taking effect. He lay in the steaming water and stared at his toes.

A thoroughly nasty possibility had belatedly dawned on him during his interview with Dalton, which had strengthened when Dalton warned off the yahoo who was intent on filling in Griffin's face with broken glass. Dalton had whispered in a language Griffin did not understand.

The steam rose, the mirror clouded over, the flat was silent, and Griffin lay in the hot water and tried to fight off the hideous black panic which threatened to engulf his faculties.

Only once before in his life could he remember this sense of hopeless, helpless, inevitable, impending disaster. And that was when he stood alongside the pregnant Brenda in the church at the age of eighteen.

Griffin blasphemed and climbed out of the bath. The water was nearly cold. He had fallen asleep. He dried himself, and flung his clothes on. It occurred to him that he was moving more freely and with less pain. The tablets were working. They were not doing too good a job on his kidneys though, which still hurt badly, and he wondered if the yahoos had permanently damaged him.

Griffin telephoned America as soon as there was likely to be someone in the office. It took a little while to track John Irving down. He was no longer, it seemed, a trade relations adviser, the incarnation under which Griffin had known him, but was now concerned with Agricultural and Soil Development. Griffin wondered what that meant. Biological warfare, probably.

'Well, George,' John Irving said into the phone at last, 'I thought your telephone people charged sky high prices for these calls. Since when did you get rich?'

There was a distinct note of reserve behind the surface banter, and Griffin did not blame him. The good odd job man, even one like Griffin who had become, if only briefly, a drinking partner, got paid and faithfully disappeared from sight. He did not ring up out of the blue uninvited.

'It's worth it to speak to you, John,' Griffin said. 'I need a bit of a helping hand.'

'I'm not working in that area any more,' Irving said. He evidently thought Griffin was touting for work.

'Nothing like that,' Griffin said. 'I need to know something, and I think you could tell me.'

'Like what?'

'I've had an offer over here from someone who says he's working for your old firm. I want to know if I should take it.'

'For Christ's sake,' Irving said. 'Information on personnel is restricted. You should know that.'

'I'm only asking for a negative check,' Griffin said. 'If someone's passing himself off as one of your people, you want to know about it, don't you?'

'To be candid with you, no, George,' Irving said. 'There are nuts all over the world doing just that all the time.'

'Well, I need to know,' Griffin said urgently. 'I could be in very serious trouble if I get this one wrong.' I already am, he thought. 'How's that musician?' he asked. 'Still playing the right

112

tunes for you?'

'You got paid, buster,' Irvine said. 'No bonus is called for.'

'You bloody grinding skinflint,' Griffin said. 'I'm not asking for blood, just a yes or no. Charge me for the service, if it'll make you feel better, and I'll pay you in booze the next time you're in London.'

Irving chuckled. 'OK,' he said. 'I'll listen. But I make you no promises.'

'Someone called Bob Dalton does the talking,' Griffin said. 'He's got two yahoos with him, introduced to me as Higgs and Denham. I'll give you their descriptions . . .'

Irving listened in silence. When Griffin had finished, he said, 'I'll have to call you back on this one.'

'Well, make it quick,' Griffin said. 'If you want that booze.'

He took two more tablets, and washed them down with the first half of a large gin. A little euphoria would be welcome but none appeared. He had the unpleasant feeling that he had walked into the biggest booby trap of his life, even worse than that agonizing affair in Germany. At least, that time, the unbearable pain had come to an end, and he had emerged with his life.

John Irving was not likely to call back for another half an hour or so. He thought it was safe to make a couple of quick phone calls. He looked up the North Kensington mews pub in the phone book, and dialled the number.

'I've mislaid my umbrella,' Griffin said. 'I was in your pub last night, and I wonder if I left it there by any remote chance.'

'No. Didn't find any brollies last night,' the landlord said. 'Sorry.'

'Oh, well, perhaps it was Harrods,' Griffin said, using his Major's voice. 'I'll try them. By the way, someone told me there was a bit of excitement your way after closing time.'

'Was there? What sort of excitement?'

'Something about cars arriving on the scene,' Griffin said vaguely. 'My friend thought it might have been the police.'

'Not as far as I know,' the landlord said. 'We didn't get knocked up, and no one's said anything.'

'He must have got it wrong. Sorry,' Griffin apologized. 'I wasn't paying much attention, to tell the truth. I was really thinking about my umbrella at the time.'

Griffin replaced the receiver. Men had knelt, looked at Tauber's bloodstain on the cobbles of that mews, and failed to make any enquiries. Which ought to mean that they had no official status. But the landlord might have been briefed not to say anything. He was no further forward.

He phoned Captain Drew's home in Devon. Drew was the one man in the world to whom he could tell the real facts, and be confident there would be no repercussions. Admittedly Drew would probably regard it as highly amusing, and laugh at him. But there was just an outside chance that Drew might feel philanthropic enough to help him, in return, of course, for cash on the nail. Griffin could use an ally with no scruples, just now. But the woman who answered the phone said that Captain Drew was abroad. She was not sure where, possibly Africa.

Griffin hung up. Drew was probably in either Tanzania, Mozambique or Rhodesia, working for either the guerillas or the counter-insurgent force, depending on which had made the highest offer. For preference, he would be employed by both sides. That was the deal Captain Drew liked best, although even he could not always swing that one. In any case, he was not available, and there was no one else Griffin would trust not to shop him to someone or another.

He smoked and waited for the phone to ring, spinning out the gin, sipping just enough now and then to lubricate his cigarettes. He was in poor shape after that beating up. He could not afford to get half pissed as well.

The grey clouds cleared and a beam of sunshine slanted through the window. The phone remained silent. Griffin finished the packet of cigarettes in his right hand pocket, and groped for the full packet in his left. His fingers encountered Dick's note, which he had forgotten. He unfolded it, and read it.

'You'll have to get some more milk,' it said. 'Do you know you're nearly out of coffee? Will give your regards to mum. We both felt a bit peckish, so you're two tins of Chunky Chicken and a packet of frozen peas light. Love, Dick.'

Just a bloody transport caff, that's all this place is, Griffin thought. His eyes travelled down the page to the PS.

'PS. Someone called after our snack. Very anxious to buy one of your posh sets, and wants to see you today. Asked him in while I tried to contact you, but no luck. He has other appointments, so you cannot reach him, but he will try and get hold of you later on. Acting as your assistant made us late, so will have to catch the train now. Do I qualify for commission on your commission? In haste. D.'

You qualify for a bloody good hiding, you stupid little bugger, Griffin thought. Who was he? What did he look like? How is he going to get hold of me later on? *What the hell did you tell him?*

He crumpled the sheet of paper savagely between trembling fingers. Dick knew nothing, and yet there was some implication in his note that he had, at the very least, made some sort of suggestion. What? Could he have inferred something? Griffin racked his brains. Nancy. Dick had picked up her name, and asked casual questions. How had Griffin answered him? He could not remember. He must speak to Dick. He stretched out his hand.

The phone rang, as his fingers touched it.

'The position is this,' John Irving said. 'The gentlemen you mentioned have no connection with my old outfit.'

'Did you check the descriptions as well as the names?' Griffin demanded, querulously.

'You must be in a bad way to ask a stupid question like that,' Irving said.

'I've known better days,' Griffin said. 'Do the profiles match any of the competition by any chance?'

'That would take time and money to find out,' Irving said. 'And with all respect, George, your problems are not ours. Whether you take the offer or not is up to you. I know you've worked for the competition as well as us,' he said, sticking the needle in.

'Only by accident,' Griffin protested.

'The accident being that you don't give a goddamn so long as

115

you get paid,' Irving said. 'OK, you're like a taxi, you're for hire, you don't care who your customer is or why he wants you so long as he's got money in his pocket, and sometimes we all need taxis. What I'm saying is this, your customer this time doesn't work for us.'

Griffin hesitated. He had swallowed so many lies that he was now uncertain if Tauber was who he was supposed to be. But he was desperate. A couple of CIA men beside him would be a great comfort.

'The deal I've been offered might be of interest to you,' he said.

'It's not my department any more,' Irving said, 'and I never discuss deals on an open line.'

'It concerns a man called Tauber,' Griffin said.

'A very fine tenor,' Irving said. 'My mother collected all his records. She especially admired his "On with the motley".'

'You might know him as Eric Groman,' Griffin said. Tauber was only Tauber, of course, because Bob Dalton had said he was.

'His records were not in my mother's collection,' Irving said.

'John, please,' Griffin pleaded. 'It's no joke at this end, believe me, and I need some help, rather badly.'

'Believe it or not,' Irving said, 'our staff in London have work of their own to do. They don't have the time to pick up odd job men who fall over their own feet.'

'For me, John,' Griffin said. 'Because we got to be good friends.'

'Get off the line, George,' Irving said. 'I've told you what you wanted to know and that's it. Our friendship just lapsed. You're wasting my time.'

Griffin swore down the phone, and again, at greater length, after he had hung up. And yet he knew that he had begged for the impossible. The CIA might be like a hydra-headed monster, but it was not in business to bail out George Griffin unless it were in their interests to do so.

The name Tauber meant nothing to John Irving, Griffin was sure of that. Perhaps the face would. Griffin briefly considered radioing Tauber's photograph across the Atlantic, but there was no time for that. Not after Dick's note, and Irving's phone call. By the time Griffin found someone who would send the photograph by radio, it had reached Irving's desk, been checked, London contacted . . . no, it would be too late, even if they moved fast. And why should they? Even if they thought 'Tauber' was important enough? And would they? Griffin realized he knew nothing except what he had been told, and if part of it was false, why not the rest? He might be dealing with a terrorist group, like the Bader Meinhof gang, who had enlisted him to find some errant comrade who knew too much and wanted out. Or simply international gangsters, paying off an old score.

He must be getting old and stupid. Irving was right. The sight of a bundle of ten pound notes was enough. He did not check, and he did not care. Anyone could buy him for five hundred pounds, because he always needed five hundred. And look where that had got him.

Despite the evidence to the contrary, he had hoped against hope that his suspicions were ill-founded. That Bob Dalton and his two yahoos were ruthless CIA men who intended to carry out their unofficial, undercover job no matter who got hurt in the process, including Griffin. Had that been so, he would have been safe to the extent that they would probably not, in the end, have killed him. But that safety net had been removed. It no longer applied. CIA men who were gunmen and killers were one thing. Gunmen and killers who were not CIA men were quite another.

He dialled the Portsmouth number.

'Oh, hullo, George,' Brenda said, placidly. 'How are you?'

'Fine,' Griffin lied. 'Has Dick got home yet?'

'Yes. About half an hour ago.'

'Good. Put him on will you? I want to speak to him.'

'He's not here.'

'Well, where is he?'

'He went out.'

'Brenda,' Griffin said, trying to stop his voice rising in frustrated fury, 'if he got home, and he's not there now, I can deduce that he went out. Where did he go? Do you know?'

'I think he went over to Jane's,' Brenda said, sarcasm, as ever, passing her effortlessly by. 'He didn't really say, but I think that's where.'

'Have you got her phone number?'

'I think so. I seem to remember writing it down once. I forget why. Oh, yes, she wanted me to give her parents a message, that was it.'

'Well, can I have it?' Griffin yelped, driven beyond endurance.

'Why are you shouting, George?' Brenda enquired. 'Is something wrong?'

'No, Brenda,' Griffin said, controlling himself. 'There's nothing wrong. Can I have Jane's phone number, please?'

'Hold on.'

He heard the phone being put down, and after that, there was silence. The silence went on for a long time. Griffin lit a cigarette and smoked it restlessly. He forgot his resolve and poured a glass of gin.

'Come on, you stupid cow,' he muttered. 'Come on.'

The silence went on. Christ, he thought, it would have been quicker to dial Directory Enquiries, except that you could never get an answer from the bastards. Just the same, he was on the point of giving up, when Brenda lifted the phone at the other end, and said, 'Hullo?'

'Have you got it?'

'I'm sorry to have been so long. I thought it was on the telephone pad, but it wasn't. In the end, I found it on the calendar, although why I should have written it there, I'm sure I don't know.'

'You've got a local directory there. Why didn't you just look it up?' Griffin demanded, getting screwed up again.

'I thought of that,' Brenda said, conversationally, 'but I was almost certain I had it somewhere, and I don't know about you, but I think it's much harder to find anything in the phone book since they altered it.'

'Never mind, Brenda,' George said, wearily. 'Just give me the phone number.'

Jane's mother answered. 'They went out about ten minutes ago,' she said, crisply.

'Do you know where?' The whole world was against him.

'I'm afraid I don't. One of the cinemas, I believe, and then they said they might go and see some friends, but who they are, I couldn't say. Shall I ask Dick to call you back when he comes in?'

'I'm not sure where I'll be,' Griffin said. 'Will you say I want to speak to him, and I'll phone again later?'

'Of course, Mr Griffin.'

He had never spoken to Jane's mother before. She sounded brisk and well educated, and that was all he had learned.

He sighed and rang Nancy.

'Everything all right?' he enquired.

'No, of course it's not all right. When are you coming?'

'Soon,' Griffin said. 'I gather Dick phoned you a while ago.'

'Just for a chat,' Nancy said. 'We didn't talk about you.'

'I'm sure you didn't,' Griffin said. 'Does he know your address?'

'Why?'

'He was talking about sending you a book or something.'

'I don't think so,' Nancy said.

'I thought he would have it. If he looked up your phone number, he could have got your address from the book.'

'You're making very heavy weather of my address,' Nancy said. 'It's not exactly a state secret, you know.'

'It's just that Dick said something about not having it,' Griffin improvised, 'and I thought later that he could have got it from the directory.'

'He didn't know where to reach me,' Nancy said coldly, 'since you obviously hadn't told him where I was living. He rang the agency first, and they gave him my home number. So he probably doesn't know my address, no.'

'Good,' Griffin said.

'What?'

'I mean I know now that I'll have to send it to him,' Griffin explained. 'Any callers?'

'Apart from the milkman, no.'

'Phone calls?'

'One from the agency about next week's nursing assignment,

119

that's all.'

'Fine,' Griffin said, relieved. He regretted privately abusing Dick. The splendid lad had said nothing after all. 'In that case . . .'

'Apart from the wrong number,' Nancy said.

Griffin's neck prickled, and his hands grew clammy. 'What wrong number?'

'Oh, someone rang up, convinced that I was a firm of dyers and cleaners.'

'Tell me about it.'

'Why? My number evidently used to belong to someone else, that's all.'

'I want to know what they said, darling,' Griffin said. 'Tell me.'

'It was nothing, for heaven's sake,' Nancy protested. 'He was under the impression I was a firm called Dobsons. In the end, he realized that he'd been using an out of date trade directory, he apologized and that's all.'

'When was this?'

'I don't know. Not long ago. Why are you so interested?' Her voice was brittle. She was letting her nervousness show. So was Griffin.

'It's all right, Nancy, calm down,' Griffin said, trying to remain calm himself. 'I'm just being careful, that's all. He's got funny friends, I told you. Now. Did you give your name?'

'He was so persistent . . . he kept saying that he was sure he had the right number, and perhaps I lived over the shop and I could give them a message. So I said no, it was a private house, and . . .'

'You did,' Griffin said, levelly. 'All right, was there anything distinctive about this fellow? Anything you could tell from his voice?'

'He spoke with an American accent,' Nancy said flatly.

'Well, that's good,' Griffin said cheerfully. 'That doesn't mean a thing. No connection at all. Still, just to be on the safe side, you'd better make sure you keep the place locked up until I get there. I shan't be long. If anyone calls, don't answer the door.

It's only a precaution. I've pretty well got things sorted out. I'll get him out of the way, and then you can forget about it.'

He knew now exactly what had happened. He remembered what he had said to Nancy in Dick's presence. And he knew that Dick, trying to help his father bring off a sale, had told his anonymous visitor that he might be able to reach Griffin later at Nancy's phone number which Dick knew.

The wrong number ploy was simply to find out Nancy's surname. They would now have looked her up in the phone book. They knew where she lived.

On the other hand, obviously Dick had not told them much about Nancy, or they would not have needed to phone her to discover who she was.

That, if one searched for microscopic small blessings, could count as a plus. It could mean that they were just checking on possibilities. There was no reason why they should assume that there was any connection between Nancy and Tauber.

Quite the reverse, if Dick had talked in the casual open way he usually did. Griffin could almost hear him. 'Well, I think he's seeing a lady friend later on. I'll give you her number. They were talking about getting married at one time. I think dad's sorry it didn't work out.'

Griffin's momentarily rising spirits fell abruptly. Yes, and Dick in his open way might have referred to the mutual friend they were both concerned about, a particularly crass and idiotic phrase he had just remembered using in his attempt to pass off his phone call to Nancy as a matter of no importance.

If only he knew exactly what his son had said. He would phone as soon as he got to Nancy's. Getting there fast, that was the first priority. Whatever was going to happen, he did not want Nancy around at the time.

He placed no great faith in the yarn he had told Bob Dalton about the Royal Garden. That had been merely a delaying tactic. Griffin was not the only one who could bribe hotel staff, to obtain information, in this case about a Swiss businessman who had a visitor answering Tauber's description, staying in his suite.

'Hullo?' Nancy said. 'Hullo?'

121

'As I just said, darling,' Griffin said, 'there's nothing to worry about. I'm leaving now.'

'And as I just said, George, except that you weren't listening, I don't like being told not to open my own front door,' Nancy said sharply. She had clearly remained unimpressed by Griffin's cheerfully reassuring noises. 'If there's likely to be trouble of that kind, I think I'd better send for the police here and now.'

'I've told you before, I'm for the high jump if you do that,' Griffin said, grimly. 'Leave it until I get there, that's all I ask. As a matter of fact,' he ended wearily, 'I might decide that it's a good idea myself. Oh, and I shall want to talk to our friend, when I get there. So be ready to stick a needle in him, or whatever you have to do.'

It would depend on what Tauber had to say, he reflected, as he checked Tauber's gun and put it in his pocket. If they called in the law, there was no way he could avoid prison, that he could see. Still, at least he would be safe in a cell.

CHAPTER NINE

Griffin drove from his flat in Maida Vale to Gloucester Terrace, where he joined the elevated motorway to Shepherd's Bush, which route involved a lot of twists and turns. One nondescript car, a Hunter, behind him was going the same way and stayed in his rear view mirror when he turned on to the spur road to Shepherd's Bush.

For once, Griffin was glad to find that he was being tailed. It meant that they either did not know about Nancy after all, or they were by no means certain where he was going, otherwise they would not bother. They would simply sit outside her house and wait for him.

He drove through Chiswick, and headed for the Hogarth roundabout, where the approach roads for the west bound M4 and the south bound M3 converged.

The Hunter disappeared from his mirror in Chiswick, and for a while, Griffin was thrown. If he was not being followed after all, it would be safe to take the fast route via the M4 to Marlow.

Just in time, as he was hesitating at the roundabout, he realized that the Hunter had merely dropped well back and let a Rover take over, an old Flying Squad trick when trailing villains which Nick had told him about.

He chose the A316. Dalton had more bloody people at his disposal than he had imagined. He drove normally, part of the traffic stream, neither too fast nor too slow. It was important he did not show that he knew they were there. In the next half an hour they must get the feeling that this was going to be easy, no trouble at all. He frowned as he negotiated the string of roundabouts past Richmond. The fact that there were two cars worried him. One car he could lose, but how could he possibly manage to

123

give two of them the slip? He decided that he could not. He would have to think again.

Once on the M3 he accelerated to the legal 70 mph limit. There was much less traffic on the motorway than he had hoped for, a thin scattering of cars and lorries heading south, but no more. There were whole stretches where you could see for miles in front and the Rover was content to hang well back, waiting to see which exit he took, with the Hunter almost out of sight behind acting as a back-up car.

Griffin cruised in the middle lane, watching for the opportunity, as the Camberley exit came up, to lose at least one of the bastards, if not both, but none occurred. He was alone on his stretch of the motorway as he passed the signs. Not a hope. Even if they were both half asleep and both stupid, which was not too likely, they would spot his manoeuvre. His hopes began to seep away. If he carried on like this, he would land up at the end of the motorway, still with two cars invisibly attached to him.

He saw his chance as he passed the notice stating SERVICE 1 MILE. A huge lorry was lumbering along in the inside lane some six or seven hundred yards ahead of him. Griffin hit the floor with the accelerator. The big Ford responded and surged forward. He spared a glance in his mirror. The Rover was also accelerating. Good.

SERVICE $\frac{1}{2}$ MILE. Ninety miles an hour on the clock, and that lorry was still an uncomfortably long way ahead. If he misjudged this, he would kiss his earthly worries goodbye inside a crushed heap of jagged metal. He began to sweat. There was no more power to be had, but he leaned forward over the wheel, as if urging the big car on, uselessly.

The huge lorry was coming up fast now. Griffin's eyes flickered to the slip road to the service station, and back to the monster's bonnet. He was overtaking now. This was the moment, if he was going to try it. Otherwise, abandon it. Griffin decided to try it.

He cut in across the front of the lorry shaving its giant radiator with inches to spare, probably giving the unfortunate driver heart failure, across the inside lane, on to the slip road, with its sharp left hand bend at the top of the incline, hit the brakes, skidded violently, and managed to slither round the corner leading to the car park without writing himself off.

He had lost the Rover, which had had no chance of imitating his idiotic manoeuvre. It would be miles before that bastard could turn round and come back again. The back up Hunter would have seen what happened, of course, and would be coming up fast, but he had a few seconds to spare, which was all he could hope for.

The tyres squealed as he braked to a stop in the car park. He was out of the car at once, and running for the complex of buildings. Now he knew why the motorway was so empty. They were all parked here, their occupants milling around aimlessly between the restaurant, the shop and the lavatories.

Griffin pushed his way through the crowd of people, swearing under his breath, but the throng would obstruct his pursuers just as much. He gained the stairs which led up to the footbridge over the motorway, and ran up them as fast as he could, urging his protesting, painful muscles on. Those bloody pills were wearing off again.

He paused for a frantic, searching glance back half way across the bridge. The Hunter was lurching at speed into the car park. Griffin did not wait to see what happened next. He could only hope they would waste half a minute searching for him, before they thought about crossing the bridge.

He clattered down the stairs, ignoring the protests of irritable parents with small children, stumbled outside, ran across the car park for north bound traffic and along the road towards the section where the diesel fuel pumps were located.

He was gambling desperately, and he had no way of knowing if his gamble would pay off. If it went wrong, he would be stranded, trapped where he was at best, bundled into a car for a bit of private, painful questioning at worst.

There was only one lorry beside the pumps an articulated monster which had already been refuelled. The driver was starting the engine. Griffin shouted, but the clatter of the diesel coming to life drowned his yell. He forced his stiffening legs on, as the lorry began to move, and managed to jump on to the step, and wrench the nearside door open.

The driver braked, and glared at him. 'What do you think you're doing, you stupid bugger?' he growled.

'My car's broken down,' Griffin managed to gasp. 'I have to get to London urgently.'

The driver framed his lips to say 'piss off', and then saw the ten pound note in Griffin's fingers.

'OK mate,' he said cordially. 'Climb in.'

Griffin thankfully relaxed into the seat and tried to get his breath back. The driver took the ten pound note from his fingers, tucked it in his top pocket and drove off.

Once on the motorway, he cruised at a steady 50 mph and chatted away in the same relaxed fashion. Griffin lied absent-mindedly, in reply to his occasional, casual questions and kept his eyes on one of the lorry's huge wing mirrors.

When the Rover appeared in the mirror, it was burning along the motorway like a racing car. Griffin dropped his cigarettes and grovelled apologetically on the floor as the Rover passed. It must have been travelling at a hundred miles an hour.

'He's in a hurry,' the lorry driver remarked.

'Yes.' The chances were that the Hunter would appear next. Griffin felt exposed on this great ribbon of concrete. His pursuers might have guessed the truth, or they might be assuming that he was using a switch car which had been waiting for him. In either event, the motorway ended eventually in a slow moving bottleneck of traffic, where they could wait and study the occupants of the crawling cars—and lorries.

Griffin studied his watch, tutted, and shook his head in an exaggerated fashion. He would be late for his appointment, he groaned, unless he could catch a train. He supposed the lorry driver could not possibly drop him off at Camberley Station?

'That'd put me behind time,' the lorry driver said. 'I could miss me bonus.'

They agreed that another five pounds would insure him against the risk, and the lorry slowed, and took the Camberley exit.

A police car was parked beside the roundabout. Its occupants appeared to be watching the traffic which was leaving the motorway. Griffin developed a fit of coughing, and buried his face in his handkerchief. Could the law know that he had shot Tauber? Had Nancy phoned them, after all?

He took an anxious glance over his shoulder as the lorry gained the Camberley road, but the police car was making no attempt to follow. God, he thought, his paranoia was becoming uncontrollable. He had enough real problems, without his feverish imagination inventing imaginary ones.

The lorry driver had acquired a small, knowing smile. 'They're after some bleeder,' he remarked cheerfully. 'Do you reckon that Rover was a police car? You know, the one that went past doing a ton,' he reminded Griffin helpfully. 'When you dropped your fags.'

'If you think you can shake me down for another fiver,' Griffin told him, sourly, brazening it out, 'forget it. We can stop at the bloody police station now, as far as I'm concerned.'

'All right, mate,' the lorry driver said. 'All right. Don't get huffy. I wasn't casting no aspersions.'

Griffin got out at the railway station, walked into the ticket office, waited until the lorry had driven off and walked out again.

Three taxi drivers were propped up against the first turn cab morosely bemoaning the lack of work. Griffin stood, waiting. They eyed him blankly and continued their conversation.

'Is this a strike meeting?' Griffin enquired at last, 'or does one of you want a job?'

The fat one of the trio got into his driving seat, and started the engine, still laying down the law about the price of petrol, inflation, and the breadline.

'London Airport,' Griffin said, for the benefit of the other two, just in case.

As they drew away from the station, Griffin said, 'I've changed my mind. Make it the Compleat Angler, at Marlow. No point in meeting that plane yet.'

'Do you want me to hang on for you?' the driver asked,

hopefully.

'No, thanks,' Griffin said. 'My brother-in-law's mother-in-law's staying there. She can take me.'

The driver's eyes glazed, and he drove in silence. Griffin watched the passing scenery and noted the returning stabs of pain in various parts of his body.

Griffin went into the bar of the Thames-side hotel, and swallowed two quick gins and a couple more tablets. He thought it would be nice to stay there, with the river rolling picturesquely past the window, and get smashed. He sighed, stood up, and forced his complaining, aching limbs into action.

He walked across the car park, and away from the hotel. Cars came and went, hotel guests twittered and chattered, and the world in general went about its business, and took no notice of George Griffin.

He strolled along slowly, like a man out for a quiet breath of air, gritting his teeth and wincing every now and then. Those damn tablets seemed to be getting progressively less effective.

He reached Nancy's secluded house without seeing anything which would arouse the suspicions of a nervous old lady. Just the same, his cheek was twitching, and his nerves were screaming with apprehension when Nancy opened the door.

'I need a holiday,' he told her.

'You need putting down,' she said, flatly. He supposed that her nerves were in no better condition than his.

Tauber appeared to be peacefully sleeping. Griffin sat down, and watched Nancy as she dabbed his arm.

'How long before he comes round?' he asked.

'A few minutes.'

'I wouldn't mind something to eat,' Griffin said. She hesitated, and, although she said nothing, her thoughts were only too clearly written on her face. 'Go on Nancy,' Griffin said; tiredly. 'I only want to talk to him. Nothing's going to happen.'

She shrugged and closed the door. Griffin took his hand from his pocket and laid Tauber's gun on his knees. It was quiet in the bedroom, apart from a few birds chirping outside the window and occasional sounds as Nancy moved about downstairs.

Tauber's eyes remained closed, his expression peaceful. Griffin yawned. He thought how pleasant it would be to settle down for about twelve hours sleep himself. He remembered how comforting Nancy had been to sleep with, in the good days before it all went wrong.

CHAPTER TEN

George Griffin had taken to life in the Army like an eagle to the air. He was not just a good soldier, he was a crack soldier, which was why he had ended up in the SAS, a small elite group which avoided publicity for the very good reason that some of its exploits would not be understood by a nation which liked to think it was at peace.

George had learned more ways to kill or disable a man, with or without weapons, than he had dreamed existed. He was an apt pupil. Some of the things George had been paid for doing would have seen him at the Old Bailey in civvy street. But then, that was the beauty of the SAS, its standards were different. It made its own rules, which coincided with George's own view of life as being largely a random series of cruel booby traps which you avoided if you could, blew up if you could not, and if you got caught, that was your fault. His brief dreams of a sedate and fulfilling family life already seemed a laughable aberration.

Just the same, for Brenda's sake, he did pursue the possibility of married quarters, and he was eventually offered a house. He was not surprised when Brenda proved to be less than enthusiastic, and, feeling that he had done his duty to his wife, he did not press the matter. He was beginning to know his Brenda now. She was quite content where she was.

He spent his leaves at home. Brenda accepted his presence, as she accepted his absence, without visible emotion. But he liked to keep in touch with Dick. It gave him a kick to see the boy grow, he looked forward each time to the pleasure of noting the physical and mental changes in the child since he had last seen him.

Brenda continued content where she was until her father gave up the unequal struggle with the spreading supermarkets. He was too honest to fiddle bankruptcy proceedings which might have left him with something. He just went bust and lost everything, including the house.

George was there when the auctioneers were selling the furniture for the benefit of her father's creditors. Brenda was weeping silently over the upright, out-of-tune piano which she sometimes played, as she put it, 'by ear', which proved, George thought, that she was tone deaf, and which she fondly hoped Dick would master. 'I mean, it's an accomplishment, isn't it?' she used to reflect frequently, although she always found the thought fresh and new. 'Once you've learned properly, you can take pleasure from it for the rest of your life. I could never cope with all those minims and crotchets and things, but if Dick can learn to play from music . . . well, I mean, you can play anything then, can't you, even if you've never heard it before in your life?'

The departure of the piano, which fetched three pounds, symbolized for Brenda the destruction of a life-style which had seemed secure and in which she had comfortably belonged. Brenda was not one to look ahead very much, and unexpected disturbances took her by surprise even more than most people. She was, George had come to think, like a harmless domestic animal, good natured, protectively taking its offspring for granted, aware of the seasons, but moving placidly from one day to the next with not much conception of tomorrow or next year.

And now she felt as lost and afraid as a cat abruptly flung out into the street and deprived of its home for no reason it could understand. He felt sorry for her.

'Come on,' he said. 'Your mum and dad'll be all right. They'll probably be better off.'

Brenda's father had got a job managing a small grocer's shop in Newbury. A tiny flat went with the job, but there would be no room for Brenda and Dick.

'I know,' Brenda sniffled, 'but I was born here. I grew up here. And it's the only home Dick knows.'

She had another resemblance to a domestic animal. Her consciousness of the impact of events on anyone but herself and her offspring was restricted to something approaching zero.

'Well, he'll have to get to know another home,' George said. The auctioneer was selling off the bed Brenda had used.

'Who'll start me off at five pounds? Come along, ladies and gentlemen, this good solid double bed, none of your wartime rubbish, why the walnut bedhead alone is worth five quid. Who'll start at five? Five? Four? Do I hear four pounds? Sorry, sir? Ten bob. Ten bob I'm bid. Any advance on ten bob?'

'What I've been thinking,' George said, 'is that perhaps now's the time for me to buy a house for you and young Dick.'

He had not been thinking anything of the kind. He had no idea where the notion had come from.

'How do you mean?' Brenda was puzzled and wary. She treated any new idea with suspicion as though it might bite.

George explained. Although he had been paying Brenda's parents for her accommodation and keep, he had been able to save quite a lot of his pay, 'what with marriage allowance and everything'. He thought he could get a mortgage, and there were those new houses they were building . . .

Brenda blew her nose thoughtfully. Her eyes began to gleam as she saw the possibilities.

'We could get a piano one day, on hire purchase,' George said.

New estates were being built on the outskirts of Portsmouth. The house was not at all like the spacious individual houses sitting high on the downs which George had once and briefly aimed for. It was semi-detached, looked exactly like its neighbours up and down the road, had all the unique design of a box outside and in, with, the builders boasted, 'not an inch of wasted space', which was true, since they had somehow crammed a lounge/diner, kitchen, bathroom and three bedrooms into its limited dimensions. But it had a pink bathroom suite, a fitted kitchen, and Brenda loved it all.

'I'll be able to grow my own flowers,' she said gleefully, looking at the patches of rubble front and rear which comprised, according to the agents, a manageable garden.

Brenda settled in, and never asked anything more out of life, except that the house should be kept functioning. In her own slow way, she polished and cleaned, and cleaned and polished, and although she never complained about Dick's muddy football boots she flared up if George put his feet up on the settee.

She formed superficial friendships with the neighbouring wives, and they visited each other when the kids were at school and discussed their children and their ailments. Brenda's speciality was her varicose veins.

'My mother always suffered from them,' she said. 'It runs in the family.'

She was convinced the condition was inherited, and became deaf when her doctor unsympathetically suggested that if she lost two or three stone it might help. The doctor noted her blank eyes and her meaningless nod, and rang for the next patient. He was a busy, harassed, National Health doctor with no time to spare for talking to people who did not want to listen. He had a packed surgery night and morning, and among those who were simply killing time, or wanted his signature on a certificate so that they could avoid work, there might be someone who was ill. Those, he would spend time on.

There were always more weeds than flowers in the garden, but flowers did eventually appear in the borders round the tiny, bumpy lawns, and Dick grew big and strong, year by year.

George continued to come home for most of his leaves, and it became taken for granted that he would sleep in the spare room. He no longer thought of Brenda in any physical way. There would have been something mildly incestuous in the idea. Apart from the few weeks a year which he spent mostly with Dick, his real life was the army. That was when he was the man he was.

The house ceased to be new, on the very outskirts of Portsmouth, and became encircled by other estates. The fitted kitchen began to fall apart, and there were always repairs to be done, which were left until he came home on leave.

On one occasion, George had rehung the French windows, which had become warped and jammed. When he finished, he gave himself a beer and sat in the kitchen, reading the evening paper, ignoring the sound of the television set, which Brenda switched on at six o'clock every night, and switched off when the programmes finished. There was nothing much in the paper, and he wandered into the lounge to ask about supper. Brenda was watching 'Coronation Street' which was her favourite programme. She never missed an episode.

He sighed and sat down. There would be no food until this was over. He watched the screen idly for a few minutes but since he never saw television except when he was at home, he was not *au fait* with the story line.

'Who's supposed to be screwing who?' he enquired. But the volume was turned up high, as it always was, and Brenda did not hear him.

He found himself looking at her, instead of the screen, really looking at her, perhaps for the first time in years.

Brenda was no sloven. She home-permed her hair regularly. She wore powder, lipstick, earrings, a cultured pearl necklace and her favourite perfume, Californian Poppy. She groaned into roll-ons religiously, and only struggled out of them, with sighs of relief, when it was time to go to bed. She sat in an armchair, unaware of his gaze, her plump legs crossed, her hands resting on the roll of fat which spilled out from the top of her roll-ons, the flesh under her chin quivering as she laughed at some electronic jest. She was beginning to look exactly like her mother. Christ, George thought, we're exactly the same age. She's thirty years old. And she'd pass for forty-five any day.

He was glad to get back to his unit. There was talk of a spell on the German border and certain interesting though unspecified duties. Eventually, he found out what that meant.

A thin mist had arrived with the first cold lightening of dawn, sufficient to conceal the nearest of the watch towers which marched along the frontier.

George and Nick were chilled to the very bone. They had carried out their night time reconnaissance, and were now in a hollow, concealed on the safe side of the broad strip of no man's land between the two countries, the lethal, mined area between East and West.

The operation was the following night. If it worked, it had

never happened, as far as the army were concerned. If it failed, the SAS would disown them.

George craved for a cigarette. He was looking forward to breakfast in the warm mess, the mugs of tea, the first satisfying inhalation of smoke.

Nick touched his arm, and silently pointed. A small, distant, vague shape had appeared in the mist. George raised his binoculars and focussed on the far off figure.

It was a man of about fifty, with a thin, worn face. He was moving slowly and steadily, following an erratic but pre-determined path through the long glistening grass. He stopped, and looked back. A woman was moving a few paces behind him. She carried a bundle and her eyes were fixed on the flattened grass which indicated the man's footsteps. Following the woman were two children, a boy and a girl. The boy was about twelve, and the girl about ten.

The man started off again, and the small file trailed behind in his wandering course.

A guide, George thought. One of those who shepherded refugees through the border minefields. It was nothing to do with George, but he wished them luck, in the still, dank morning.

A trace of moving air caressed George's cheek gently. Christ, he thought, a breeze now is all they need. He scanned the area with his binoculars, but the watch towers were still hidden. Nick was watching, fascinated, too. They had their own route across, a mile to the south, but that was straighter and easier, thanks to some discreet defusing which had been carried out at night. This guide knew his stuff. The location of every mine to within inches must be printed in his mind.

They were making good progress. Three-quarters of the way across. The man, the woman, and the two children moved through the thin wraiths of mist like silent ghosts.

The silence was broken by shots. The little girl collapsed and fell to the ground without a sound. The boy turned back instinctively to look at his sister. More shots. Blood sprayed from the boy's head and he fell backwards.

The guide was shouting and gesturing to the woman to follow

135

his example and run. Bullets whined after him, but he made it to a clump of trees, and dived into cover.

The woman stood where she was, a frozen statue, looking back at her dead children. George hunted with his binoculars, and found the source of the bullets. A frontier guard, patrolling on foot, who had chanced to see the refugees through the mist. He was aiming at the woman with an automatic rifle. For some reason, he lowered his gun.

The woman had put down her bundle. Slowly, deliberately, she walked back towards her children, taking a straight line, ignoring the dog leg of flattened grass.

The explosion hammered George's eardrums. Soil showered down a few yards away. A foul cloud of black smoke gently drifted upwards. Where the woman had been was scorched, blackened grass ringing a shallow crater.

George focussed the binoculars carefully on the frontier guard, who slung his automatic rifle over his shoulder, and walked away.

'Come on,' Nick said. 'I'm frozen.'

'I'll know that bastard again,' George said.

They crossed the border the following evening, and found the farmhouse without incident. They were wearing ordinary civilian clothes, the pockets of which contained their normal paraphanalia, including week-end leave passes. If challenged before making contact, they were two innocent, if thick, squaddies who had somehow wandered over the border to sample the local beer. Bored British soldiers sometimes did just that in search of a bit of variety and excitement, and although, if caught, they might be reminded that they were unwelcome visitors, it would probably not amount to much more than being worked over in a routine fashion with rifle butts.

After they had made contact, no such line of retreat was open to them. They either got back over the border, by one of the planned routes on which they had been briefed, or, in all likelihood, not at all.

George had no idea who the walking parcel, whom they were supposed to collect and deliver, was. Not long after, he found out the hard way that his name was Hans Grunwald, which meant nothing to George. Years later, when it no longer mattered, he asked Captain Drew about the man.

'Oh, he was a staff officer with scruples,' Captain Drew said. 'He knew about the Russian plan to move into Czechoslovakia and crush the Dubcek regime and he didn't like it. He thought that if the West knew in advance, they'd do something about it. He was like most people with a conscience—incredibly naïve. The West did sod all, of course.'

'So getting him over, and all the bloody aggro I went through, was all a useless waste,' George said, resentfully.

'It seemed important to somebody or another at the time, I seem to remember,' Captain Drew said vaguely.

George only ever caught one glimpse of Grunwald at the farmhouse, an erect, severe man of fifty, staring into the kitchen fire, waiting. George drew Nick outside again.

'There's something I want to see to,' George said. 'We're timed to leave in two hours. I'll be back by then.'

'You'd better be,' Nick said. 'You know what our orders are. I'm not bloody waiting for you.'

George turned to go.

'And do it quietly or not at all,' Nick said softly. 'We don't want any search parties out. So don't take any chances.'

George did not intend to. It was dark, but the streets of the nearby garrison town were busy and lively. He had chosen his clothes with care, to pass as one of the locals, and no one looked at him twice.

There were two cafes frequented by soldiers. The frontier guard was in the second one. He was about twenty-three years old, fair haired, with a laughing, handsome, open face. From the careful way he caressed a wayward wisp of hair back into place, he seemed to be proud of his appearance.

George waited. From his deductions, the frontier guard should be leaving to go back on duty soon, but, unless he went alone, George was ready to slip back to the farmhouse. The minutes ticked by, and George thought he must have got their duty roster wrong. He was ready to pack it in, when the frontier guard stood up, laughed at something, slapped a comrade on the back, settled his hat precisely into place and left.

George followed the frontier guard, who was whistling a carefree tune, along the road, and out of the town.

Halfway back to barracks, the frontier guard stopped to relieve himself. George took him then.

He caught one glimpse of the whites of the man's startled eyes in the dim, cold moonlight, his mouth half open in surprise. Then George rammed a handful of soil down his throat. He wanted to do it while the guard was conscious, but cries of pain ringing out in the stillness he could manage without.

He jerked his knee savagely up into the guard's genitals, and felt the dribble of urine seep through his trouser leg. The guard choked and groaned as he doubled up. George put a lock on him, and broke each one of his fingers, starting with his trigger finger.

With some regret, he ended the man's agony, but it was necessary for him to remain unconscious for a long time. He dragged the limp figure to a clump of bushes, scooped the dirt from his mouth and throat, and left him face down under a pile of leaves. George did not want him to choke to death. He wanted him to come round in a few hours time, and then try pulling his boots on, much less shooting children.

It was all over in less than a minute, but George knew that he was going to be late back at the farmhouse, unless he ran, and a man running along quiet roads could attract attention.

He had studied large scale maps of the area, and he carried the knowledge of every inch of it in his head. He knew it was risky, but he decided to take a chance and return to the farmhouse across country. The chance did not come off.

The first part was safe enough, but a few hundred yards from the farmhouse, he had to cross a finger of land which was part of a restricted area. He slowed down, and moved cautiously, but he failed to see the patrol until the challenge rang out.

George changed direction at once, and ran away from the farmhouse. They did not waste any more breath. Two shots shattered the stillness. They either missed, or they were warning shots above his head.

George stopped in his tracks. He had achieved his purpose. Nick would have heard the shots, and left at once with his walking parcel. It was up to him to deliver it now. There was nothing more George could do, and there was no point in getting shot. His remaining duty was to kill enough time for Nick's benefit with rambling explanations about being a squaddy interested in the local beer.

Boots crunched towards him. George raised his hands on high, and turned to begin his explanations. A rifle butt swung into his temple. Sound and sight turned into silence and blackness.

When the blackness began to clear, George groaned, opened his eyes and tried to blink them into focus. His head was throbbing, and, for some reason he could not understand, his jaw was aching abominably as well.

They stood around and looked at him impassively, waiting with quiet patience until he had come round properly.

He was in a cell. In the middle of the cell was an old fashioned dentist's chair. George was strapped into the chair. He could move his fingers and his toes but nothing else. His head was clamped firmly into position. A prop between his teeth forced his jaw wide open. He tried to open his mouth wider to spit it out, and could not.

The one in the white coat was polishing his glasses absently. At some signal from the one in officer's uniform he perched his glasses on the end of his nose, inspected his drill, peered closely at George's teeth, which were strong and white and contained no fillings, selected a front one he liked the look of, and started work.

The drill was also old fashioned, and set to run at a low speed. For a few seconds, George could simply hear the growl as the drill bit in, and then the pain hit him.

He discovered that a man with his mouth propped wide open cannot scream in agony, in a full-throated way, except within his own head. Otherwise, he emits choking gargles, and the tears stream down his face.

He discovered what an eternity of torment in hell meant. There was no limitation of time, only forever, unending, the unbearable pain, unremitting, unceasing. It went on and on and on, and you called on Christ for help, screaming inwardly please God, please God, and nothing happened. You were locked for ever and ever into unthinkable torture, all existence, all consciousness concentrated on one point of impossible, flaring agony, while the drill delicately bored and searched. There was no future, there was no past, there was only a present which would never end, never, never, never, no matter how much tormented tissue cried out for mercy, mercy, mercy.

The dentist stopped. George fought for strangled breath, craving, savouring, the ending of eternity. The dentist blew thoughtfully on his drill, and squirted ice cold water into the cavity he had created. George hit the straps with enough force, he would have thought, to snap steel chains, but his rigid muscles made no impression on the thick leather. He was due to remain where he was, clamped into position, for as long as it suited them.

Two goons removed the prop from his mouth. Sticky saliva dribbled down George's chin, joining the hot sweat which was flooding down his face. The dentist cleaned him gently with a tissue and threw it away.

The one in officer's uniform was, George now recognized, a major in Intelligence. He lit a cigarette, inhaled, and spoke in perfect English, the smoke catapulting from his lips as he talked.

'The experience is unpleasant,' he said. 'Remember what it was like, please. It can be repeated as often as necessary.' He was holding George's week-end pass. 'We shall ignore this piece of camouflage,' he went on, 'but I shall address you as Griffin for the purpose of convenience. You may even be the Griffin you purport to be. We shall establish this in due course. You will now tell me what operation you are engaged in, and who and where your comrades are.'

George had caught two glimpses of the wristwatch strapped to the dentist's hairy wrist, once before he started to drill, and the second time, blurred through tear-filled eyes, when he had stopped. So George knew that eternity had, in fact, lasted about a minute and a half, and that it was just after midnight.

He also knew that the frontier patrols would have been

strengthened after his capture, and that, in any case, Nick would not risk escorting his charge over the border by the quick direct route they had intended to use. His job was to see the man across without any avoidable risk of being shot at.

He would use the alternative crossing point to the south, but that involved a drive in a safe car, which was at their disposal if they needed it, which would take two hours because of the necessary double backs away from the frontier.

Assuming he crossed safely, it would be, at the earliest three am before he reported what had happened by telephone to Captain Drew. Drew would then drive to the frontier post, say that an absentee called Griffin was thought to have illegally crossed the frontier, and request his arrest and return.

Three hours to go. It could be six or seven or eight, if Nick ran into any delays.

'I'm sorry, sir,' George said. 'I don't quite understand.'

He needed to keep the Major talking. He could not stand any more of that drill. He would cough up everything he knew, shop Nick, shop anybody. The bastards knew what they were at, when they demonstrated first and asked questions second.

'I think you do understand, Griffin,' the Major said, courteously.

'I know I shouldn't have done it, sir,' Griffin said. 'I shall be on a charge now, when I get back. But I'd heard what the cafes were like over here, and I nipped over to try the local beer.'

'Who with?'

'No one, sir,' Griffin said. 'One of my pals was going to come with me, but he backed out. He said he knew someone who'd got six months detention for illegally crossing the frontier, and he . . .'

George got no further. The two goons, reacting to a nod from the Major, forced his mouth open, and jammed the prop back in. The dentist stifled a yawn, adjusted his glasses and started drilling again.

The grinding drill bored into already inflamed nerves, and George moved back into his private personal hell, where he moaned and screamed inside his own head, alternately called on

God to help him, and blasphemously cursed Him for allowing any human being to endure the unendurable.

When the dentist stopped again, the throbbing agony continued. Only gradually did it die down sufficiently for the veil to clear a little from George's eyes, or for the Major's voice to penetrate his consciousness.

'Answer me,' the Major demanded.

'I'm sorry, sir,' George mumbled. 'I didn't quite hear . . .'

'You were sent over to meet Colonel Grunwald, weren't you?'

'Colonel Grunwald?'

'Where was your meeting place? Who came with you? Where are they now?'

'I don't know any Colonel Grunwald,' George said truthfully. 'I've never heard of anyone of that name. The truth is that someone bet me five pounds I wouldn't cross the border and drink a glass of beer in a cafe . . .'

They jammed the prop back in his mouth again. For a moment, George could not understand why the pain was less awful, practically bearable. Was he, by some miracle getting used to it? Could he stand it after all? Then as the ferocity escalated to its former incredible pitch, he realized that the dentist had started on the adjoining tooth.

After forever, the dentist stopped and released the head clamps. George was choking on his own vomit. They turned his head, and he spewed into a bucket. They cleaned him up, the Major asked some more questions, and they started again.

George no longer tried to glimpse the dentist's wristwatch during the intervals. Time was no longer measurable. A month was thirty seconds, years were shown as minutes, an hour would never pass, time made no sense in the eternity which he inhabited.

His senses began to desert him. Sheer insanity was not far away, and part of him welcomed it and embraced it, while another part of him fought to comprehend what the Major was saying.

He knew that his replies were growing more rambling and incoherent. He was gripped by twin fears, terror of the drill and

142

fear of betraying Nick.

He struggled to retain some remnant of logical thought. Nick had not been arrested or they would not continue with this. The Major was growing bored. There was a whole wonderful, heavenly five minute respite, when the Major sent out for schnapps and chatted idly to the dentist.

The dentist drank three glasses quickly, and started again.

George received the greatest gift he could have wished for. He fainted. They brought him round, while his tortured mind sent out unavailing protests. No, please . . . God, let me die . . . please God, let me die . . .

The measured, calm, English voice kept on asking questions. George repeated his story, over and over, hazily gambling with vague thoughts which came from a brain which might have belonged to a lunatic.

The frontier guard . . . they had not discovered the frontier guard . . . or at least, they did not connect his injuries with him . . . otherwise they would be questioning him about that . . . wouldn't they? . . . or were they being clever? . . . waiting for him to incriminate himself . . . after all, they had all the time there was, long since creation and long after, they had eternity . . . how was he to know?

'It was a bet,' he breathed, in a strangled whisper. The Major had to bend close to hear him now. 'I went into a cafe . . . afterwards I took a wrong turning and lost my way . . . I was trying to get back to the frontier . . . before that I was in a cafe . . . there were soldiers there . . . I can tell you what it's called . . .'

One of the goons went off, in response to an order, presumably in order to check, but the dentist started drilling again anyway, and the Major kept on asking questions.

George began to faint at ever more frequent intervals and they wearily brought him round again, and the mechanical questions were repeated. By now, George's answers were as fixed and imprinted as the tracks on a record. He could not have told them the truth if he had tried.

He felt the blessed release from pain coming as he began to faint once more. He waited for the automatic reaction, the slaps, the icy water, the thumb lifting his eyelid. But nothing happened. He drifted deeper. Voices murmured soothingly and gently in the background, but nothing happened. Just before black oblivion received him, he thought this is what it's like . . . this is death . . . oh, God, thank you . . . thank you, God . . .

When he came round, he was still in the cell, but the dentist's chair was not. It was daylight. The flashing agony of the night before had been replaced by its inheritance, a dull, constant, aching pain from the battered, protesting, living tissue which, in its fixed, unvarying way, was almost as intolerable.

The Major walked in, and offered him a cup of coffee and a couple of tablets. George looked at them vacantly, and then up at the Major's face.

'For the discomfort,' the Major explained.

George swallowed them with a mouthful of coffee, wincing as whatever was left of his teeth protested against the hot liquid.

'You are under arrest,' the Major said. 'Come.'

George tried to stand up, and fell back on to the bunk. The two goons propped him up, and walked him out.

Military Police were waiting in a jeep at the border crossing. They bundled him in, exchanged courtesy salutes with the Major, and drove off.

A mile along the road, out of sight of the border, a limousine staff car was waiting. Captain Drew was in the back smoking a cigarette. George transferred himself to the limousine, sitting beside the driver, and they moved off.

'What did they do?' Captain Drew asked.

'I haven't looked yet,' George said.

He turned down the sun visor, opened his mouth and looked at himself in the vanity mirror.

'Christ,' he lisped, appalled, 'I look like bloody Dracula.'

'There's a very good dentist in Hamburg,' Captain Drew said. 'He'll fix you up.'

Drew was in his late thirties, and had the handsome, fresh good looks of a twenty-five year old. Only the thin, ironic lips modified the innocence of his face.

'Is Nick OK?' George asked.

'He doesn't think much of your stupid stunt,' Captain Drew said. 'And nor do I. You deserve to be courtmartialled.'

'Why?' George enquired. 'Since I didn't receive any orders, I couldn't have disobeyed any, could I.'

'Don't be impertinent, Griffin,' Captain Drew said, languidly. 'I can fix you any time, and don't you forget it. I'm good at cooking up phoney courtmartials.'

George thought he was probably speaking the truth, and they drove on for some time in silence. The driver, judging by his lack of interest, appeared to be stone deaf, but then he was SAS as well, and the members of that group had their own code superimposed on top of Queen's Regulations.

Captain Drew lit another cigarette. 'As it happens,' he said, 'by pure chance, you'll get away with it. Information came in after you'd left, and it was too late to warn you. The gentleman you were supposed to collect had come under suspicion.'

'A Colonel Grunwald, according to them,' George said. 'Who's he?'

'None of your business,' Captain Drew told him. That question was only answered much later, when they were both in civvy street. 'They had a fair idea what he was up to, and they were watching the border in this area even more keenly than usual. So, but for your fatuous little private feud, the odds are you'd all have been nobbled. Nick had his difficulties, even using the southern crossing, but still, it worked out. You can consider yourself lucky though.'

'Oh, yes,' George said. 'I do.' He explored the remnants of his front teeth with his tongue, and reflected on his luck.

'Since I had to retrieve you,' Captain Drew said, 'you'll have to go on a charge of course. Crossing the border like that, merely to boast about drinking their beer, is not only foolish bravado, it's a serious breach of regulations. You should have known better.'

'I shan't do it again,' George said, 'without written orders. You can take bets on that.'

'You're an insolent lout,' Captain Drew said. 'I begin to doubt your fitness for such a fine, disciplined body as the Special Air

145

Service.' He looked at the passing countryside for a few moments. 'By the way, what did you do to him?' he asked casually.

'He'll recover,' George said. 'But he won't be gunning down children for a while.'

'You're a fool,' Captain Drew sighed tiredly. 'The way they're trained to think, anyone heading West is mere fodder for target practice. The whole border's manned with such people. What good do you imagine duffing up one of them's going to do?'

'It made me feel better at the time,' George said.

He was allowed to go to Hamburg before he faced his charge. The dentist proved to be an artist.

'Also, ninety per cent as strong as the original teeth,' he beamed, when it was over. He was proud of his work.

George looked at his new crowns, and agreed with him. The bill, the dentist told him, was already paid. When he got back, George expressed his appreciation, to Captain Drew, for the army's generosity. Captain Drew looked at him blankly.

'Are you raving, Griffin?' he enquired. 'If you wish to use an expensive, private dentist for your disgusting teeth, instead of the admirable free service at your disposal, that's your business. But the army would most certainly contribute not one penny towards your self-indulgence.'

George had been so pleased with looking like a normal human being again, that he had forgotten that the operation had never happened. He wondered briefly how Captain Drew had fiddled the money to pay for it. Then he remembered that Captain Drew was the Officer's Mess treasurer, and good at bamboozling service auditors.

Nick had proved less successful in one of his ventures, although, admittedly, his enterprises were devoted more to serving himself, on occasions, than his Queen and country.

'I'm on my way,' Nick said, as he packed. 'Buying myself out, while I've still got an impressive service record I can brandish at prospective employers. My sources tell me the SIB are closing in, and I don't want to be set up by those suspicious bastards.'

146

George supposed that Nick's role in a complicated fiddle concerning duty-free cars supplied to service personnel which somehow found their way into civilian hands was on the verge of coming to light. The Special Investigation Branch took themselves, and their quarry, seriously though, and the tentacles of the fiddle stretched back to the UK.

'They might still be able to do you,' George said. 'Even in civvy street.'

'No, they won't,' Nick said. 'First of all, I am, of course, totally innocent. Secondly, I've made arrangements.'

George discovered what that meant when the arrests were eventually made. Nick had covered his tracks, and left someone else holding the baby. He was a heartless bastard.

'What will you do?' George asked.

'I fancy the Royal Mint as first choice,' Nick said. 'Closely followed by the Bank of England.'

It turned out, in fact, to be the police force, where Nick found it just as possible to coin money on the side.

George was wheeled up before the Colonel, where he received a reprimand, but no loss of rank. His crime was crossing the border. No mention was made of Grunwald, or the frontier guard, or the night he had spent being interrogated in an old-fashioned dentist's chair.

'The Old Man thinks you did well,' Captain Drew said, as they walked away from HQ. 'Keeping your mouth shut like that.'

'Unfortunately, it was propped wide open most of the time,' George said. 'That was the trouble.'

'Facetiousness is one of your problems,' Captain Drew said coldly. 'Curb it. Especially when the Old Man puts it to you that you should apply for a commission which he intends to do.'

'What? Just after collecting a reprimand?'

'That will be counterbalanced by glowing, if hypocritical comments from people like me,' Captain Drew said. 'Also, honest praise from the Old Man, since he knows you less well. Up to you, but it's there if you want it.'

George thought about it, and laughed. 'Sorry,' he apologized. 'I was thinking of the last time I nearly moved out of the ranks. I was eighteen at the time, a porter in a chain store.'

'Well, you're lucky to get a second chance,' Captain Drew said. 'You're nudging the upper age limit for a commission already. This is the last opportunity you'll get.'

George considered the idea. On the whole, he liked it. It meant regarding the army as a permanent career, but why not? He knew where he was in the army, he was a good soldier, he was at home. He had no desire to do anything else.

'If you need a hint to take back to the Old Man,' he said, 'I'd like to have a go.'

'Good,' Captain Drew said. 'We'll have a mammoth piss-up the day you put your pips up.' They walked on in silence for a while: 'Oh, by the way,' he said 'we're moving to Buckeberg in three weeks' time, in case you want to say an extended goodbye to your German girl friend.'

George nodded indifferently. He did not think he would mention the move to his local girl friend, who was becoming something of a drag. As for Buckeberg, it was just another place. Where he was stationed next was of no importance.

In that judgement, George was wrong. Six months from that day, he was not sporting his Sam Browne and his new won pips. He was unsuccessfully trying to sell typewriters in civvy street, thanks to visiting a house in Buckeberg.

George's natural proclivities had let him down again.

148

CHAPTER ELEVEN

Buckeberg had been quiet and peaceful after the excitements of life on the border. At first, George Griffin relished it. Soon, he became bored. Shortly afterwards, he took up an activity which assuaged the tedium. Not long after that, Captain Drew suggested a night out in Minden.

They were in a restaurant, and well into their second bottle of Moselle. Both were wearing civilian clothes.

'This is my version of farewell to the troops,' Captain Drew said. 'I've been offered a golden handshake under the latest defence cuts.'

George stared at him. 'You're leaving the army?'

'I've had a good run,' Drew said. 'But I've served Queen and country long enough.'

'What have you got lined up?'

'I shall grow roses and meditate,' Drew said piously.

'Balls,' George said. 'You wouldn't quit if you didn't have some swindle going.'

Drew sighed into his wine. 'You are a basic person, George,' he said, with distaste. 'Still, I suppose it's my fault for mixing socially with other ranks.'

'What is it? This swindle?' George enquired, ignoring the flannel. He reached for the bottle of wine.

'There are various openings,' Drew said cryptically. 'Ways in which I might occupy my leisure time. Various rural and urban pastimes I could take up. If you need the occasional odd job after you've bought yourself out, you must get in touch.'

George froze. 'After I've done what?'

'You're spilling the wine,' Drew told him. George restored the bottle to the vertical. 'Bought yourself out of the army,' Drew said. 'Before you get courtmartialled. Or possibly accidentally shot during the next battle exercise when they're using live ammunition.'

George would like to have supposed that Captain Drew was having him on. But Drew's sense of humour did not usually stray in such directions.

'The last time you showed any interest in my future,' George said, 'you were urging me to apply for a commission. Which I've done. I'm waiting to hear about it.'

'Alas, George,' Drew said, 'you're not officer material after all, I fear. Regretfully, but there it is.'

'When did you decide that, you bastard?' George demanded, annoyed.

'I didn't,' Drew said, unruffled. 'But Major Hawsey is a jealous man. He doesn't like his wife being poked by a corporal like you for some reason. In fact, I gather he's taken considerable exception.'

Cheryl Hawsey was a reasonably attractive woman, in a lacquered kind of way, and her cool, off-hand county manner concealed, it had turned out, an eager interest in fundamentals. But only the boredom of Buckeberg had led George to try his luck, and much of the excitement, as far as he was concerned, had come from having an affair with an officer's wife, and the risks involved in bringing Cheryl to the boil under her own roof. Now those risks had, it appeared, come home to roost.

On the other hand, Major Hawsey, although a stuffed shirt, was little more than a glorified quartermaster. He carried no weight with fighting men and, given his prissy personality, was most unlikely to draw public attention to events by bringing formal charges. George relaxed and breathed more easily as he put this point of view to Captain Drew who, he suggested, was exaggerating. There was no danger to his prospective commission, let alone any chance of being courtmartialled.

'That's the trouble with being an ignorant bum like you,' Captain Drew sighed. 'You don't understand the ways of officers and gentlemen. Major Hawsey is feeling decidedly peevish, not to say vindictive, about the whole thing. He's after your hide, and unless you get out fast he'll have it.'

'Come on,' George said. 'Can you see him giving evidence at any courtmartial? No, and nor can I.'

'I said you could be courtmartialled,' Captain Drew said patiently. 'What the offence might be is another matter. Screwing Cheryl, no, there I agree with you.'

'A cooked-up charge?' George shook his head. 'The old man would never let one of his lads be fitted up like that. The SAS counts, and bloody quartermasters don't.'

'Your trouble,' Captain Drew said, 'is that you will regard the SAS as a kind of private bandit gang, a sort of superior mafia which looks after its own.'

George grinned. 'Well?'

'We're still part of the British Army,' Captain Drew said, 'believe it or not. Major Hawsey himself may be about as important as dog shit, but what you're too illbred to know is that he's an undistinguished member of an old and very distinguished military family. One of his cousins is a Brigadier who carries a lot of clout with the Special Investigation Branch. And another is a Colonel in the Commandos, the same unit, as chance would have it, whom we join for manoeuvres next month. Now that's your real mafia, Georgie boy, and you're due to be fixed, believe me, one way or another, unless you get out while you've still got two legs to walk on.'

George had lost his grin long before Drew finished speaking.

Just the same, he hesitated for some time. He had no wish to return to civilian life. He had got used to the army, or at least, the SAS.

But things began to happen. He was tipped off that the SIB were around and seemed to think he was tied in with Nick's transport fiddle. A group of beery commandos picked a fight in a bar in Minden one night, and George only escaped relatively undamaged by diving through a window. A round exploded in the breech of his gun while he was carrying out target practice on the range, and a fragment left his cheek bleeding profusely. This could well have been pure accidental chance, but George decided not to risk the battle exercise with live ammunition.

151

'I want to buy myself out sir,' he told his colonel.

George arrived back in London, as a civilian, without the faintest idea what he was going to do. He found a room, and a job, selling typewriters.

'Just until I get myself sorted out,' he told Brenda on the phone.

'I don't know why you had to leave the army, she said uneasily. Brenda still disliked unexpected changes.

George toiled around Inner London, and learned the humiliation of making cold calls. Driven on by visions of handsome commission, he persevered, bluffed his way past suspicious receptionists, arranged demonstrations, gave forth with the spiel from the sales manual, and even managed to sell a few machines, enough to pay his rent, and keep him going.

What he needed was one big sale, and then it seemed as if he had clicked. He happened to call on a big firm of solicitors just when they were considering re-equipping throughout with electric typewriters. George could see his bonanza, the freedom that enough money provided, and devoted himself to bringing off the sale.

He cultivated the senior partner, got on drinking terms with him, showed him what the machine would do, and worked ceaselessly, until it came to him that he was spending endless hours in the solicitors' office, drinking his whisky, and talking about most things except typewriters.

The realization came one evening, after they had seen off one bottle of whisky, and were about to embark on another. George was marginally less pissed than the solicitor, and pointed out that their splendid social relationship would be enhanced rather than diminished once the contract was signed, and he laid the document firmly on the desk.

'I'm sorry you brought that up, George,' the solicitor said, sadly. 'I like you. It's a pleasure to talk to you. I look forward to our little sessions together.' He topped up George's glass, and belched. 'But if you're going to push me . . .'

'I'm not pushing you, Clarence,' George said. 'But don't you think it's time we got this sewn up?'

'What's a bright fellow like you doing working for this shower?' the solicitor enquired plaintively. 'You can sell yourself, George, and that's good. That's what a salesman's supposed to do. But you must know that what you're trying to flog is a dead horse. Yours is the worst machine on the market, bar none.' He smothered a hiccup. 'I'd like to help you, George, I really would, but I can't buy rubbish like that.' He shook his head dolefully. 'Have another drink.'

They had several more drinks, while George tried to get over the shock. He realized how naïve he had been. He knew nothing about typewriters, and had accepted the sales manager's evaluation. 'Always remember, you're selling the best machine there is.'

'Bollocks,' he muttered.

'Now don't take it to heart, George,' the solicitor said. 'Even the best saleman must have something decent to sell. If you were with IBM now . . .'

But IBM would not give George Griffin, no education, no experience, no qualifications, well over thirty, the time of day.

He knew that he would have to find another job. When the solicitor staggered out to the lavatory, George took some blank sheets of his notepaper and put them in his briefcase. Lousy his typewriters might be, but they could come in useful before he abandoned them.

George acquired more blank sheets of notepaper from various well known firms on whom he called. The solicitor's business heading eventually topped a soberly glowing reference extolling the morals, merits, and financial standing of their valued client, Mr George Griffin. It was with the aid of this document that George acquired the unfurnished flat in Maida Vale for which there was keen competition.

Notepaper from the other firms became warmly phrased references which George used as necessary. One such paean of praise got him a job selling life insurance in which he briefly prospered, and was later left penniless when the company collapsed owing him five hundred pounds commission.

George was beginning to feel that life had it in for him. He fired off a barrage of phoney references to various large and

153

prosperous companies, but although they were impressed, they had a bureaucratic tendency to require documentary evidence of qualifications, which George was in no position to forge. In the end, and with deep foreboding, he took another sales job, this time, encyclopaedias.

But, by chance, George had found his niche. The books were not the best available, but they were not the worst either. With something to sell, he became skilled at conning that segment of society which liked the idea of a short cut to knowledge packed up handily under posh bindings. The rate of commission was good, and he was a free agent, able to work when he felt like it. Or to be more exact, he was not obliged to work if he did not feel like it, for example after a heavy night.

He furnished the flat in Maida Vale, and for some time preserved the mutual fiction that he was working in London while visiting his family at infrequent weekends. Brenda seemed to accept the new arrangement, but eventually he wondered if she would agree to a small variation. He drove to Portsmouth on a Wednesday to find out.

Brenda was surprised to see him, and a little worried. 'Is something wrong?'

'No,' George said. 'Let's have a sherry.'

'It's only one o'clock,' Brenda said, alarmed by the suggestion. She reached for the sherry bottle at six o'clock prompt, never before.

'Come on,' George said. 'Be a devil. Live it up.' He overcame her scruples, and they sat together in the small, polished living room. George kept her glass topped up, and in this way managed to get half a bottle down her.

'You'll get me drunk,' Brenda said.

'Rubbish,' George said. 'You've only had a couple.'

'Is that all? I feel quite light headed.' She giggled. 'It's rather nice, though.'

George judged that the moment had arrived, and began talking. His nostalgic reflections took in the moment they had met, how young they were at the time, and the reason they had got married.

Brenda was nodding dreamily. 'We didn't know about the pill in those days,' she said, wisely.

George was a bit surprised that she had heard about the pill at all, but he agreed, and added for good measure that they were just a couple of innocent kids who did not know what they were doing.

'No more than children,' Brenda said. 'That's what we were.'

George let his mouth go on manufacturing words, and thought that they were both exhibiting a high degree of hypocrisy. He remembered the eighteen-year-old George Griffin very well indeed, and that youth knew exactly what he was doing. He was bent on screwing any girl who would have him, and Brenda happened to be willing. For her part, whether she had realized it or not, she wanted to be married and pregnant, or pregnant and married, and in which order did not much matter.

That was what he thought now, anyway, but he did not feel any resentment. In her limited way, Brenda was a nice old bird, who meant no harm to anyone, and he did not want to cause her any pain.

He thought he had though, when, after pointing out how much of their married life had been spent apart and how this state of affairs seemed to suit them both, he went on to conclude that perhaps they should extend the logic of the situation and uttered the word 'divorce' for the first time.

Tears sprang into her eyes, and she dabbed at her nose with a lace fringed handkerchief.

'I'm only trying to be sensible,' George said uncomfortably. 'There's nothing to cry about.'

'What about Dick?' Brenda sniffed.

'I'll maintain him of course, and when he gets to university I'll make sure he's all right for cash.'

They both took it for granted now that Dick would go to university. They had got over their astonishment that the boy was cleverer than most.

'Yes, but what about this house? I love this house,' Brenda wept. 'I don't want to leave this house. I thought I could stay here for ever.'

'So you can,' George said. In the face of her tears, he abandoned his as yet unspoken suggestion that they should sell it, take half of the proceeds each, and she should move into a flat. 'I'll go on paying for it. You won't have to move.'

'But can you afford all that?' Brenda asked, tremulously. 'I mean keeping me, and Dick, and paying for the house, and your flat . . ?'

'Of course I can,' George said. 'I'm doing it now, aren't I?'

He felt strong at that moment, able to support anybody. Brenda dried her eyes and raised no further objections. She made tea for him and even kissed him when he left.

As George drove towards London, he thought that, provided Brenda was not obliged to change her modest little life-style, she not only did not object to a divorce, she welcomed it. She had everything she wanted, and she did not need a husband. A husband was something of a nuisance.

George felt quite pleased with himself. He thought that he had sorted matters out neatly and painlessly. The pain set in later, and was mostly financial.

Prices seemed to go up faster than George's earnings. Also, he spent more, developing a taste for dining out, gin, and night clubs. The female factor in his life remained as constant as it always had been, but somehow they seemed to come more expensive as time went by.

George became more or less permanently hard up, especially when he established the Sinking Fund. It was only with the advent of the occasional odd job that he was able to balance the books for most of the time.

Captain Drew fortuitously reappeared in George's life at a night club. It was a high class night club, which did not employ hostesses. Instead, the go-go dancers changed into slim-fitting dresses after their act, and allowed lonely guests to buy them champagne. That way, punters who were so minded felt that they had struck lucky with a glamorous lady from the world of show business, to whom it was a pleasure to give a present. It was not like buying it.

George was there on business, entertaining the chief buyer for the Tanker division of an oil company. George hoped to persuade him that the crew of every tanker in the fleet deserved the educational uplift and edification of a luxury set of encyclopaedias in the ship's library. It was a bold stroke, but George was hopeful of success especially if he got the chief buyer drunk enough, and cut him in on a big enough percentage.

Late on, the chief buyer excused himself, and did not come back. Half an hour later, he was found asleep in the lavatory. The commissionaire shovelled him into a taxi, and George was left moodily contemplating the bill, and the undulating upper curves of the go-go dancer with long blonde hair.

Five minutes after the act finished, she arrived at his table, wearing a low-cut dress and a smile. A waiter hovered with a bottle of champagne at the ready. That was when Captain Drew turned up.

'We'll have the champagne,' Captain Drew said. 'But we shan't need any company.'

'I wouldn't dream of intruding,' the girl said. 'Pardon me, I'm sure.'

Captain Drew eyed her up and down. 'Actually, darling,' he said, 'on a second look, I've had second thoughts. Come back in ten minutes when my friend will have gone. I can afford you, and he can't.'

'Actually, darling,' the girl said, 'piss off.'

Captain Drew sat down. 'Why do they have to talk?' he wondered. 'Especially in that ghastly accent.'

'She talks sense,' George said, moodily. 'You heard her. Piss off.'

'I knew you'd be pleased to see me,' Captain Drew said. He dusted the immaculate sleeve of his immaculate suit with immaculate fingers. 'God, you're an elusive chap. It's taken me all evening to find you. And here you are spending money like water. You must be very prosperous these days.'

'Not especially,' George said. The chief buyer, he knew, was much married. His wife would require explanations from her drink-sodden, vomit-stained husband, who would look for someone to blame. The leading contender was George Griffin, and

157

that would be the end of his bold conception. The tanker crews would be deprived of the educational benefits they might have acquired, and George's bank balance would not benefit from commission running into four figures, earned in one evening. He sighed. It had been such a neat idea, lost now because one stupid bastard could not hold his drink.

'I thought I told you to get in touch with me,' Captain Drew said, 'if you fancied the occasional odd job.'

'I didn't fancy chopping logs or digging ditches down in Devon for you, thank you,' George said.

'I wouldn't dream of employing you for either,' Captain Drew said. He picked up George's bill, and glanced at it. 'By God you do yourself well,' he said. He fanned ten pound notes across the bill. 'Suppose I picked this up?'

'Why should you do that?' George enquired suspiciously.

'To encourage you to consider a little proposition, for which you would be paid two hundred pounds in crisp oncers.'

'Doing what?'

Captain Drew smiled across the dance floor. The girl with the long blonde hair smiled back. 'I do believe the little lady is relenting,' he said.

'She's seen your wad of tenners,' George said. Like the girl, he felt more friendly towards Captain Drew himself.

'Rubbish,' Captain Drew said. 'She finds me irresistibly attractive. I'd like you to go soon, George, so let me brief you quickly. Not that there's much to say. All I want you to do is meet someone for a beer.'

The beer was served in a litre tankard in a beer hall called the Zillertal, on the Reeperbahn in the city of Hamburg. George sat there waiting. He knew this big, cheerful, noisy place well. He had been there several times when his unit was stationed in Germany.

Eventually, a plump, talkative German introduced himself. They went back to George's hotel room. George handed over the documents from the briefcase. They shook hands. The German went. And that was all.

George lay on the bed and worried. The whole thing smelt. No

158

one got paid two hundred quid for this. So what was he really being paid for?

Captain Drew had driven him to London Airport that morning, handed him the briefcase, and given him instructions. George had his own ideas about that briefcase, but he only had time to give it a cursory inspection before the flight was called. Suddenly, the whole thing looked very risky, and George sat in his seat on the plane, hugging the briefcase, and wishing he did not happen to need two hundred pounds rather badly, in which case he could have backed out smartly.

He went through a bad few minutes at Hamburg Airport, when Customs seemed to pay a lot of attention to the briefcase, but in the end, he was passed through courteously.

Once in his hotel room, he locked the door, and went to work on that briefcase. An hour later, he admitted defeat. It was exactly what it seemed to be, no false panels, no false bottom, just an ordinary briefcase, of the kind turned out weekly by the thousand, nothing more.

He took out the bundles of documents, and spread them on the bed.

'Important contracts,' Captain Drew had said. 'I'm a director of an import/export agency.'

Balls, George had thought. Camouflage for what's really in there. But there was nothing else except those documents. He studied them hopefully, but they were in German, and he learned nothing. George could speak the language passably, but reading legal German jargon was beyond him.

George was convinced there was some fiddle going on, but, whatever it was, he could not spot it. The obvious only occurred to him, belatedly, back at London Airport.

Captain Drew met him, took the briefcase, and handed George an envelope containing the balance of his fee as they walked across to the car park. Captain Drew switched on, revved the engine and waved goodbye. It occurred to George that the man was in something of a hurry and anxious to get away from the airport for some reason.

George cursed his own stupidity, wrenched open the door of

the reversing car and scrambled in beside Drew.

'You can give me a lift,' he said.

'I'm not going your way,' Captain Drew said.

'Oh, yes you are,' George said dangerously.

'Get out you pig ignorant bum,' Captain Drew said.

'Right,' George said. 'And I'll take this empty briefcase with me, shall I? Mine's getting a bit dilapidated. I could use a new one.'

Captain Drew controlled himself, and drove down the spiral leading out of the multi-storey car park.

'I'll drop you off at Osterley tube station,' he said. 'I have to get to a meeting, and I can't be late for it.'

I'll bet, George thought. He cuddled the briefcase, which bore no initials and looked like ten thousand others, and which he strongly doubted was the same one he had taken to Hamburg. Some Kraut he had never met had switched it while he was out of the hotel room, sitting in the Zillertal, nursing a beer.

Captain Drew pulled up at the tube station. George caressed the briefcase. 'The documents were a blind,' he said. 'Someone switched briefcases in Hamburg. This one has a false compartment. What's in it?'

'None of your business,' Captain Drew said.

'I think it is,' George said. 'Let's take a look.' He opened the briefcase, and started looking for the concealed catch.

Captain Drew cast an alarmed glance at the people passing by. 'For Christ's sake,' he said.

'I hear, or I see for myself,' George said. I see anyway, if I don't believe you.'

'Diamonds,' Captain Drew said softly.

George choked. He believed him. He also had little doubt that the stones were stolen. He remembered the absent-minded way in which he had walked through the green Customs channel, and shivered. 'You set me up to smuggle diamonds for two hundred lousy quid?' he protested.

'There was no risk,' Captain Drew said impatiently.

'What? I could have got five years inside,' George said.

'Rubbish,' Captain Drew said. 'This country is crippled by an

160

excess of red tape and bureaucrats. They interfere with the free flow of market forces. Especially a section of Customs and Excise known as the Investigation Branch, who are,' he said with feeling, 'as miserable a bunch of vindictive, lousy bastards as I've ever yearned to take a sub-machine gun to. But millions of people a year use London Airport and the evil, suspicious swine have to concentrate on what they call "known travellers". I am one, but you're not. There was no chance they'd give you the works.'

George was not convinced. He felt that he had a grievance. He complained loud and long. In the end, Captain Drew reluctantly handed over another hundred pounds, grumbling about the erosion of profit margins caused by greedy, grasping buggers like George, who had, by his rapaciousness, priced himself out of a lucrative future, and drove off.

This was largely rhetoric born of momentary irritation. George did many more odd jobs of various kinds for Captain Drew, although after that first time, he always insisted on knowing the background. Captain Drew did not object. In fact, George sometimes thought ruefully, the man rather enjoyed cooking up elaborate and convincing stories concerning what lay behind George's latest piece of courier or delivery work which bore no relation to the truth whatever.

Captain Drew's import/export business proved to be extremely flexible, sensitively responsive to the demands of world trade and Captain Drew's bank balance, but in the end it specialized in the export of men.

'I'm giving you first offer,' Captain Drew said.

'No, thanks,' George said. 'I'm getting too old to be shot at in unpleasantly hot climates. I had all that when we were in the Far East.'

'You're too valuable to be cannon fodder,' Captain Drew said. 'That's for the natives. You'd be a military adviser, with the rank of captain, with a small bunch of picked men to help you, ex-paras and so on. A twelve-month contract, five hundred a week, tax free, and five grand in cash when you finish your tour.'

The money tempted George sorely, as nice round figures

always did. But he said reluctantly, 'I don't think so.'

'Please yourself,' Captain Drew said, off-handedly. 'That's the plum job I have to fill. If you don't want it, plenty will.'

George experienced a sharp pain at the thought of all that money going to some other, more undeserving person, but he shook his head again. He had long since ceased to believe in fairy godmothers, and in his experience money invariably had to be earned, but especially big money. Five hundred a week, meant danger of a kind which George increasingly disliked. Five thousand at the end of a twelve month tour was generous, so generous that George thought that they did not believe there was much chance of it being collected.

George was sorry to turn it down at the time, but he was glad later, when he heard what had happened to the ex-marine who took his place, and whose life drew to a slow and agonizing end.

Captain Drew had felt that he was doing George a favour, and he was rather put out. 'I shall be fully occupied on this project,' he said, stiffly, 'so don't expect any more odd jobs, will you.'

'OK, George said. I shall have to freelance.' He had met John Irving and a number of other people in the trade who thought well of him by then.

'Contacts you've made through me,' Captain Drew said. He frowned thoughtfully. 'I think I should charge you ten per cent on your earnings.'

George smiled, although he knew that Captain Drew was not joking. 'You can try and get it,' he said amiably.

CHAPTER TWELVE

The Sinking Fund had done well while John Irving was stationed in London. George was sorry to see him go. It had been a fruitful period, after a dodgy start.

'Sure, George,' John Irving said, 'you've done a little fetch and carry work on the side for Captain Drew, but I need something more than a fall guy, which was how he used you.'

'I know it,' George said with feeling. 'But I didn't fall.'

'True,' John Irving said. 'Just the same, anyone I use has to be able to operate, without help, in difficult situations. I don't know if you're in that league, George.'

'I am,' George said, 'for the best possible reason. I have a lot of commitments. I need the loot.'

'Sell more encyclopaedias,' John Irving suggested.

'Tax-free loot,' George said. 'It adds up faster that way. Easy money, that's my motto.'

'Easy, yes,' John Irving said. 'Apart from the chance of being beaten up, shot or dumped into some foreign gaol.'

'I don't think about those aspects,' George said. 'It would confuse the issue.'

He was lying, of course. The possibility of being hurt haunted him almost as much as his pressing need for money.

They were drinking in the bar of the Savoy Hotel. George was trying to get John Irving to give him some little odd job to do on a trial basis. It cost him a meal and a bottle of Mouton Rothschild before he succeeded.

'Well, it so happens,' John Irving said, chewing thoughtfully, 'that you might be suitable for one little chore, if you can handle it. You're not known, you're not on anyone's files. The right guy is proving hard to find.'

'You've found him,' George said, promptly. He almost added 'How much?' but decided to leave the bargaining until Irving had committed himself.

'Ever hear of a conductor called Balescu?'

'Tram or bus?' George enquired. John Irving was not amused. 'Sorry. Orchestral, I presume. No.'

'He was allowed out on a tour with his wife. That was a year ago. They claimed political asylum at our embassy in Paris. They're still there.' He sipped his wine appreciatively. 'We have a problem. Balescu had to leave his four-year-old daughter behind. He won't travel to America and he won't talk, until we get her out. He thought that once he'd defected, they'd let her join him. He's a simple soul in some ways.'

'Talk?' George asked, puzzled. 'Talk about what? How to interpret someone's ninth symphony. What use is he to you?'

'Balescu is not only a distinguished musician,' John Irving said patiently, 'but for several years he was Minister of Culture. He took government seriously until he became disenchanted. Politically, he has a lot to offer us. Militarily too, maybe, like Warsaw Pact contingency plans in the event of . . . various possibilities,' he ended vaguely.

George was quite happy to lie on the beach in Mamaia and sun himself. He had driven across Europe, through Hungary, along the Balkan Highway to Bucharest, on to Mamaia, and he was tired.

Admittedly, the loudspeakers strung along the beach were distracting, with their mixture of music and what he imagined to be pep talks, and he could not get used to the male Rumanian habit of sunbathing while standing up, head tilted back to the sky, eyes closed, motionless. Why did so many of them have pot bellies? Poor diet perhaps? He yawned and closed his eyes. He would never find that out. All he had to do was wait.

At the end of a week George had a rich, golden tan, and he was bored. He was also becoming concerned. All the arrangements hinged on a ten-day holiday. On the ninth day, a dark haired, attractive woman wearing a demure bathing costume sat down beside him. Nearby a little girl splashed in the water

'How do you do,' she said. 'I am Anne, your wife.' She smiled slightly.

'Glad to know you,' George said. There was no one within range of their low-pitched voices. He nodded at the little girl.

'Is that my daughter, Carol?'

'Yes. We leave tomorrow. You will pick us up at the railway station in Constanza, at eight o'clock. Get a good night's rest. It will be a long drive.'

'Are you under surveillance?'

'I don't think so. We shall find out tomorrow.'

She moved away, and joined Balescu's daughter in the water. George thought that her voice, with its softly accented English, was a pleasant one.

The idea was so simple as to be obvious. Too damned obvious, George had thought. He had come in over the Hungarian border. He had in his possession an additional perfect British passport, although not in his own name, which showed that he was an architect, that he had a wife, Anne, aged thirty-one, and a daughter Carol, aged four. It was also decorated with the appropriate visas and entry stamps. They would leave, *en famille*, across the Yugoslav border.

'For Christ's sake,' George had said, appalled, 'they'll have records, they'll check, they'll know I went in under another name without any bloody wife and kid.'

'Too much documentation can be counter-productive and lead to inefficiency,' John Irving had said. 'But if you'd rather call it off . . .?'

George grumbled, but he did not call it off. He only hoped John Irving knew what he was doing.

His hopes were bolstered somewhat when, on the sixth day in Mamaia, he ran out of cigarettes. He went to the Carpatsi office, and bought a pack of American cigarettes. Before this transaction was completed, a clerk had filled in a long form with four carbon copies, given him the top copy, and directed him to the cashier's desk. The cashier was more economical. She merely filled in an invoice with two carbon copies.

When George walked out with his pack of cigarettes after

165

twenty minutes form filling, he thought that perhaps John Irving was right. Presumably all those pieces of paper would be filed somewhere, by busy clerks. Any country which had that much paper washing around in the system might well not have an instant check on who arrived where and departed with whom.

From Mamaia, they had to cross the Danube, and drive back to Bucharest. Then they took the road to Turnul Severin. After that, they were to cross the mountains to Timosoara.

'We shall avoid most of the Post Controls, but not all,' Anne said.

George nodded. He had become accustomed to being stopped, well inside the country, and his papers inspected. He was not sure what purpose it served, apart from keeping the locals in order. The guards did not speak English, and although they studied his papers with fierce concentration, he very much doubted if they could read English either. He guessed that they were merely looking at the bits filled in at the border to make sure he was on the authorized route. The road they were taking, although not heavily used, was all right for tourists.

George drove as hard as he could, but the sun was low as they passed through Turnul Severin, and daylight gave out in the mountains. The road was slow, and, George thought, somewhat dangerous. He concentrated on the beam of his headlights. The little girl had long since gone to sleep on the back seat. She had large, luminous, serious eyes, and seemed like a good kid.

It was midnight when they got to Timosoara, a grubby nondescript town not far from the border, where they were to stay overnight.

That was where the first thing went wrong. The hotel clerk, who spoke little English, disclaimed all knowledge of any booking. Anne, who was holding the sleepy child in her arms, could hardly intervene and sort things out. She was supposed to be English, with no knowledge of the language.

George did not have to pretend in that respect. He was hot and sweaty, and his clothes were sticking to his back.

'I reserved a room weeks ago,' he kept on saying.

The hotel clerk shook his head obstinately. 'No booking.'

Anne managed to get near enough to him to whisper, 'Carpat-si.'

'I booked it through Carpatsi,' George told the clerk. 'Carpat-si.' Which was true.

This had an electric effect. The clerk made a phone call, and came back an apprehensive man, apologizing profusely. That was strange, because Carpatsi was only the name of the State Tourist Organization. Moreover, the clerk grinned, dinner would be served on the terrace, but at once, never mind the time. Could they bath first? But of course.

They put the child to bed, and ate on the terrace, under the stars. It was really quite romantic, George thought, if one could ignore the overpowering smell emanating from the nearby urinal.

'I happened to notice,' George said, as they finished a bottle of light, pleasant wine, 'that there's a double bed in the room. Natural, I suppose, for an old married couple.'

'We shall behave just like an old married couple,' Anne said. 'We shall sleep soundly, back to back.'

George was rather put out to find that she meant it. Here he was, the hero of the hour, taking the child to its parents and Anne to freedom. It would be fitting, surely, for him to receive some small favour in grateful recognition. But Anne was not having any. George spent a restless night. He kept waking up after disturbing dreams. Anne slept like a log.

As they approached the border, George stopped, and handed Anne a pair of binoculars.

'Take a look,' he said, got out, lifted the bonnet, and busied himself giving the radiator water which it did not need. When he got back in, Anne's face was set.

'We shan't get across,' she said. 'There are secret police there.'

'Are you sure?'

'I've been in their hands,' Anne said. 'I'd know their kind anywhere.'

George took a look for himself. Tall watchtowers, manned by soldiers, strode along the border. Beyond the frontier post lay a bare stretch, about half a mile wide. Beyond that was the Yugoslav border.

He focussed in on the group of buildings. Besides the usual border guards were three men in plain clothes. They just seemed to be waiting. A black car was parked to one side. George lowered the binoculars. Including the two nearest watchtowers, there were five machine guns which could be brought to bear in a few seconds.

'Does Carol speak any English?' he asked. Anne shook her head. 'All right. If they're looking for us, why haven't they picked us up already?'

'Perhaps the information came through after we'd left the hotel. Perhaps they don't know for certain. Perhaps they're not even looking for us. It doesn't matter. We could have got past the border guards, but the secret police, no.' She glanced at the child, in the back seat, and gave her a reassuring smile. 'Take us back to Timosoara, and we'll catch the train to Bucharest.'

'Hang on, hang on,' George said. Far off, a lorry was passing through the Yugoslav border. 'You're not where you're supposed to be, so what happens if you go back now?'

'For myself, a labour camp. For the child, foster parents, good party members. We only got this opportunity because we lived quietly for a year, and supervision became lax. But one lapse, and they'll make certain.'

'Do you want to take a chance?'

'Is there a chance?'

'Get down and keep down,' George said. 'Tell the child to lie on the floor.'

The lorry was half way across no man's land, surrounded by a cloud of dust. George started the engine, and drove forward, quietly and sedately, trying to judge the distance. He had to arrive at the right point at exactly the right time. His hands were clammy on the steering wheel. He wiped them on his shirt.

His slow moving car was a hundred yards from the border when they raised the barrier to let the lorry through. George hit bottom gear and the throttle at the same time. The rear wheels spun, bit hard, and the car accelerated like a rocket.

He went past the lorry on the off side, using its great bulk as a shield. The barrier which they were trying to lower again, hit the roof with a bang, but he was underneath it and past.

He started to zigzag, throwing the car from side to side in gut wrenching lurches, just as they started shooting. The rear window went, splattering glass into his hunched shoulders. He prayed they would not find the petrol tank.

A rear tyre burst, whether from a bullet or the way he was driving, he never knew. The engine was tearing itself to pieces, howling like an agonized animal, but he kept the throttle jammed to the floorboards. Bullets hammered into the body-work. He caught a glimpse of the Yugoslav guards running, and hoped they would not start shooting as well. The barrier was looming up. He ducked as they hit it. The windscreen burst into a thousand pieces, he jammed on the brakes, the car skidded, hit a concrete post sideways on with a terrifying crash, considered turning over, thought better of it, and dropped back on to its wheels.

There was silence, apart from the dying hiss of the engine. The shooting had stopped.

The Yugoslav gaol was smelly and unpleasant. When John Irving walked in, George had never been so glad to see anyone in his life. The way he had been treated so far, he felt that he would be lucky to get off with a thirty year sentence.

'OK action man,' John Irving said. 'Let's go and find a cold beer.'

George said, 'Gin and tonic for me.'

'By the gallon,' John Irving said. 'You're entitled to drink yourself stupid.'

'How come you pull weight in this place?' George asked, as they walked along dark, stone corridors.

'Through our commercial section,' John Irving said. 'Which is building a chain of hotels for them. You are a drunken British architect, employed up to now on the project. We've promised we'll deal with you, but they don't want to see you again in this country, so don't come back.'

'I won't, George promised. There had to be more to it than

169

that. The Yugoslavs were a sturdily independent people, who were far from simple, and their relations with their Eastern neighbour were delicate, since, if the Russian armies ever chose to strike at Belgrade, that was where they would come from. All the more reason why they would be highly unlikely to swallow a yarn like that. He supposed that John Irving now owed them a favour of some sort.

Outside, it was warm and sunny. They walked towards Irving's car.

'How are they?' George asked. He knew that the woman and the girl had not, mercifully, been wounded, but they had both been badly shaken.

'They're OK now,' John Irving said. 'They're both on their way to Paris.'

George was rather sorry to hear that. He remembered the way Anne had squeezed his hand, with a small smile, before the Yugoslavs marched him off. He thought there had been a different look in her eyes. He thought that a man could build on a look like that.

'That Anne,' he said 'is a very attractive lady. Who is she? One of yours?'

'No,' John Irving said. 'She's Balescu's mistress.'

The money which changed hands soothed George's disappointment. In between the ensuing odd jobs, he led the relatively normal life of a Maida Vale flat dweller, who was out at work every day, and out on other matters most evenings.

Saturday afternoons, he went to the launderette. He was returning from one such expedition, carrying a bag of washing, when he saw a particular Victorian wall clock for the first time, from behind, wrapped in brown paper. It was under Nancy's arm as she struggled, lop-sided, up the stairs.

'I'll take it,' George said, politely.

'It's all right,' Nancy said, flustered.

'Come on,' George said. 'Give it to me.'

'Well, all right,' Nancy said. 'Thank you.' George took the clock, which was heavier than it looked, and tucked it under his spare arm. Nancy rubbed her ankle. 'I'd have been all right,' she explained, 'but I tripped over that bike as I came in.'

'I wish I knew who it belonged to,' George said. 'I'd let his tyres down if I was certain he was smaller than me.' Nancy laughed. He noticed that she had a pleasant laugh.

Griffin never did find out which resident it was who made a habit of leaving his bicycle just inside the entrance to the block of flats.

George knew Nancy by sight. She lived in the flat next to his, but he had never spoken to her before. They exchanged idle conversation while he carried the clock up the three long flights of stairs, and waited while she fumbled for her front door key. She had bought the clock in the street market at Church Street, Marylebone.

'Very nice,' George said, as he lugged it into her living room. 'Can I put it up for you?'

'No, thanks,' Nancy said. 'I can manage now. Besides, I want to oil it first. Well, you've been very kind . . .'

'No trouble at all,' George said. He looked at his watch.

'Can I offer you anything? Coffee or a drink?'

'Not now, thanks,' George said. 'Some other time, perhaps.'

George was due to meet an out of work actress of whom he had high hopes, which were never, as it happened, fulfilled.

After that, they smiled and nodded, and sometimes exchanged comments on the weather whenever they happened to meet.

Nancy, he discovered was a theatre sister at St Mary's Hospital, Paddington, and she came and went at odd hours which sometimes coincided with his own nocturnal excursions. Later, she told him that she had taken up agency nursing, which was more flexible with better money, and was working at a private clinic off Wimpole Street.

Eventually, at two o'clock one morning, when George was dry-mouthed and fed up and only too pleased to sit and relax with a pleasant woman whom he was not trying to make, they did have coffee together.

He thought that she was in her late twenties or early thirties. She had a small, neat figure which showed, but was not revealed. She was not conventionally beautiful and her large eyes were too

171

open and candid to be overtly sexual. But she had a warm, wide smile, and George thought casually that it was the sort of face to which brooding scowls and frowns would be foreign and he could understand any man who thought it would be pleasant to have around.

After that first coffee, they behaved like good neighbours. George fixed her waste disposal unit when a tea spoon went down it and gummed up the works. She offered him a meal and he accepted.

Nancy left her keys with him one day when the Gas Board were due to come and overhaul her cooker. Predictably, no one arrived, and it was George who rang up later and blasted an indifferent girl at the other end to no effect whatever. Nancy sat and giggled during this performance, and later they talked and idly watched television.

George decided that he liked Nancy, which was an unfamiliar feeling where women were concerned. It was good to have a friend of the opposite sex, to whom he could talk, just talk without calculating his chances of getting her into bed.

Nancy's husband was called Victor. He was a senior steward with British Airways, who flew the long Far Eastern routes. George only met him a few times from beginning to end. Victor was about thirty-five, a heavily built, impersonal sort of man, who said little.

Nancy neither volunteered to talk about her husband, nor avoided talking about him. They had been married for eight years.

Once, George asked if they had not wanted children.

'We did,' Nancy said, 'very much. But it wasn't possible.' That was all she said, and George assumed that she was sterile. It was much later that he discovered that she was not, that it was Victor who could not father a child, that it was Victor who would not even discuss the possibility of adoption.

George was never very clear how or why it happened. He had no conscious intention, of that he was sure. Yet considering the way the words died after that accidental touch, the seemingly inevitable, anguished ecstasy that followed, it seemed that he

172

must have wanted her desperately without knowing it. And she him, there was no doubt about that.

When George felt able to speak again he said into the wisps of her hair which fell across his mouth, 'I love you.'

Her hand caressed his back gently and languidly. 'There's no need to say that,' Nancy said.

'I know,' George said. 'But I do.' He was amazed to find that he did. He wished there were words which had not been cheapened by over use, and searched his mind but he could not find any. 'I love you,' he said again experimentally. It sounded all right after all. He liked saying it.

Nancy liked hearing it too. He knew that from the way her arms clenched round him. But she fought against it. Not much perhaps, and pretty ineffectually, but she tried. 'No,' she said. 'It makes it all too complicated.'

'We could get married,' George said.

'I'm married already.'

'You could get a divorce.'

It all seemed very simple at the time as they pressed against each other in the tumbled bed in the dark room. The complications arose afterwards.

Victor posed the first one. A week later, back from Japan, he hammered on George's door at midnight. Nancy had insisted on telling him herself.

When George opened the door, Victor came in like a runaway lorry, smelling of whisky, eyes flaming, intent on pounding George into a pulp.

George did not want to harm him, but short of acting as a human punchbag, which he did not much fancy, he had very little choice. Victor lacked George's professional training, but he was beserk with rage, stronger, fitter and two stone heavier.

Clinically, without any ill will, and taking care not to damage any of the furniture, George did what was necessary for his own safety and physical wellbeing without inflicting too much needless pain.

That done, he propped the winded Victor up in a chair, bathed his bleeding mouth, forced some whisky down him and watched him collapse into a sobbing, wretched hulk.

Later, he listened to Victor talk with defeated resignation, and felt unwilling compassion and admiration for the man's essential decency and concern for Nancy. It was true that Victor was pretty stoned by then, slurring his words and maudlin.

'You'll look after Nancy,' Victor pleaded. 'You'll take care of her.'

'I'll make sure she's all right.'

'You swear it?'

'I swear it,' George swore solemnly.

'On your solemn oath?'

'On my solemn oath,' George said, wishing that the man would pass out.

The next day, Victor, pale and unsteady, moved out, taking his clothes with him in suitcases. Before he went, he finalized all the arrangements for the divorce with Nancy.

'He couldn't have been any fairer,' Nancy gulped, weeping for the past.

George had to admit that no one could have been fairer than Victor. They would sell the lease of the flat and its contents, and they would each take half the proceeds. They would also divide equally all their savings, insurance policies and so on.

'It's all so sad,' Nancy sobbed. George only knew one way to console her, and she clung to him gratefully.

With Victor gone, however, Nancy slowly became less sad and more practical. She was pleasantly surprised to find how much money would be due to her, enough, she pointed out, to buy a house, if they moved out of London.

'In your name though, since I'm not contributing anything,' George said, overcome by all the fairness which was flying about.

It was Nancy who found the house near Marlow, although George approved whole-heartedly. It was an easy drive for him into London, and handy for London Airport should any odd jobs crop up, although he had not found an opportunity to mention that side of his life to Nancy.

Victor kept his word, and sued for divorce, although the courts were so busy ending marriages, it appeared, that it would be some time before George and Nancy could be married. Meantime, Nancy bought the house near Marlow. She moved in, and spent her time happily decorating and searching for cheap but good furniture. She would go on working, she told George, until they were married and could think of having their first baby.

Sometimes George stayed at Marlow, but not often. Nancy was prudish about physically living with him all the time. George found this amusing, but also rather charming, and he did not really mind driving back to London in the small hours. In any case, he was then on the spot for his next day's calls.

At one o'clock one morning, as he turned on to the slip road leading to the M4 his headlights illumined a pair of jeans, a rucksack, and an outstretched thumb. He pulled up.

'Where are you heading?'

'Where are you going?'

'London. Maida Vale.'

'Right on the button.'

As far as George could tell, in the unflattering, overhead sodium lighting along the M4 she looked like an attractive pixie. She chattered away as he drove, and quite brightened the journey.

Approaching Maida Vale, George asked 'What part?'

'Well, actually, I need to make a phone call. The people I hope to stay with don't know they're going to have the pleasure of my company. Can I use yours?'

George felt that it would be churlish to refuse after being pleasantly entertained. He took her up to his flat, and pointed to the phone. 'Help yourself.'

'Can I make some coffee first? I'm dying of thirst. Would you like one? My name's Maisie by the way.'

Her face was indeed that of a pixie, twinkling and laughing, with pert—or were they impertinent—eyes. Her figure could have belonged to a boy, except for the firm, pointed swelling of her breasts. George tried not to look at them.

They sat over coffee, talking. George contributed brandy. It was some time before he remembered the phone call, and reminded her.

'I was lying,' she said. 'I don't know anyone in Maida Vale, except you. The truth is, I haven't got anywhere to stay tonight. Can I borrow your couch? I promise I won't run off with your priceless silver.'

'No chance of that,' George said, 'but . . .'

'But is a word I never use,' she said firmly. 'And whenever I hear it, I take it to mean yes. Thank you very much. Where's the loo?'

Short of chucking her out, George did not quite see how he could refuse. He gave her a couple of blankets, and said good-night.

He was yawning when he came out of the bathroom. He stopped dead in mid yawn.

'The couch wasn't very comfortable,' she said. 'You don't mind too much do you?'

The sheets were pulled up as far as her waist. George found it hard not to look at her appealing charms. He swallowed. 'I'll have to take the couch,' he said.

'Why? I don't care.'

'I'm engaged,' George told her.

'Really? I assumed you were married.'

In the cold light of many dawns after that, George wondered why. There was no good reason. He was not short of loving, Nancy saw to that. He did not need anyone else, he did not even want anyone else. And yet, when it was on offer, he took Maisie as fiercely as if he were a sex-starved adolescent. Why? Because she was available, and because she might be different? There could be no other answer. George wondered what was wrong with him.

She was certainly different. There was no affection in her case. What she gave was a sinuous, single-minded desire reminiscent of an energetic snake, and George responded in kind.

The first light of morning brought, as well as dawn, remorse and good intentions, which temporarily collapsed in the face of a repeat performance, after which they returned, enhanced and strengthened.

'This is ridiculous,' George said, drained. 'I'm going to marry

176

a perfectly nice woman. What's more, I'm in love with her.'

'Congratulations,' Maisie said, indifferently. 'But let's not have the scene where you wallow in guilt. There's no point. I'll be gone by the time you get back.'

George was yawning as he climbed the long flights of stairs that night. He had canvassed two large blocks of flats, sold one ordinary and one de luxe edition, driven to Marlow, rubbed down two doors ready for painting, half made good the plaster in one wall, and responded with all the limp enthusiasm of a rag doll when Nancy kissed him gratefully.

'I'm exhausted,' he said. 'I need an early night.'

'It's all this driving to and fro,' Nancy said. 'Never mind. It'll only be for another month or two.'

His stamina was waning, George thought. He was getting too old for complications. A nice, settled married life, that was all he wanted now.

The dark empty flat was comfortable, reassuring and restful, as George let himself in. He looked forward to a cup of coffee, a last cigarette, nine hours sleep, and the erasure of last night's idiocy.

He came to a stop, his hand outstretched, half way to the kitchen light switch. His nostrils twitched. What was that slight perfume which hung heavy in the air. Bath oil?

Maisie was in his bed. She opened her eyes sleepily. She must have good circulation, George thought. She never seemed to pull the bedclothes above her waist.

'What the hell are you doing here?' he enquired.

'I might be getting a job,' Maisie said. 'They said they'd call me. Yours was the only number I could give them.'

If Maisie had a profession, apart from unconcernedly wrecking other people's lives, it was that of photographic model, although she did not work very often. When she did, it was usually as the occupant of a bubble bath.

George never did find out much about her. She appeared in his life, as she was, without a past, stayed as long as it suited her and departed when she felt like it.

Nor did George much want to know about her. He was never

quite sure if he felt anything for her, apart from the one thing. Maisie had a lazy, justifiable arrogance about that. She could turn George on whenever she chose.

'There are other phones in Greater London,' George said. 'Millions of them.'

'I like the fringe benefits attached to this one,' Maisie said, writhing against him.

'You could get that too,' George groaned helplessly. 'No trouble at all.'

'You're good at it,' Maisie told him. 'The best I've had for many moons.'

Even allowing for flattery, George could not help being flattered.

Maisie would go, she promised, just as soon as she could get herself fixed up elsewhere. It was a promise she kept, although not, as it happened, until six months later.

But it was only a matter of days before Nancy began to look at him strangely, and ask one or two apparently casual, yet in reality, searching questions. George laughed it off, and when the questions recurred in another form lied with heartfelt sincerity.

'You'll have to go,' he told Maisie.

'I'll find somewhere at the weekend,' she said. She probably meant it, but it was marginally too late.

At five o'clock on the Friday afternoon, a key clicked in the lock, and Nancy walked in as she had every right to do.

They were not even in bed.

Nancy looked at the untidy piles of clothes on the living room floor, threw the keys in George's face, and walked out again.

Her aim was good. A thin trickle of blood was running down George's forehead.

Maisie padded across the room in the nude, fished a bottle from her handbag, sat down, and started to paint her toenails.

'I suppose I could be an unknown nymphomaniac,' she reflected, 'who forced my way into your flat, and insisted on stripping off.' She blew in the direction of her foot. 'But that wouldn't really explain your condition.'

'Nothing is going to explain this,' George said miserably.

There was no way he could talk himself out of this. Nancy still carried a fair load of guilt about Victor. She was a straight and honest woman who had cheated. For her to be able to live with that, the result had to be above board, permanent and worthwhile. She wanted a faithful husband she could trust, not a randy bugger who couldn't keep his hands off anything on offer. That reduced her to the same level. George knew precisely what he had done.

'Well, in that case,' Maisie said, 'I may as well stay on after all.'

CHAPTER THIRTEEN

Tauber opened his eyes, gaining fully alert consciousness at once. He noted the gun, his strange surroundings, and recognized Griffin. Under the bedclothes, his powerful body tensed.

'I would imagine,' Griffin said, 'that this gun would make a hole you could shove your fist in. So just relax. All you're required to do is talk.'

Tauber allowed his muscles to ease, but he declined to talk.

'What's your real name?'

'What are you doing in England?'

'Who's your contact with British Intelligence?'

To each repeated question, Tauber presented frozen eyes, and closed lips.

Griffin palmed the photograph of Dalton, and pitched it on to the bed-clothes. 'Do you know that man?'

For a few moments, Tauber ignored the small photograph. Then something about it seemed to capture his attention. He picked it up and studied it. A strange look, a look foreign to those killer's eyes, fractionally changed his expression, and stayed there. A look of fear.

'Is his name Dalton?'

Tauber shook his head.

'Who is he?'

'Who are you?' The accent was thicker than when Tauber had spoken to him in the mews, an occurrence which either seemed a minute ago, or a thousand days, Griffin was not sure which.

'Let's abide by the rules of the game,' Griffin said. 'I'm holding the gun, and I'm not particular whether you get killed or not. That means I get to ask the questions, not you. You just answer. So who is he?'

'I am very thirsty,' Tauber said. 'Could I have something to drink?'

'Later,' Griffin said. He indicated Dalton's smiling, open face. He spoke slowly, emphasizing each word. 'That joker is willing to pay me to deliver you to him. I don't see why I shouldn't. Do you?'

The way small muscles were twitching under the skin of Tauber's face, he seemed to be against the idea.

'Don't bottle it up,' Griffin said. 'I'm open to reason. And think yourself lucky you even get asked. If I'd wanted, you could have been collected when you were unconscious. Just remember that.'

'You must forgive me,' Tauber said, politely. 'But it would help if I knew who I was talking to.'

'I make one phone call, and you talk to him,' Griffin said, pointing at Dalton's photograph. 'I'm the one who can hand you over, that's who I am. So let's not have any bull, eh?'

There was a pause. Griffin knew enough about Tauber's breed of man to be able to guess at the thoughts which flashed through his mind.

He would have been briefed with a cover story, and a fall back cover story. Assuming there was some truth in Dalton's version, Tauber would have constructed a few of his own, to be dealt out in emergency.

During the brief silence, Tauber considered the possibilities. He did not know who Griffin was, but he knew who he was not. He was not part of any organization, or there would be no debate going on. That meant that there were options open, other than the one Tauber disliked. He opted to play by Griffin's rules.

'Right,' Griffin said. 'Who's this so-called Bob Dalton?'

'My superior officer,' Tauber said.

'In whose army?'

'No army,' Tauber said. 'Not exactly.'

'Why does he want you so badly?'

'I have certain plans, of which he might not approve,' Tauber said drily.

'What happens to you if he gets you?'

181

'I expect he would like me to go home,' Tauber said.

'And once back in the dear old mother country,' Griffin said, 'you spend quite a long time repenting the error of your ways, after which you get to be dead. Yes?'

'Something like that,' Tauber agreed.

'Let's have a little more detail,' Griffin said. 'This is what I've been told. You check it out.' He thought the answers he would get would be somewhere near the truth. The butt of the gun sat comfortably and reassuringly in his hand. His forefinger rested on the feather light trigger. The safety catch was off. He felt pleasantly relaxed. Tauber's angle was rather different. Tauber was looking at an ugly, black round hole from which, with one sharp cough, could emerge his instantaneous death at any second. Tauber had a strong vested interest in not making him irritable or jumpy. 'First,' Griffin went on, 'that you're a good hit man, highly thought of in the trade.'

'I have played the role for which I was trained,' Tauber said, 'in the struggle for democracy and freedom.'

Griffin ignored the cant, all-purpose words, and took that for assent. 'Second, that you were in London to deal with an East German defector.'

'It was my assignment to interview a person of that nationality,' Tauber said.

He talked like a civil servant, Griffin thought. In fact, that's what the man was, a civil servant who happened to kill people for a living. 'Third, that you're setting up a cross-over deal with British Intelligence.'

'I am at the peak of my career,' Tauber said, modestly. 'But mine is a young man's profession. In a little while, I shall be too old to go on working in the field. I am not an administrator by nature. I could only look forward to some sort of clerical position in which I would lose my present fringe benefits. I have to consider the future. This seemed to be a suitable moment to make contact and hold discussions. I have no family ties at home. Provided I could negotiate suitable terms, my prospects would be much improved by placing myself at the disposal of some organization over here which might be interested.'

182

God, inside this brutally powerful ape, this machine-like killer, was a little bureaucrat worried about approaching middle age, losing his perks, and financial security.

Somehow, the embarrassing Tauber had to be got rid of, and to someone who would not mind the fact that he was in a slightly damaged condition. Bob Dalton? Complete the deal, and collect the five hundred pounds due to him on delivery?

Yes, but would Dalton pay? Or was it not at least possible that, once he had Tauber, the goons would be turned loose on George Griffin instead?

Griffin thought that it was more than possible. It was distinctly likely. Dalton wanted Tauber, but once that was achieved, he might well regard Griffin as superfluous to requirements. Dalton was not, as it had unhappily turned out, a CIA man who would feel some kind of loose constraints concerning a British subject who had done him a service. Suppose their positions were reversed? Suppose Griffin were over here to get Tauber back, and had used Bob Dalton? Would he, George Griffin, pay Dalton another five hundred pounds and send him on his grateful way with a warm handshake, a merry wave, the hope that they might work together again one of these fine days and a pressing invitation to look in for drinks the next time he happened to be passing through Omsk or Tomsk or wherever such hospitality was dispensed when at home?

Griffin would not. Griffin would do something else. And so would Bob Dalton.

'I want the phone number you use to contact British Intelligence,' Griffin said.

Tauber shook his head. 'The only British organization I have been in touch with,' he said, 'is a trading organization.'

'That'll do,' Griffin said.

'Certain details of my contract are not finalized,' Tauber said. 'I would not wish to prejudice the outcome by premature acceptance.'

'You're not bargaining for goodies like life-long protection, a pension and a house in Canada any more,' Griffin told him. 'Forget that day-dream matey. You're playing for your life, take

183

it or leave it.'

Tauber, whose trade was ending life, valued his own. But he stared at Griffin in cold silence, reluctant to abandon his vision of affluence on his own terms.

'Make up your mind,' Griffin said. 'Otherwise I phone Bob Dalton and tell him to come and collect you.'

Tauber was not to know that angry, purple bruises tormented Griffin's flesh beneath his clothes and that his anxiety not to expose himself to Dalton again certainly equalled Tauber's. Reluctantly, Tauber spoke.

Griffin memorized the number. 'All right,' he said. 'You can get dressed now.'

Nancy had prepared sandwiches and a pot of coffee. A log fire was burning cheerfully, banked up with coals. She eyed Tauber warily, and then started as she saw the gun in Griffin's hand.

'What the devil do you think you're doing with that thing?' she demanded angrily. 'Have you gone stark raving mad?'

'It's his,' Griffin said. 'And I'd rather I held it than him if you don't mind.' Tauber had staggered a little when he was pulling his trousers on, but he soon recovered, and as far as Griffin could see that iron body of his was functioning quite well enough to be murderously dangerous were he not deterred by the risk of being shot. Griffin waved the gun. Tauber sat down, and started to eat. 'It's all right, Nancy,' Griffin said. 'He's decided to surrender to the authorities.'

'Good. I'll phone the police now,' Nancy said promptly.

'I'll do it,' Griffin said hastily. 'It's a special number.'

He chewed on a bacon sandwich as he sat by the phone. He had some bargaining to do himself. He would certainly need protection from Dalton and his goons, but he was undecided how much to ask for over and above that. He was doing his country a service, after all. Moreover he had lost five hundred pounds. He was entitled to that much, surely. Also, there was the wear and tear on his body and nerves to be taken into account. Griffin decided to demand a thousand pounds.

He swallowed the last of his bacon sandwich, and swilled it down with a mouthful of coffee. It was all over, and he might

184

come out ahead of the game yet. It had not turned out too badly after all.

He lifted the telephone, but he did not dial. He listened and his face went slack. Somewhere down in his stomach, a hole seemed to have opened up in his guts.

Slowly, he put the receiver back on its rest. Tauber had stopped eating, and was staring at him. Nancy glanced from one to the other, and caught the infection of fear.

'What's wrong?' she enquired shrilly.

'Your phone's out of order,' Griffin said, lying automatically.

The bastards had cut the line. They were out there, waiting. This quiet, pleasant, gracefully furnished warm living room had turned into a trap. And the trap had sprung shut.

Nancy lifted the receiver, and listened for herself. Like any other telephone subscriber dependent on the high powered technology and efficiency of the Post Office, it did not surprise her to find that the line had gone dead without warning. It was irritating but commonplace.

'There's a call box at the cross-roads,' she said.

Griffin remembered walking past it. He guessed it was about half a mile along the winding, leafy lane, just by the farmhouse.

'It's not far,' Nancy said impatiently. 'You turn right towards Marlow.'

'I know,' Griffin said. 'But I think vandals have been at it.'

'Then you can use the farm telephone,' Nancy said. 'They won't mind.'

Griffin considered the permutations, none of which had any immediate appeal. Go himself? And leave Nancy with Tauber? He dismissed that at once. Even if he left her the gun, she would certainly never use it. He would come back to find Tauber gone, at best, and a dead Nancy as well, at worst.

Send Nancy? But there was the delicate matter of striking a deal for a thousand pounds, before telling them where to come.

Suppose they all went in Nancy's car? He glanced through the living room window at the sylvan scene outside. The sun-dappled, rolling fields stretched into the distance, forming the kind of rural picture which had inspired countless now despised and forgotten Victorian watercolour artists. The woods, trees, and hedgerows dotted around formed a delightful setting fit for any chocolate box. They also provided enough cover for a battalion, let alone Bob Dalton and his yahoos. Griffin thought that it would be safer inside, at least until it grew dark. But something had to be done before then. Dalton could afford to wait, but Griffin could not.

That savage working over and the too frequent pain killers were telling on him, Griffin thought, with sour, resentful anguish. His mind was not functioning properly.

Nancy picked up her handbag. 'Well, if you're not going, I am,' she said, with finality.

'Just a minute,' Griffin said. 'I'm trying to think.'

'Don't bother,' Nancy said, bitterly. 'Whatever it is, I shan't like it. I've lost count of the number of times I've wished I'd never met you, but never more than since you brought that creature here.' Tauber eyed her, blankfaced. 'I don't know why I ever agreed to help you. I knew it was wrong, I knew I was being a fool. I suppose it was because I once . . .' She hesitated for a moment, like one trying to avoid the use of hateful words, '. . . because I once believed the lies you told, and I was stupid enough not to want to accept that it was all as cheap and meaningless as it seemed. But it was, and in my heart I know it. I want you out of my house for good. So you can either take him and get out now . . .'

'You don't understand,' Griffin said.

'Or I go and phone this minute,' Nancy finished.

'You don't know the number,' Griffin said, practically.

'Nine nine nine will do nicely,' Nancy said. 'It'll get the police here, and that's all I want.'

'All right, you go and phone,' Griffin said, capitulating, because she seemed to know what to do, and he did not. 'But not the law. This is too big for local coppers. I'll tell you what to say.'

He transferred the gun to his left hand, and kept Tauber covered, while he wrote a note. He gave it to Nancy. She read it slowly and carefully, and looked at him with contempt.

'So it's all about money,' she said. 'I should have known. I've read about things like this in the newspapers, but I never really believed they happened. Who's buying him? Some gang of thugs?'

'He's a defector,' Griffin said, tiredly.

Nancy laughed. It was a harsh, unpleasant sound. 'Still true to your philosophy, George,' she said scornfully. 'If you're going to lie, make it a really big one.'

'He's telling the truth,' Tauber said. 'I wish to defect. There are people who want to stop me. My own people.' He studied Griffin with no particular liking. 'I would expect him to try and get money, but he is selling me to his own government.'

Nancy shook her head, now thoroughly bewildered. 'Well, I must admit that sounds like you, George,' she said. 'Not to do something half-way decent except for cash. But how on earth did you ever get mixed up in anything like this?'

'I wish I hadn't,' Griffin said sincerely. 'Can you memorize what's on that note word for word?'

'Yes,' Nancy said, after a pause.

'OK,' Griffin said. He took the note from her, and threw it into the blazing fire. 'Take the car, don't let anyone stop you, and make the phone call from the farm.'

That way, he thought, she should be safe enough. He watched through the window as she walked to her car, got in and drove off. Nothing else happened. He could see no one out there. No untoward sounds broke the stillness.

Griffin relaxed a little. He began to feel embarrassed and silly, like a man who had panicked over nothing. After all, telephones went out of order all the time, and, life being what it was, never more often than when you needed to make an important call. He had jumped to frantic conclusions without any evidence at all. The odds were that Bob Dalton had not the foggiest idea where he was.

He knew that no matter how accurately Nancy repeated the message, he would not now get the thousand pounds he had hoped for. The people at the other end would agree and then renege on the deal later. They would have tried to do that anyway, of course, but had he been able to speak to them himself, he would have been able to make somewhat more complex arrangements than simply giving them Nancy's address.

Blind panic had cost him money and he was regretting it now. He would probably get something though. He wondered how much. None of his odd jobs had ever been on behalf of his own country and he had no idea how generous they were likely to be. Not very, he suspected. Scrooge, after all, was an Englishman.

'Put that down,' he said to Tauber, wearily.

Tauber had taken advantage of what he took to be Griffin's wandering attention to pick up a knife, and Griffin did not think the man intended to cut any sandwich with it.

Tauber sullenly dropped the knife. It clattered on a plate. Tauber would still rather work out his own deal, of course. Like Griffin, he stood to lose this way, but Griffin could summon up no fellow feeling for this anonymous-looking thug.

'Sit down on the hard chair by the wall,' Griffin said. 'Put your hands in your pockets and keep still.'

Tauber did as he was told. Griffin sat facing him. The log fire crackled comfortingly, and the coals underneath glowed. The pendulum clock ticked in a friendly fashion and its insides wheezed asthmatically as it geared itself up to strike the half hour. It was still working, Griffin thought, idly. The telephone began to ring.

Griffin could hardly have jumped further if a bomb had gone off without warning. He sat staring at the insistent phone, his heart racing like an engine out of control. Tauber seemed to be equally startled.

And then Griffin experienced a surge of genuine happiness. The phone had been fixed! It had merely been out of order after all, probably a fault in the exchange.

He lifted the receiver. 'Hullo?'

'Ah, George,' Bob Dalton's friendly voice said. 'Listen carefully for a minute or two, will you, old chum? Your lady friend, who is still in good health at this moment in time, will be arriving any second now. She has an escort with her, so she'll be perfectly all right, provided you're hospitable enough to let them both in. I'd prefer to settle our business affairs without any excitement or

188

loss of temper. Are you in agreement to that suggestion, Georgie boy?'

'Yes,' Griffin said. Their timing was immaculate. Through the window, he could see Nancy driving up. Beside her, sat one of Dalton's yahoos. She got out, followed by the yahoo. Her features were strained, and her face was deathly white.

'Fine,' Dalton said cheerfully. 'See you soon.' There was a click. Dalton had used a portable unit to make his call at the point where he had cut the wire. Griffin knew how it was done. He had been trained in the technique himself.

Tauber was on his feet, having accurately assessed the score. 'Give me the gun,' he said, thickly.

Griffin saw no merit in that proposal. 'Sit down and shut up,' he said.

Tauber ignored him, and moved into the kitchen fast. There was the sound of the back door being unbolted. Griffin let him go. There were only a few seconds left in which to flog his tired brain into action.

Should he hide the gun somewhere? But even while his eyes searched the room, he thought better of it. They would not believe for one second that he could have controlled Tauber without a persuader. They would not bother to search. They would enquire, while the heavy boots tore into his guts. His insides flinched involuntarily at the very thought. He did not want to take another beating, ever again, until the day he died. In the circumstances, that unhappy event was liable to be in the rather near future.

Should he try shooting it out? Provided his hands stopped shaking in time, he stood a reasonable chance that way. He was good enough with a hand gun to bring it off, given a bit of luck. But there was Nancy. Poor Nancy, who had merely been stupid enough to help him when he needed it. What right had he to take any chances with her life?

The footsteps on the path stopped, and the front door rattled. Time had run out. Griffin unlocked the door.

The yahoo came in cautiously, using Nancy as a shield, and Griffin was glad that his gun was reversed, that his finger was not squeezing the trigger. The odds were that he would have hit Nancy.

'Put it down,' the yahoo said. Griffin obeyed. The yahoo pocketed the gun.

There was a strangled grunt from the direction of the kitchen, and Tauber came in backwards, his hand to the left side of his face. The other yahoo followed, an automatic pointing at Tauber's stomach. Griffin supposed that the barrel had been laid across Tauber's cheek by way of encouragement.

Everyone stood around waiting, presumably for Dalton. No one said anything. Nancy groped for the back of a chair, and sat down. She was breathing deeply but shakily. Griffin wondered if she was going to faint. Her yahoo escort checked Griffin for any more firearms, perhaps for something to do, and moved away, satisfied.

Griffin asked Nancy if she was all right. He wanted to find out if they would object if anyone broke the silence, but no one seemed to care. Why should they? Nancy put trembling fingers to her face, but did not reply.

'Did they pick you up before you managed to phone the River Park Hotel?' Griffin asked.

'They were waiting,' Nancy managed to say. 'Just round the first corner . . . there was a car across the road . . .' She gestured vaguely.

'Well, Bob Dalton wouldn't have been there anyway,' Griffin said. He willed Nancy to look at him, but she clasped her hands in her lap and sat with her head bowed.

Griffin moved, very slowly, very carefully, towards Nancy. He was aware of the yahoos watching him, of their pointed guns following him. He wanted to touch her, to try and comfort her, to convey his aching regret for having selfishly involved her for his own ends, for not having left her alone, as he should have done, left her to forget about him and find the good, decent, peaceful life to which she was entitled.

The nearest yahoo did not appear to mind as he put his arms around her. That meant she had been searched, and they knew she had no weapon she could pass him. Nancy stiffened as he touched her, and recoiled sharply. 'Did they knock you about?' Griffin asked gently.

Her yahoo escort chuckled. A black evil rage welled up thickly inside Griffin. He studied the yahoo as he had once stared through binoculars at the face of a young border guard on a misty morning, soon after dawn. The yahoo, by way of being a mind reader, chuckled again.

Outside, a car drew up, a big Jaguar, and Bob Dalton got out. A Jaguar? Griffin had expected a Rover or a Hunter. He puzzled over that for a moment. They must have had some reason to switch cars.

Dalton walked in. 'Sorry to have been so long,' he said cheerfully. He lifted the phone, listened, and replaced the receiver. 'All in good working order again, ma'am,' he told Nancy. He looked at his watch.

'Well, there he is, old chap,' Griffin said.

Dalton stared at him.

'Tauber,' Griffin said. 'You owe me five hundred quid.'

'You're kidding,' Bob Dalton said.

'That was the deal,' Griffin protested. 'Half a grand in advance, and half a grand on delivery.'

'Ah, but you didn't deliver, old son,' Bob Dalton said. 'I've had to collect.'

Griffin shrugged. 'That's your lookout,' he said, impatiently. 'All you had to do was sit tight and wait. No need at all for all this racing round the countryside.' He waved at Nancy. 'Still less for frightening this lady,' he said indignantly. 'Since she was on her way to phone you.'

It was not going to be any use, he knew that, but at least they were talking, and nothing unpleasant was going to happen while conversation was taking place.

Bob Dalton laughed, and shook his head with delight. 'You're a one, George,' he said. 'You really are a one. You missed your vocation, old son. You should have been a high-class con man.'

'He'd told me what to do,' Nancy said, distinctly. 'I was to phone the River Park Hotel, and ask for Bob Dalton. I was to give him this address.'

Griffin stared at her with admiration and gratitude. She had taken it in after all, despite her condition. Would it work? Was it conceivable?

'So there you are,' Griffin said. 'I've carried out my side of the bargain, and I'd be obliged if you'd stop pointing guns at me. Just cough up the five hundred quid, and get Tauber out of here. I've seen enough of him to last a lifetime.'

Bob Dalton was put out. He had developed a frown. 'So what have you been up to, George?' he enquired, his voice an ugly rasp. 'Playing both ends against the middle?'

'Tauber got damaged,' Griffin said, patiently. 'He needed running repairs. He only recovered this afternoon. As soon as he was OK, I tried to phone you, but of course you'd cunningly cut the wires.' He looked at Nancy. 'She was on her way to the phone box when you picked her up.'

The yahoo escort was looking pleased with himself. 'He fed her the River Park Hotel and your name before you arrived,' he told Dalton.

Dalton's face cleared. 'That's more like it,' he said happily. 'That sounds more like our George.'

'Balls,' Griffin said, violently. 'I asked if you'd picked her up before or after she phoned.'

'Who were you really supposed to call, darling?' Bob Dalton asked.

'I was to get through to the River Park Hotel and ask for Bob Dalton,' Nancy said. 'I was to give him this address.'

'I think she'd tell us if we insisted,' Bob Dalton said.

The yahoo escort regarded that as the off, abruptly barged Griffin sideways, and laid practised hands on Nancy. Dalton extended one foot without bothering to take his hands from his trouser pockets. Griffin tripped over it, and fell to the floor. Nancy was bent double. She was screaming.

Griffin clawed himself to his feet. The sounds Nancy was making echoed shrilly inside his own head. Bullets or not, he had to stop those awful noises.

Dalton sighed, and employed what appeared to be his favourite contribution. He kicked Griffin in the stomach.

Griffin fell down again, coughing and retching. His tormented, bruised, beaten flesh exploded into sickening arrows of pain.

Through tear-filled eyes, he saw that the second yahoo, the one who had a personal grudge against Griffin, was caressing the trigger of his gun like a restless lover. He was paying no attention to Tauber at all. All the stuffing had gone out of Tauber as soon as Dalton had entered the room, even though Dalton had scarcely glanced at him. Since then, Tauber had sat, grey faced, not moving, hardly blinking. He looked like a dead man already.

Griffin heaved himself up again, and stumbled blindly forward.

'All right,' Dalton said impatiently. 'All right.'

Griffin sat down, crouched over the contracting spasms in his guts, and tried not to be sick.

The yahoo, who was enjoying his work, removed his hands from Nancy reluctantly.

'Anyway,' Bob Dalton said, 'I know who she was going to phone.' He lit a cigarette, exhaled smoke, and watched the wisps rise into the air. 'British Intelligence, yes?' He looked at Griffin, eyebrows raised.

Griffin hesitated. Nancy was curled up, moaning softly.

'Lies cause trouble, George,' Bob Dalton said.

Griffin nodded. They could be no worse off if he told the truth. 'I happened to find out that you weren't CIA,' he said. 'That seemed like a lot of trouble. Tauber gave me the number of his contact.'

He was not prepared for Bob Dalton's reaction, which was one of icily controlled fury.

'Jesus Christ,' Bob Dalton said viciously. 'Do you think I don't know? Don't insult me by expecting me to swallow pathetic little lies like that.'

'I swear to God . . .' Griffin began, baffled.

'You welshed on me, George. You've been in touch with them from the beginning. Did you screw them for more money? Is that it?'

'I haven't been in touch with anybody,' Griffin yelled. This was nightmare compounded by lunacy.

'No? Not Tom Bradley, in his flat off Queen Anne's Gate? George, you were tailed there.'

'He wanted to buy an encyclopaedia,' Griffin said. Had Dalton gone mad?

Bob Dalton shook his head in exasperation. 'You never give up, do you.'

Griffin's mouth was suddenly dry. Fragmentary recollections about Tom Bradley came back to him. If Bob Dalton believed that he had been crossed from the very beginning, Griffin was in the same position as Tauber. Dead, now, as of this moment.

'We talked about books,' he said carefully, 'and nothing else. Bradley had made an enquiry through my head office. He happens to live in my area.'

'One thing you're not, Georgie boy,' Dalton said, 'is stupid. Tom Bradley heads a very private outfit which has its resemblances to mine. We've never met, but I know him, and he knows me. So when I find you're meeting Bradley, I know you're selling me out, all the way.' He stubbed his cigarette out. 'Books,' he snorted. 'For the first time, you disappoint me, George. You're not class after all. You're second rate.'

Griffin sat there, dumb, feeling like Tauber, only worse. At least Tauber had asked for what was going to happen to him. He, George Griffin, had simply behaved like the biggest fool of all time. Not stupid? Dalton was wrong there. He was stupid to the point of congenital idiocy.

Griffin groaned inwardly. Not only had he failed to spot what Tom Bradley was, he had been so obsessed by his fears of Bob Dalton that he had cleverly shaken off the very people who might have saved him and Nancy. Those two cars on the M3, the Rover and the Hunter, had been Tom Bradley's people. Dalton, having found out where Nancy lived had simply sat and waited for him, and he had duly, and like the rankest amateur, obliged.

Nancy seemed to have recovered somewhat. Griffin wished he could ask her to forgive him, but there were no words in anyone's vocabulary which he could use. All she owed him was contempt and hatred.

Dalton went over and spoke to Tauber for the first time,

speaking softly in a language Griffin did not understand. Tauber's eyes did not move, his face remained blank.

'What happens to him now?' Griffin asked.

'What he would expect. He'll be flown home, and tried as a traitor.'

'How will you get him out? As a sick diplomat?'

'The arrangements don't concern you,' Bob Dalton said.

But it would be that, or something like it. That would explain Dalton's anxiety about dates and times, his reference to arrangements made. A special flight would have been cleared with the Foreign Office, a plane with 'medical' staff and all the necessary drugs to take one of their cultural attachés home for treatment for some nervous disease.

Not that Tauber's future was uppermost in Griffin's mind, at that moment.

'Part of your arrangements concern me very much,' Griffin said.

'I think it would be best if you were to accompany us,' Bob Dalton said. 'Part of the way.'

Griffin did not need any elucidation of the second part of that statement. It was what he expected.

'Look,' he said, 'you've got Tauber. As it happens, I wasn't going to cross you, not in the beginning anyway, and as far as I was concerned, Tom Bradley was just another prospect. All right,' he said, seeing the expression on Dalton's face, 'you're never going to believe that, so forget it. But Nancy's just an innocent bystander. I dragged her into it, but she didn't know what was going on, or who Tauber was. You've done your job, you've got what you want. You don't need her.'

Bob Dalton hesitated. He seemed uncertain.

'Come on, Dalton,' Griffin said urgently. 'You're a professional. A good pro doesn't do any more than he has to.'

Bob Dalton thought about it. The escort yahoo was looking at him with an intent expression on his face.

'I think the lady should also come with us, part of the way,' Bob Dalton said at last.

The escort yahoo looked pleased.

Griffin felt that he wanted to vomit. He had to try something, but he needed movement, the faintest glimmer of a chance, God knew what, but something. There was never going to be an opportunity in this room with everyone static like this.

He stood up. 'Well, let's get moving,' he said.

'Sit down, George,' Bob Dalton said, tiredly.

Two guns were pointing at him. Griffin sat down.

'I have a phone call to make in half an hour,' Bob Dalton said. 'So you can wait where you are, in comfort, until then.'

Griffin took out his cigarette case, and opened it. There were four cigarettes left. He took one out and lit it. He closed the cigarette case, and put it back in his pocket.

He was due to be killed. Not here. Somewhere else. So was Nancy. In her case, by the time the sadistic escort yahoo had finished with her, she would probably welcome it.

In the cigarette case, one nine millimetre bullet. Against that, three trained gunmen, armed with efficient, automatic weapons. Sharp, alert, fit men with fast reactions. And Griffin sat there, his guts coiled in angry protest, the rest of him aching abominably, his co-ordination beaten out of him. He was continually swallowing bile and his cigarette tasted foul, but he forced himself to go on inhaling, as though he desperately needed the solace of a cigarette.

He wanted to give up, let whatever was going to take place happen to him, and cling to the one remaining hope that it would not take too long when they began on him. But there was Nancy.

He thought wildly of using the one bullet he had on her, choosing his moment, before it started. That way, perhaps, he could save her the final agony. But the bloody thing was defective. There was something wrong with it, which he had not had time to try and fix. Fired at close range, it had not harmed Tauber seriously. He could not rely on it to end her pain instantaneously.

And yet, if he could not guarantee that, what use was his one bullet against three hard men? How could he inflict any more than a trivial wound on even one of them?

Bob Dalton sat, relaxed, his lips pursed as though whistling, although no sound came out. The escort yahoo was studying

196

Nancy's legs. The other yahoo explored his broken teeth with his tongue and stared at Griffin hungrily.

Somehow, this tableau had to be broken, the distance between Griffin and those guns had to be closed. He stirred restlessly and glanced at his watch.

'There's twenty-five minutes before you make your phone call,' Griffin said. 'Suppose I help Nancy make coffee all round?'

'No one moves about,' Bob Dalton said, 'least of all you, George. That way, you won't be tempted to try anything foolish. And don't be so transparent, old son. You tax my patience when you act like a trainee at combat school trying to be clever.' His eyes ran over Griffin in a thoughtful way. 'I've assessed you now, George,' he said. 'I could write a report on you. You're quite good when the opposition's not expecting it. But it's one shot or nothing. You're over the hill, and to make matters worse, you're in poor physical condition. You drink too much, with the usual result, you don't think as fast as you used to. A situation such as we have here, you're not much use at all. In fact, I'd back one of our cadets against you.'

The escort yahoo snorted with approval. The vindictive yahoo just kept staring at him. He caught Nancy's eyes, and realized that the expression which flickered momentarily there was, humiliatingly, compassion.

Not that he could fault Dalton's judgement. That was the trouble, the man was one hundred per cent right.

Funny how it had crept up on him, how he had imperceptibly declined from a hard bitten, hard drinking soldier, one of a select handful of crack troops, to a paunchy lush, the like of whom could be seen propping up the bar in any pub in London.

He complained about his morning cough these days, bemoaned his tendency to run out of breath if he exerted himself unduly, tended to postpone decisions which he would once have made instantly. He was aware, and yet he had not noticed it happening. And now, the attributes he had once possessed, and which he desperately needed, were gone. Vanished. In the past.

Bob Dalton made his phone call, precisely at the intended time. He spoke a few words, listened, and then hung up.

197

'We leave in five minutes time,' he said.

Griffin thought he could anticipate how those five minutes would pass. He took out his cigarette case, and put a cigarette in his mouth. He noticed that his hands were shaking.

The vindictive yahoo picked up the poker, weighed it in his hand like a man selecting a tennis racket, appeared to be satisfied and placed it in the fire making sure that as much of it as possible would get the benefit of the coals underneath the logs.

Nancy stirred uneasily. The atmosphere, heavy with the yahoo's hatred had become almost as explicit as words.

'Why don't you let her wait in the car?' Griffin asked, in as off-hand a tone as he could muster.

Bob Dalton nodded, and the other yahoo took her outside. Griffin's heart was pounding, but his breathing, while quick, was very shallow. He steadied himself, and took a couple of deep breaths. It did not help much. This was it. This was like being in that dentist's chair again, waiting for the drill to start, only worse.

At least there were only two of them now, but Bob Dalton, although he had not bothered to take out his gun, was certainly armed.

He looked at Tauber. When it happened, would there be any help from him? But in Bob Dalton's presence, he was utterly cowed. He was hardly aware of what was going on around him. His dull eyes were not taking in what the yahoo was doing.

The yahoo stirred the logs with the toe of his boot. Bob Dalton looked at his watch again.

'I don't want blood and shit all over the place,' he said impatiently. 'Just so that he travels quietly, that's all.'

'He can go quiet afterwards,' the yahoo said. He peered intently at the poker.

'After what?'

'A kind of vasectomy,' the yahoo said.

Bob Dalton looked interested.

Griffin began to shake. If begging for mercy would have done any good, he would have pleaded on his bended knees.

The yahoo took the poker from the fire. Eight or nine inches of it were glowing a brilliant red, and the yahoo seemed content. He turned and advanced towards Griffin. The poker was in his right hand, while the automatic in his left hand pointed steadily at Griffin's stomach.

Griffin stood up. His knees would hardly take his weight. The yahoo's eyes were lively, bright and alert. Whichever way Griffin went he was ready for him. The red hot poker glittered and sizzled gently on some fragments of charred wood. Wisps of smoke rose lazily.

Griffin was shivering uncontrollably. He stared at the finger-thick, glowing metal as though hypnotized. He made no sound, but inside him was that shriek of animal terror he had heard once before. 'Oh, God no . . . mercy . . . please have mercy . . .'

He forced his leaden, reluctant feet backwards. But that only led him into the corner of the room. This madman was ready to shoot if necessary, but not to kill. Not yet. A disabling shot, perhaps, but no more. He was going to take the most dreadful, most appalling revenge even his perverted mind could have invented.

The yahoo kept coming. Suddenly, he swung the poker. There was a swish, and the forgotten, unlit cigarette flew from Griffin's lips. He felt the searing heat singe his mouth. The yahoo smiled, pleased with his skill.

Griffin stumbled over the edge of a white rug. In the second that he was off balance, the yahoo let loose again, aiming at the side of his head. Griffin flung up his left arm, took the force of the blow and collapsed with a moan. He thought that his arm was broken.

His vision blurred. All he was conscious of was pain again, the pain which he loathed and hated and feared. His arm, his scorched lips, and then he smelt the smouldering cotton of his shirt, and he shrieked as the iron burned into his belly.

All he could see was the yahoo's face, intent, lips parted in the second before he leaned hard on the poker.

Griffin extended his trembling right hand, which still held his cigarette case, pressed the concealed catch and fired the single nine millimetre bullet which it held. The bullet tore into the yahoo's throat.

In the same instant, Griffin desperately rolled sideways as the yahoo's finger instinctively tightened on the trigger, felt the bullet smash into the floor beside his ribs, grabbed for the gun, missed it and without waiting, dived across the room as Bob Dalton's hand travelled fast towards his waist band.

Griffin hit Dalton head first. His skull felt as though it had been smashed by a hammer. Something happened to Dalton's face, and the man screamed, and fell over backwards. Griffin wrenched the table up with his good arm. Crockery went flying.

The other yahoo came through the front door, firing as he came, twice at Griffin. Both shots embedded themselves in the table which Griffin held before him like a shield as he flung himself towards the yahoo, hit him, and smacked him against the wall with a crunch.

Griffin turned, and kicked Bob Dalton's hand viciously as it came away from his waist band. The gun spun across the room. There was no time to go after it. The yahoo whom he had hoped was safely unconscious under the table was only half winded, and had quite enough breath left to pull a trigger.

Griffin closed on him using the kind of methods, head, knee, thumb, at which his body was expert, as long as it held out. He was hampered by his almost useless left arm, but just before his muscles were about to cry enough and give up, the yahoo went still.

That moment arrived when the yahoo's arm was dislocated and Griffin had his gun pressed up under his chin.

Griffin pulled himself to his feet, exhausted, dizzy, fighting to get a decent, whole breath of air into his lungs. During the thirty seconds or so which it had lasted, he had hardly been aware of the sounds around him, but he was conscious that Nancy had come in.

'Where's Dalton?' he gasped.

'In the car,' Nancy said.

Griffin heard the engine start. He dragged himself to the door. It would be a pleasure to pick off Dalton. From the porch he could practically do it blindfold.

'Drop it,' Tauber said. 'And stay there.'

Griffin had forgotten about Tauber. But with Dalton's departure, and Dalton's gun in his hand, the man had come to life again. Griffin spread his fingers and let the gun drop to the floor.

CHAPTER FOURTEEN

Tauber surveyed the scene. It appeared to please him.

In the far corner, one yahoo lay twitching, choking on bubbling blood. Nancy's eyes widened. She crossed and knelt beside him.

'Leave him alone,' Tauber said. Nancy ignored him. Tauber squeezed the trigger delicately. The yahoo's body twitched violently, one last time, and then went still for good. Nancy flinched, withdrew her hands from the yahoo and knelt where she was, her face blank and empty.

The second yahoo was holding his dislocated arm with his other hand, and staring at Tauber.

Griffin's left forearm felt as though it were on fire. He ran his tongue over his swollen painful lips. He was finished, useless. This was it.

'George Griffin,' Tauber said, quietly. He made it sound like a two-word epitaph.

'You could be on a stretcher, doped to the eyeballs,' Griffin said, 'on your way home for corrective therapy. You would be, if I didn't have this preference for staying alive.'

'But you would have let them take me,' Tauber pointed out, 'if you thought you could have saved your own lousy skin that way. Moreover, if it hadn't been for you and your liking for money, they'd never have found me.'

Griffin had to admit that his logic was impeccable. He wondered if Tauber could be made to see reason before he became bored with talking.

'The phone's working,' Griffin reminded him. 'You can make contact now, and complete your arrangements.'

'There's no hurry,' Tauber said.

'You're not thinking straight,' Griffin said. His sense of balance seemed to be going. He was afraid that he might faint at any second, without warning. 'These yahoos, they won't give a damn. They'll give you a putty medal. But if you knock me off as well, you'll be in trouble.'

'Why?' Tauber enquired. 'Since you were working for them?' He glanced at Nancy speculatively.

'She wasn't,' Griffin said. It was becoming hard to find words, to delve them from his mind. Harder still to say them.

Tauber said, 'When bullets start flying around, there are bound to be accidents.'

'One last little hit job before you retire,' Griffin said, bitterly. There was something in Tauber's face that made his flesh crawl. 'Does it give you a kick if it's a woman?' But there was no way he could translate his terrible, helpless anger into useful movement. It was all he could do to stand up.

'Not all women,' Tauber said, in a detached tone of voice. 'It depends on age and appearance.'

Griffin sought desperately for words, arguments, insults, anything which might serve to deflect Tauber for a little longer. But he could find none. His mind was an empty vacuum capable only of waiting passively to die.

It was Nancy who moved. She stood erect and walked towards Tauber.

Griffin saw, incredulously, that she was behaving exactly as if she had been summoned into a ward to deal with a difficult patient.

'I've heard quite enough,' she said tartly. 'More than enough. I suggest you stop talking such utter nonsense and try and understand the consequences of your actions.'

Tauber looked startled at first, and then amused. Nancy stopped a few feet away from him, close to the telephone.

'I've had some experience with unbalanced people, and you,' she told Tauber, 'are almost certainly a psychopath and possibly psychotic. You should have been placed under restraint long ago, for your own protection and everyone else's.'

Tauber did not like that. He lost his smile, and the gun moved, deliberately, until it was pointing straight at Nancy. Griffin realized, hazily, that her manner was deceptive. Her voice was clear, her words incisive, but bottled up inside, as in a pressure cooker, was raging hysteria. She was getting it wrong, she was going too far, her courage was suicidal. But there was nothing he could do.

'However, I doubt if your indifference to suffering extends to yourself,' Nancy said, contempt edging her voice higher. 'So you'd better follow what I'm saying carefully. I'm going to lift this telephone, and send for the police. I advise you to put that firearm down now. If you use it on me, you will certainly be tried for murder, and you'll spend the rest of your life in a prison for the criminally insane.'

Darling, don't, Griffin tried to say. You don't understand him. Killing is a job of work as far as he's concerned, which he also happens to enjoy. He's survived this long because he can cover his tracks, and he can do it again now . . . he's right about that . . . they may not believe him, but there'd be no percentage in putting him on trial . . . they want him to talk . . . he'll get away with it because he knows things they want to hear . . . my darling, don't . . . please don't . . .

But no words came out.

Nancy lifted the receiver. Tauber let her dial nine once. Then he took a deep breath, shifted his aim with loving care, and an expression of deep peace and fulfilment relaxed his features.

Griffin summoned up the last, final reserves he possessed. Lurching on legs which threatened to collapse any second, he managed to shuffle forward like an old man until he was between Nancy and Tauber's gun. He heard the dial move round as her finger released it. The second nine.

'You first then,' Tauber whispered with dreamy quietness.

'You've left it too late,' Griffin said.

Car engines were switched off. Tauber hesitated. 'Outside,' Griffin said.

Tauber's eyes went to the window. There were two cars, a Rover and a Hunter. Casually purposeful men were moving round the house. Nancy frowned, not understanding. Griffin put the receiver back.

Tauber understood, though. He sighed, slid the safety catch on with mild regret, and placed the gun on the mantelpiece.

Tom Bradley came in the front door, the others through the back. Bradley looked around him without much surprise.

Griffin sat down heavily. He did not lose consciousness, not quite. He was aware of Bradley making crisp, brief phone calls, that he was doing a fast cover up job, which involved private clinics, safe places, and a service mortuary, but it all seemed to be taking place somewhere in the distance, the way a dozing man half hears a conversation in the next room.

Later, he opened his eyes, and Bradley was talking earnestly and at length to Nancy, on whom what he said seemed to be making an impression. Griffin closed his eyes again. He could not be bothered to listen.

Someone was taking his jacket off. Griffin let them do it.

'Time to go,' Tom Bradley said. 'Do you want a stretcher?'

'I think I can walk,' Griffin said. He could, just about. He was now alone with Bradley. Everyone else had gone.

'Your cars on the M3,' Griffin said, compressing, unable to frame complicated thoughts. 'I found that out too late. How did you get on to me?'

'A painfully time consuming process,' Tom Bradley said. 'By way of a lorry driver who told the police about his hitchhiker, Camberley Station, a useless dash to London Airport, and finally a taxi driver who'd packed up for the day and gone home, the one who dropped you at the Compleat Angler. Then we guessed, from letters in your flat. A pity it all took so long.' He looked at the upset furniture strewn around, shattered glass and ornaments, and a huge, congealing, sticky blood stain on the white rug.

Griffin nodded. 'Where's Nancy?'

'We'll see that she's comfortable for a day or two,' Tom Bradley said. 'We've got some cleaning up to do. Make this place fit to live in again.'

Bradley's voice receded into the distance again. Griffin took two more steps towards the door and slid quietly to the floor.

Far off, he heard Tom Bradley say 'We're going to need that stretcher after all.'

CHAPTER FIFTEEN

'What did you do to your arm?' Brenda asked.

'Fell down some stairs,' Griffin said. His forearm was in plaster, but he could move his fingers.

'I suppose you'd been drinking,' Brenda sniffed. She looked at him more closely. 'What's wrong with your lips? It looks as though you've burned them.'

'I fell asleep with a cigarette in my mouth,' Griffin said. They had efficiently dealt with the other burn, which was, thankfully, confined to his stomach, in the clinic.

'George, really,' Brenda said. 'I don't know about you, I really don't. If you go on getting drunk all the time, you're going to kill yourself one of these fine days . . .'

Griffin switched off until she had finished.

'I suppose Dick's gone back,' he said, eventually.

'Well, of course,' Brenda said. 'He was only home for a couple of days. He got your message and he tried to phone you, but he couldn't reach you.'

'Oh, it wasn't very important,' Griffin said. 'I'll drop him a line.'

'Will you be staying?' Brenda enquired. 'Because if so, there's something wrong with the boiler.'

'As a matter of fact,' Griffin said, 'I'm feeling a bit tired. I could use a rest. I thought I might hang on for a week or two, if that's all right with you.'

There was a pause, as if she was thinking it over. Griffin was surprised. She always seemed to take his comings and goings for granted.

'The house is always here,' she said at last, peering down over her chin at her pearl necklace. 'It's up to you.'

Griffin wondered if that was an invitation. He wondered if he wanted to take it up, if it was.

For a few days, he spent most of his time in bed, sleeping a good deal, but sometimes lying on his back, staring at the ceiling for hours at a time.

He was getting on. He had lived at least half of his life, and probably a much higher fraction than that if he continued putting the gin away as he had been doing. Leaving aside the endless cigarettes. Quite apart from the probability of a sudden termination, as each odd job became more dangerous due to the inexorable slowing down with each passing year. Perhaps he was getting too old for all this racketing around.

What did he want?

There was the money side of it.

But even taking the Sinking Fund into account, he was only permanently short of cash because of the way he lived, a way which meant maintaining two establishments, and considerable ancillary expenses on women.

He was a good salesman. He thought the firm would transfer him to Portsmouth. That would save a bomb.

No more odd jobs. No more getting hurt. No more fear. Settle down. Live like everyone else. Accept the inevitable, creeping advance of middle age. Stop pretending he was still young.

Brenda wasn't too bad. Never said anything worth hearing, but then he did not have to listen. Nor sleep with her. She did not want that any more than he did.

Incredible to think of the passion he had once felt for her. Unbelievable now. And where had all that got him? Not only Brenda, but the others. Who wanted it any more, compared with peace and quiet and comfort and security?

In her slow pottering way, Brenda looked after his comfort. Her cooking had improved a lot over the years. No more sitting in launderettes. No more tinned food. No more queues of stained crockery and dirty glasses, waiting to be washed up. Clean clothes to order. Good food. Waited on hand and foot.

Dick could get married any time. Start a family. That would turn George Griffin into a grandfather. Fact. That was what he

208

would be. Time, surely, to slow down and take it easy. Accept that he was what he was.

The weather changed for the better, and Griffin transferred himself to a deck chair in the garden, where he sat in the sun, eyes closed, dreaming, feeling the warmth on his face.

'You haven't fixed the boiler yet,' Brenda said.

Griffin fetched some tools, but he did not need them. All the thermostats were wrongly set. Brenda would never understand thermostats.

'It's OK now,' he called.

'Good,' Brenda said. 'Now I can have a nice hot bath.'

At the end of seven days, Griffin said, 'Well, thanks for the square meals and all that. I'll be off now.'

'Oh, all right,' Brenda said. 'Do you know why the fridge isn't working?'

'Yes,' Griffin said. 'It's defrosting.'

He still got a twinge of pain when he changed gear, but otherwise his arm seemed to be much better. He thought he would avoid the motorways, and make his way across country to Marlow.

Strange, the effect of being driven to the limit of one's endurance. For a few days, he had been prepared to resign from living, give up. Settle down to be a moving vegetable, let the meaningless years pass and finally slip into death like getting into bed.

No. So he was over forty. What about it? He still had some good years left. He could still want a woman as a woman. He wanted Nancy.

The way she had seen it through. The way she had confronted Tauber when Griffin was drained and beaten. The two or three minutes she had gained by her courage had saved both their lives, Griffin knew that. He wondered if Nancy realized it. God, what a woman.

He loved her, and he was sure that, deep down, she returned it. He would explain to her about his crazy itch for Maisie. He would make her understand.

Perhaps no explanation would be necessary. She would open

the door, and he would say 'Hullo Nancy,' and she would say 'George, darling!' Griffin tried to stop pursuing that line of thought. It made him feel quite weak at the knees. He laughed, and blew his horn for no reason, out of sheer exuberance. He was George Griffin, and he was alive, thank you very much, and he knew what made life worth living.

He walked up the path and knocked. Nancy opened the door.

'Hullo, Nancy,' Griffin said.

'Oh, hullo, George,' Nancy said.

Griffin stepped inside, and put his arms round her. Somehow he missed her lips, and kissed her cheek instead. He could smell the light fragrance of the flower-like perfume she used, and which he had come to prefer above all others.

'I don't think you know Doctor Carter,' Nancy said. 'This is George Griffin.'

'How do you do,' Griffin said.

'I've heard a lot about you,' Doctor Carter said. He was a tall, solid-looking man in his middle thirties. He was holding a glass of beer.

'Would you excuse us, please, doctor?' Griffin said. 'I want to talk to Nancy.'

'Yes, of course,' Doctor Carter said.

'No, don't go,' Nancy said, quickly. She was fiddling with something on her left hand. Griffin saw what it was.

'Engaged?' he queried, stupidly.

'We bought the ring this morning,' Doctor Carter said.

'Congratulations,' Griffin said.

'Thank you,' Doctor Carter said.

'Simon's at the hospital in Maidenhead,' Nancy said. 'But he also has an appointment at Guy's, so he's away for a few days, sometimes.'

'I see,' Griffin said.

'Look, I know you're old friends,' Doctor Carter said, 'so if you'd prefer to talk privately . . .'

'No, no, it's not important,' Griffin said. 'When's the happy day?'

'Next Friday,' Nancy said.

'No point in hanging about,' Doctor Carter said, cheerfully.

'True,' Griffin said.

Nancy saw him to the door.

'Sorry,' Griffin said, quietly. 'You didn't tell me you had someone else.'

'You didn't ask me,' Nancy said.

The flat was stuffy, and airless. There were half a dozen bills in the letter box. Griffin threw them to one side, and opened the windows.

He had remembered that he was nearly out of gin, and bought a couple of bottles on the way. He sat down, poured himself a drink and lit a cigarette.

When the doorbell rang, he was surprised to find that it was six o'clock, and that half a bottle of gin had gone. He opened the door. It was Tom Bradley.

'My spies told me you were back,' Tom Bradley said cheerfully. 'Had a good rest?'

'Yes, thanks,' Griffin said.

'Good. Just a couple of things. I shan't keep you long.' He produced Griffin's elaborate cigarette case, which fired a single nine millimetre bullet. 'Just out of interest, where did you acquire this?'

'When I was in the SAS' Griffin said. 'A souvenir. I took it off a dead man in Indonesia. It was made in Formosa.'

'Not a new idea of course,' Tom Bradley said. 'But I haven't seen this type before. Very unusual. Just as well for you, actually. Your friends would have spotted it if it had been the Czech or East German model, and you'd never have got the chance to use it. You won't be surprised to learn that you're not going to get it back again, I presume?'

'I wouldn't be surprised,' Griffin said, 'to learn that you were going to hang a few phoney charges on me.'

'No need to look for phoney ones,' Tom Bradley said gently. 'But we prefer the discreet approach. Do you want the Riot Act?'

'I can read it myself,' Griffin said. 'The revised version for gullible idiots.'

'Fine,' Tom Bradley said. 'That understood, I have raised your case with our financial controller, pointing out that, admittedly by accident, you performed a small service, in the course of which you suffered minor injuries. He agreed to an ex gratia payment.'

He handed Griffin an envelope. Griffin opened it. Inside was one hundred pounds. He thought of protesting about British miserliness, but, after all, he had not really expected anything from that quarter. Also, Tom Bradley could still do him at any time, if he felt like it.

'Did you ever catch up with Bob Dalton?' he asked.

'No. He got on to that special diplomatic flight. A great pity. He'd have been really worth having. Rather as if the KGB nobbled me,' Tom Bradley said. 'God forbid.'

'Let me give you a drink,' Griffin said. 'I think I've got some scotch somewhere.' The evening ahead of him suddenly yawned endlessly. Tom Bradley seemed as if he could be agreeable company.

'Sorry,' Bradley said, shaking his head. 'Things to do, no rest for the wicked you know. One thing though, George, before I go. We know a lot about you now, so in future, watch it, right? And stop calling yourself a major. You never rose above the rank of corporal.'

'I was thinking,' Griffin said, 'now that we know each other, should there happen to be any little odd jobs you want done, you might remember me.'

'Not very likely, I fear,' Tom Bradley said. 'No slur intended on your professional abilities, nor do I wish to make too much of a point about patriotism and loyalty, and all that bull. But you're altogether too cavalier about who you work for. I don't think I could trust you, George.'

'I thought Bob Dalton was CIA,' Griffin protested. 'That's our side. Well, more or less.'

'I was referring to a somewhat more serious occasion,' Tom Bradley said cryptically. 'Well I think that's all, so if you'll excuse me . . .'

Griffin changed his mind about the money. A hundred quid was damn all, compared with what Tom Bradley had got. Tauber was worth a hell of a lot more than that.

'Is Tauber talking to your satisfaction?' he enquired, as Bradley moved towards the door.

'Quite likely,' Tom Bradley said. 'Though not to us. We sent him back home. Did a swap. On Saturday, actually.'

'You did what? But he had all sorts of information, things which could lead you to deduce future enemy policy and . . .' His voice languished and died as he saw the expression on Bradley's face.

'You must have been fed that by Bob Dalton,' Tom Bradley said, laughing heartily. 'Really, George, you do get taken in easily. I should be careful if I were you. No, Tauber doesn't know anything. We thought we could use him for one reason only, and that was to get back one of our own people, who unfortunately got himself kidnapped in Berlin. Rather a good man, who's now in London, and would be suitably grateful to you, if he knew of your existence. You really must stop believing everything you're told.'

'You can tell your plumbers that, another time, they'll get their faces filled in,' Griffin said, reminded. 'I suppose they were yours?'

'Most people fall for that one,' Bradley said, consolingly. 'I'll send back the keys we had made.'

'I'll have the bloody locks changed, thank you,' Griffin said. 'I don't trust you either, mate.'

Tom Bradley was still chuckling as he left. Griffin's face was red. He had been conned by everybody, but everybody. And what the hell did that crack about not trusting him mean, anyway?

For a few moments, he could not imagine, and then it came to him. If they really did know a lot about him now, as Bradley had stated, perhaps they knew about the time he had hired a boat in Portimao and gone sailing. John Irving seemed to have done, from his waspish remarks about taxis.

That was perhaps the simplest and best paid odd job George

had ever done. At the arranged point, out of sight of land, George had met a trawler. A man had climbed on board. George took him back to Portimao. They walked through the streets together, the man got into a car, and that was that. A cool grand, and an expenses paid holiday on the Algarve for nothing.

George had seen the man's face again, later. That was on television. The man was making a speech in Oporto. George had wondered at the time if, for his grand, he had done quite a lot to set off the Portuguese revolution.

Oh, to hell with it. He topped up his glass, and looked at his watch. Twenty past six. He had to get out, do something, be with somebody. The boozer? A club?

On the other hand, he now had an unexpected hundred quid, in cash.

He looked up the Marylebone number in his diary, and dialled. 'Hi' he said. 'This is George Griffin.'

'Oh, hullo, George,' the divorcee whose tits might or might not have been bestowed on her by nature said. 'I thought you'd got lost.'

'I've been abroad on business,' Griffin said. 'Look, I know this is terribly last minute, but I was supposed to take a client to dinner tonight. Now he's cancelled, which leaves me with a fat expense account doing nothing . . .'

It was surprisingly easy, perhaps because, even while he was talking to her, Griffin did not really care. 'I was rather thinking of L'Ecu de France,' he said.

'I quite like the Mirabelle,' she said.

Yes, she bloody would.

He arranged to pick her up at eight o'clock, rang the Mirabelle and booked a table, bathed, and put on clean clothes.

In the corner of his underwear drawer were a few letters. They were the only personal letters he had ever kept in his life, the ones, presumably, from which Tom Bradley had learned Nancy's address when his minions searched the flat. He sat down and read them through. Nancy wrote as she talked. The letters were warm, open and loving. When he had finished the last one, he went into the bathroom, held them over the loo, and set fire to them. He flushed the charred remnants away.

Then he went out.

His phone started ringing at one o'clock in the morning. Griffin stumbled, naked, into the living room, and picked it up. 'Hullo.'

'I tried to reach you earlier, but you were out,' Nancy said. She sounded keyed up. 'I don't know why you came here today, or what you wanted to talk to me about, but after Simon went, I thought . . . I thought I'd better find out before . . . before I do anything drastic.' It was a rehearsed speech he realized, the way someone talked when they had thought about it, over and over. 'Simon's a nice man,' she said 'and I know I can rely on him. I don't think I could bear to be let down again, George. Do you understand what I'm saying?'

Griffin opened his mouth to tell her that he understood what she was saying, and that she need never have any doubts about him ever, ever again.

'I'm going to make some coffee,' the divorcee said. 'Do you want some?' She had the sort of refined voice which carried well.

She was standing in the doorway, yawning gently. Her tits were real, as it happened. They were the only real thing about her.

'Nancy,' Griffin shouted into the phone. 'Nancy'. But the phone was dead.

'Who's Nancy?' the divorcee enquired, without much interest.

'Get out, you whore,' Griffin said, wearily. 'Go home.'

'Charming,' the divorcee said.

Griffin sat where he was, long after the door closed behind her. When he began to shiver, he crawled back into bed. There was still a trace of her perfume on the sheets. The wrong perfume.

Wrong everything.